Lilac Lane

By

Ann Swann

5 PRINCE PUBLISHING AND BOOKS, LLC
PO Box 16507
Denver, CO 80216
www.5PrinceBooks.com

ISBN 13: 978-1-63112-061-9 ISBN 10: 1631120611
Lilac Lane
Ann Swann
Copyright Ann Swann 2014
Published by 5 Prince Publishing

Front Cover Viola Estrella

First Edition/First Printing July 2014 Printed U.S.A.

5 PRINCE PUBLISHING AND BOOKS, LLC.

Other titles available from Ann Swann

~~~

All for Love

Stutter Creek

Acknowledgements:

I would like to acknowledge everyone at 5 Prince Publishing including my fellow authors. I am privileged to be surrounded by such generous and creative people.

Also a great big thank you to my kind and caring editors, Connie Kline and Michelle Gilmore as well as a special "Yeehaw" (that's Texan for "Good job!") to our wonderful cover artist, Viola Estrella. She gets it right, every time.

And finally, to my readers, a huge note of thanks, especially to those of you who keep asking when the next book is coming. Without you, I'd probably still be outlining.

Dedications

This book is dedicated to my mother.
She really did wield a mean hammer.

Lilac Lane

Chapter One

"I really like it, don't you?" Ella asked.

Nick, her ten-year-old son, looked up at her. "It's okay, I guess." His expression said more than his words.

Ella hugged him to her side. "It will be all right," she said. "Stutter Creek isn't that far from Albuquerque. It's just a little resort town. Skiing in the winter, camping and fishing in the summer. It backs right up to the National Park, you know. That's why it's such a tourist town."

Nick didn't say anything.

"Don't worry," she rattled on. "We'll be going to visit Nana all the time, and I'm hoping she'll come to visit us a lot, too. We'll even fix up the spare bedroom just for her."

She ruffled his dark hair and climbed the porch steps of their new rental. It was a quaint old house that had seen better days, but the realtor assured her that all the important stuff, like plumbing and wiring, had been recently updated. It was only the exterior that needed a little TLC. "Well, *that* we can do," Ella had replied. "I've painted a few houses in my time. My dad was a carpenter. One of my greatest joys was helping him finish out the houses he built." Maybe if we paint it we can get a break on the rent, she thought. But she didn't say anything. They had more than enough to worry about at the moment.

"I don't see why we had to move anyway," Nick pouted, interrupting her reverie. He trudged up the steps behind his mom.

He'd been very brave the whole time they were packing and moving, but now that they were here, it had suddenly become real.

Ella felt her spirits slump. "I know, sweetie, I wish we could have stayed put, too. But this little diner—they call it

The Drugstore—just beckoned me." She glanced down and smoothed the hair she'd just tousled. She never came right out and told him they moved specifically to hide from his stepfather. She just tried to make it sound like one big adventure. "We could never have bought anything like this back home. The prices here are half what they are in the city. And there is only one other eating establishment in the whole town—if you don't count the convenience store—and I don't." She squeezed his shoulder. "I hope you understand. I just didn't want to keep waiting tables forever. I want more, for me and for you."

Nick shrugged and plopped the box he was carrying on the sofa. Fortunately it held only books.

He's just a child, she thought. *Am I doing the right thing?* She remembered the bright red handprint on his cheek the day she'd left him in Anson's care. It was the day she'd been called into work unexpectedly. Up until then, her mom had always kept Nick. When Anson tried to tell her Nick had been disrespectful, thus giving him *cause* for a face-slap, she'd become so distraught he wound up shoving her across the kitchen. When she told him to leave, he'd simply laughed and shoved her again. This time, her face hit the doorframe. Then he went back to the bedroom and packed *her* suitcase. But Ella was no one's victim. She called the police and had him arrested. She never slapped her child, she certainly wasn't going to stand idly by and let someone else do it. When the officers arrived, Anson was convinced he could talk his way out of going to jail.

"The boy's just worthless," he'd told the senior officer. "He ain't mine, you know. Takes after his mother. Or maybe his old man; who knows? That worthless piece never even claimed him. Now I see why. Too bad I didn't know this before I took them in and gave them a home." He was talking to the gray-haired cop as if they were sharing confidences over coffee. He seemed to think every man felt the way he did. Ella assumed it was the beer talking. Once he got started drinking, things usually got ugly. But this was the first time they'd gotten physical.

She remembered standing in the doorway with Nick safely ensconced behind her. "Does he need to see a doctor?" the younger officer asked.

Glancing back at Nick, the red handprint standing out on his face like day-glo under black light, Ella shook her head. "No, he'll be okay as long as we get away from that madman." Her eyes were crusty where she'd accidentally wiped blood from her cheek into her lashes.

"I'll need you to come to the station and file an official report. But first, the hospital for an x-ray." The officer nodded toward her swelling cheek. "I'm no doctor, but I think you've got a fracture there."

Tears spilled from her eyes when he said that. They mixed with the smear of blood and left red trails down her face. "I feel so stupid," she said. "How could I have let this happen?"

The officer was kind. "You didn't let it happen, and you didn't cause it. You're going to follow through and get him put away." He hesitated as if gauging his next words carefully. "And you won't back out when it comes time to testify. You won't go back to him and make all this night's work be for nothing, right?"

Ella looked at him as if he were crazy. "Of course I won't go back to him. I'm not *that* stupid."

"You'd be surprised how often it happens," the officer replied. "You would be surprised."

The paramedics came, but Ella insisted she could drive herself to the hospital. She didn't want to start off her single life with a huge ambulance bill hanging over her head.

As she took her keys from her purse, she saw the senior officer snap the cuffs on Anson.

"You've got to be kidding me!" he yelled in between curse words. "I'll sue the whole department. I'll have your fucking job! What's your badge number? It ain't no crime to swat a smart mouth kid. Especially not one as worthless as that punk." When he said that, he turned and looked right at her and Nick.

They'd been trying to get out of the house without having to confront him.

"Worthless," he bellowed, struggling against the cuffs. His face turned the exact shade of an overripe plum, eyes bugging out as if they would leap on Nick and Ella and finish the beating. "Both of 'em. Not worth shit!" He lunged forward, catching the officer off balance.

"Hey!" The gray-haired cop leapt on Anson's back and took him to the floor.

"I'll kill 'em," Anson was screeching. "They'll be sorry they did this to me!"

The younger officer shielded Ella and Nick and hurried them outside. "A woman from Children's Services will meet you at the hospital to look after him and take your story."

That terrified Ella. "Let me call my mother. She'll meet us there, too. She'll help us. I know she will. Please, don't let anyone take my boy."

The paramedic patted her hand. "Settle down," he'd said. "No one's going to take your boy."

But Ella wasn't listening.

She was pressing her mother's picture icon on her cell phone.

Ella swept the painful memories to the back of her mind and crossed into the kitchen where she deposited her own box full of dishes and various utensils. "As soon as we get the rest of these boxes unloaded, we'll go to The Drugstore, then explore a bit."

The movers had done all the heavy work, but Ella hadn't trusted them with her grandmother's china. She also had several more boxes in the Jeep that contained photos and artwork taken from the walls of their old house. It had been a cramped ride to their new home, but now that they were here, in the mountains, Ella was thankful they had the Wrangler. The roads were beautiful but steep. Even the driveway leading up to the house was narrow and uneven.

We'll rent for a while, she thought. And if it doesn't work out, we can always go back to Nana's house. The thought stuck in her craw, though. Not only did she hate the thought of going back to mama, but Anson had made such ugly threats when she had him arrested, she was afraid to be anywhere near him, even if he was in the county jail. It was obvious how much he had grown to despise both her and Nick. He blamed her for every bad thing that had happened—even though he was the one who hurt them.

Her hand went to her cheekbone. There was a permanent indentation there; small, hardly noticeable, but what would it have looked like the next time she did something that displeased him? And what would Nick look like the next time he "swatted" him? How long before it escalated to closed fist rather than open-handed slap?

She couldn't believe she'd fallen for someone so mean and hateful. Of course, he hadn't been either of those things in the beginning. She recalled all the news stories of wives who had married men who turned out to be psychopaths in disguise. When the wife disappeared, the authorities almost always looked at the husband first. One woman disappeared right off the cruise ship while they were on their honeymoon. Another disappeared when she discovered her husband had been lying about being a med student. Her body was later found in the local landfill. And what about that poor pregnant woman whose husband sunk her body in the ocean? She had been eight months pregnant.

It's hard to really know someone, Ella thought. Especially when they seek to deceive.

Bing-bong.

"Is that the doorbell?" It was the first time she'd heard it from inside the house. Her first inclination was to call out, "Come on in!" but her second thought was to yell at Nick not to answer it. She compromised by hurrying toward the door. "Just a minute, I'm coming!"

When she rounded the corner between the kitchen and the living room, she could see a woman standing outside the door.

She opened the screen. "Hello?"

The woman held out her hand. "Norma," she said. "From next door, well, you know, down the road." She grinned and indicated the direction with a wave of her hand. All the houses in this area were set back from the road at the end of their own stumpy, humpy driveways. Each one occupied several acres separated from each other by tall pines and junipers.

"Nice to meet you." Ella took the proffered hand.

Norma swept streaky gray hair off her forehead and smiled. "Saw you two unloading boxes and thought I'd stop by and offer to help. My husband is a long-haul trucker, hardly ever home. So I know how welcome an extra pair of hands can be."

Ella returned the woman's grin even though she wondered how Norma could possibly know it was just the two of them. *How does she know I don't have a husband lurking around somewhere?*

"Hope you don't think I'm too forward," Norma said, as if she'd read Ella's thoughts. "Your realtor is my second cousin. She told me to check in on you guys and make sure you were getting settled." She held up a small brown bag that Ella hadn't even noticed hanging from her arm. "Brownies," she said.

Ella laughed and stepped aside so she could come in. "Nick will love those. Thank you so much. And trust me, we'd welcome another set of hands if you're sure you don't mind."

Norma passed the bag to Ella and patted her arm. "Just point me in the right direction."

Ella called Nick to come in and meet their new neighbor, and then she showed him the brownies.

"Pleased to meet you," Nick said politely. "Do you have any kids?"

Norma shook her head. "Sorry, buddy. My only daughter is grown and gone. She hasn't even blessed me with grandchildren yet."

Nick's face fell.

"But don't you worry." Her voice was sympathetic. "We've got a wonderful little school here in Stutter Creek. You'll make lots of friends. Besides," her face grew thoughtful. "I've got a godson who is just a bit younger than you. His name is Danny and he just turned eight." She glanced at Ella. "I'll be glad to introduce the two of them— well, all of you, of course, when you're ready. Beth and John are excellent parents. In fact, Beth is a teacher at Stutter Creek Elementary."

Ella shot her a look of thanks, then led the way to the kitchen. "Nick is in fifth grade," she said. "What grade does Beth teach?"

Norma clucked her tongue. "Can you believe she teaches fifth grade? Will wonders never cease?"

"That is wonderful," Ella replied. "I can't wait to meet her."

She waved a hand toward the kitchen. "We haven't bought any groceries yet." She opened the bag containing the homemade brownies. "But as soon as we finish unloading the Jeep, I'll run to town and get some milk to go with these."

"Couldn't I have just one," Nick wheedled, obviously won over by the cook. "I don't have to have milk."

Ella smiled. She'd thought that would be his response. He was just like her when it came to chocolate. "Of course you may." She handed him a still-warm square and pinched off a little taste for herself. "Sit at the table, kiddo," she instructed. "I have no idea where the napkins are. Hmmm, these are *delicious*."

Nick sat at the table and sunk his teeth into the first moist bite.

Together, the two women backtracked to the Jeep and began carrying in the rest of the boxes.

It was easy to put the cartons in the appropriate rooms. Ella's mom had insisted on labeling each one with a giant Sharpie while helping them pack up the house back in Albuquerque. "Half the work is done in the preparation," she'd said. Ella hated to admit it, but it had made unloading things a lot easier. Even the movers had commented on it.

When the boxes were stowed away, just waiting to be unpacked, Norma insisted it was time for her to go. But she invited them to come over for a visit. "Just stop by anytime," she said. "It's the first one on your right when you head back toward town."

"Can we drop you there on our way to the grocery store?" Ella glanced out the front window. "I don't see your car."

Norma shook her head, gray-streaked curls bouncing. "I walked. It's my greatest pleasure, walking these hilly roads. Good for my heart and my hips." She winked at Ella. "Besides, it's only a mile."

Ella gave her a brief hug. "I'm in awe," she said. "Once we get things all figured out, maybe I'll just join you sometime."

"I'd love that," Norma replied. "And Nicky, too. We've got lots of wildlife in these old woods. And I know a trail that goes straight from my house to yours."

Nick's eyes lit up. "I'd like to see that. We lived in town before."

"Well, that's a date then. The first chance you get, you two stop by and we'll go exploring."

"Sounds wonderful," Ella said.

Norma walked down the porch steps then turned and gave a little wave. Just past the edge of the drive, she headed into the woods. Ella could see the beginning of the trail—in another moment, Norma was invisible.

Wow. Guess the woods are thicker than I thought. That gave her a moment's pause. Finding such a bargain for rent seemed ideal yesterday, but now she wasn't so sure. *Yep. We definitely have to explore that trail. Face the unknown. Otherwise, I'll be imagining all sorts of things lurking there.* Anson's face popped into her head. But not him, she thought. He's in jail. And when he does get out, he has no way of finding us.

Grabbing her purse and keys, she swept away tendrils of brunette hair that had escaped her ponytail.

"Remind me to pick up the ingredients for a caramel pie," she told Nick as they drove into town. "I'll make one for Norma to thank her for coming over and helping us get settled."

"And for the brownies," Nick added, patting his midsection comically. "I liked her. I can't wait to check out that trail. You think we could camp out in the woods behind the house? Please?"

Ella laughed. "I'll bet we can before it gets too cold. But I guess we'd need a tent, right?"

Nick laughed, too. "And sleeping bags, and a lantern, you know to see by, and—"

Ella rolled her eyes. "And more money to buy all this stuff!"

She pointed to a neat white house with butter colored trim on the right side of the road. The house sat back behind a lush garden of fall mums, bright purple kale, and shiny green holly bushes graced with tiny red berries. "Must be Norma's house," Ella said. "Wonder how long it takes her to walk a mile anyhow?"

Nick shrugged. "I'll bet I could run to her house and back in no time!"

"I'll bet you could," Ella replied. "I'll bet you could."

*

After a fruitful visit to town, they returned to their new home filled with a sense of hope. Maybe it's going to be okay, she thought. *It will all depend on Nick and how he settles in at his new school.*

They put the groceries away and Ella helped her son figure out the controls on the bath/shower combination. At home (*I've got to stop thinking like that, this is home now*), they'd had separate tubs and showers so this was something new, something he'd only seen the few times they'd stayed at hotels over the years.

"It's kind of old, isn't it?" Nick said.

Ella looked at the ancient showerhead. She thought he was being very careful not to sound as if he were whining or complaining. "Yeah," she agreed. "It is old. Almost as old as me." She grinned and twisted the knob that changed the water from the tub spout to shower. "But we can deal with that. After we buy up all that camping gear, we'll go down to the Ace Hardware store and get one of those great big shower heads that make it feel like you're showering in the rainforest!"

Nick smiled. "That sounds good, mom. We can fix a lot of things, can't we?"

Ella hugged him fiercely. He was trying so hard to be good, and positive. "That's right, baby. We can fix everything. Change things, do whatever we want. With no one to answer to."

Except for the landlord," said Nick, the voice of logic.

"Well, yeah, there's that." She chucked him beneath the chin and started out of the steamy bathroom. "Better hurry," she called back. "Who knows how long the hot water will hold out."

Nick mumbled something and closed the door. She heard the metal rings scrape the metal rod as he pulled the shower curtain closed.

"Cold!" he screeched.

Oh, no. Don't tell me the hot water heater is faulty.

She pushed the bathroom door open a crack. "Is it freezing? No hot water at all?"

"Psych!" Nick giggled. "Gotcha, Mom!"

Before Ella pulled the door shut, she said, "You'll pay for that mister. Just you wait." She paused dramatically. "Hmmm, wonder what would happen if I flushed the toilet about now?"

Nick squealed, "No, Mom, no!"

Ella laughed evilly and made certain he heard her when she pulled the door shut. "Don't mess with the master," she whispered happily. It was so good to have her cheerful kid back. For too long now, he'd become more and more withdrawn, even morose. And she hadn't known what to do. Until Anson had forced her to figure it out.

After they both had showered and got into their pajamas, Nick helped her make up their beds.

They shared one more brownie—with milk—and brushed their teeth. Then she tucked him in and read him a silly poem from *Where the Sidewalk Ends*.

"Love you." She leaned down to kiss the quarter moon scar on his forehead. It was just a small one, a reminder of his first day in first grade when he'd taken a header off the monkey bars.

"Love you, too," he mumbled, squeezing the stuffed football pillow his Nana had given him on his last birthday.

Ella poured herself a small glass of wine and waited until she was certain he was asleep before she called her mother to check in. "Hey, Mom! I can't *wait* for you to come visit. I just love this house. The kitchen is a big old square with plenty of room for that antique table you gave me, and the counters are that really old white Formica stuff with the gold vein running through it—so retro. It makes my red Fiesta ware really stand out. I never would have thought it could be so – so – *chic*."

Her mother laughed. "Hi, El. Glad you love it. I can't wait to come for a visit."

"Oh, and we met the neighbor lady today and she actually brought over homemade brownies and helped us unload the Jeep. Can you believe it?"

"You sure there's nothing wacky about them?"

"Wacky?"

Her mother laughed. "The brownies, dear. The brownies."

Ella pressed the phone to her ear. "Oh, Mom."

"Just a small joke, that's all. I'm glad you two are settling in, I hope you've found a real, genuine small town. The way they used to be—"

"Mayberry," Ella interjected.

"Mayberry," her mom agreed. "By the way, the number you called me from isn't your cell phone. What's the deal?"

"Oh, that's why I called. The mountain's cause such spotty cell reception the realtor advised us to keep the old landline. Here, write down this number." She recited the ten-digit number. "And there's a land line at The Drugstore, too. Let me give you that one as well."

Her mother wrote both numbers down and stuck them under the little picture frame refrigerator magnet Nick had made for her in Sunday school. It held a small 2x3 of his latest school photo. She intended to program the new numbers into her own cell phone as soon as they were through talking.

"Okay, now. Tell me all about the drugstore and the town and your house. I want to hear everything." She plopped down in her favorite chair, momentarily forgetting all about the numbers on the fridge.

After chatting with her mom for awhile, telling her all about the town and The Drugstore, Ella finally relaxed. "Guess I'd better get off the phone now, Mom," she said. "I think it costs a lot more to talk long distance on a landline than on a cell phone."

"Oh, that's right," her mom agreed. "It certainly doesn't take long to get spoiled to new things, does it?" She laughed and said goodnight.

They hung up and Ella went to her new bedroom, sticking her head into Nick's room along the way. He was sleeping peacefully.

She smiled and resisted the urge to go in and plant one last goodnight kiss on his forehead.

*

It was after midnight when Nick appeared at his mom's bedside like a little phantom, still clutching his football pillow. His hair stuck up in little whorls and corkscrews.

"Something woke me," he said. "Sounds like someone walking around, up there." He indicated the ceiling with a thrust of his chin.

Ella came awake quickly, as only a worried parent can. "Let's go take a look." She climbed out of bed.

"You go," Nick said. "I'll wait here." He sat on the edge of her bed.

She wanted to say okay, just stay here and let Mama handle it, but she was afraid if he didn't sleep in his own room tonight, on their very first night, he might expect to sleep with her from now on.

"I need you with me," she said. "As a backup."

Nick sighed. "Okay...but what if it's a ghost? It's an old house, it's probably haunted."

"Nope. No such thing as ghosts." She spoke calmly even though his words raised automatic chill bumps on the backs of her bare arms. "Old houses just creak and groan when the night air cools the wood. Nothing to worry about." She took his hand. "Ghosts are only in books and movies. Not in real life."

She hugged him briefly and together they went back to Nick's room where they turned on all the lights, checked under the bed, in the closet, even checked each window lock. "See, everything's okay." She turned back his covers and fluffed his pillow. "Ready to try it again?"

"Will you stay until I fall asleep?"

Ella looked at her brown-eyed boy trying so hard to be brave. "Of course I will."

He climbed in and she sat on the edge of the bed and scratched his back through his PJs.

After a few minutes, his breathing deepened and she knew he was asleep again.

That's when the noises started back up.

They *were* coming from overhead.

Chapter Two

"I really don't think I like the sound of this." John's strong white teeth were tightly clenched on the fishing line he was tying onto his lure.

Beth laughed and flung her own line back into the water. Her feathered lure danced on the surface like a dragonfly. She tugged it back across the water slowly. Beth didn't really like *catching* fish, but she loved being out with her two best guys while they fished. She also loved cooking and eating the fish they caught. "C'mon," she cajoled. It'll be fun." She played with her line, reeling it in ever so slowly. "Besides, it's for the school."

John grimaced and floated his new lure over the water. "I knew you were going to say that. Rent-a-Gent. Sheesh." He yanked his line. "Got a bite!" He played the fish out for a moment, and then smoothly pulled it toward shore. "Danny," he yelled. "Bring the net!"

The boy had just placed his own catch into the wicker creel. "Coming, Dad!" He grabbed the short handled net and hurried toward the big man. "Is it a big one?"

John's line went slack and he slapped his thigh in frustration. "I think it was," he said. "I think it was old Granddad. The oldest fish in the whole lake!"

Danny laughed and slapped his own thigh in imitation. Anyone could see the hero worship on the child's face.

John's Anatolian shepherd, Turk, dashed out of the woods, barking.

"Too late, buddy." Beth patted the dog's head. "Another one got away." She delighted in watching Turk attempt to help them pull in the fish whenever Danny got one in the net. The dog was careful not to knock the boy over; he'd been the child's absolute protector since the day they had adopted Danny three short years earlier. But she was afraid it was just a matter of time before Turk got a fishhook in his mouth.

"Darn thing got my new lure," John said. "I think I'm done for the day. How many we got so far, Dan?"

"Four," the boy answered. "Not too shabby I'd say." He grinned and flung his arms around Turk's thick neck. "There may even be enough for you to have a taste you old pig." He gave the dog a hard squeeze and skipped back to the creel. Fishing and camping were his two favorite things in the world—as long as they were done with his dad.

The transformation in the boy was nothing short of miraculous. When he was only four, his biological father, a serial killer, had abused him almost to the point of death, and then he had left him for dead. Turk and Beth had found him in a cave—she was actually a prisoner of the killer at the time—and John had saved them all, with a little help from a friendly spirit who just happened to be Beth's late father.

Now, the child was growing up the way children are meant to grow up, with firm and loving parents, lots of fresh air every day, surrounded by good people and a great village. And Turk was as faithful as the boy's own shadow.

"Now," Beth said on the way home, "we were discussing Rent-a-Gent, the fundraiser to get new equipment for the school playground."

"You know I'll do it," John said. "For you and for the kids." He lowered his voice, and whispered, "But you'll owe me." He treated her to a comical leer.

Even after three years of marriage, Beth still found herself blushing at the insinuation.

"Whatever you say, Big John." Using his old nickname made them both crack up.

"What's so funny?" Danny demanded. He'd been lollygagging along behind them. "Was it a knock-knock joke?" His new passion was knock-knock jokes.

"Yes it was," Beth said, allowing him to catch up. "Knock-knock..."

"Who's there?" Danny responded.

"Dwayne," she said.

"Dwayne, who?"

"Dwayne the baftub, I'm dwowning!"

"Oh, I get it," the boy said with a giggle. "Knock-knock, Mom."

"Who's there?"

"Banana!" he crowed.

"Oh, no. Not banana!" She and John both groaned dramatically. "Anyone, but banana!" They knew this old joke, and they always made a big deal of it for Danny's sake. It was his favorite.

It was only a short hike back to their cabin. They continued telling knock-knock jokes all the way home. It only took half a dozen.

Chapter Three

Ella raised herself from the edge of Nicky's bed and gazed up at the ceiling.

The noises had stopped.

Just an old house settling, she told herself just as she'd told Nick a few minutes earlier. *Just old wood creaking.*

She gave herself a little mental shake and went back through the house, checking every door and window to make sure they were locked.

In the hallway outside the kitchen was a plain wooden door that opened onto the narrow attic staircase. The door had an old-fashioned lock that required a key. The realtor had actually stuck the key into the lock so that Ella would know where it was.

Heart thumping, Ella turned the key to lock the door, then she removed it and tested the doorknob to make certain it would no longer turn. She couldn't make herself go up there this late at night with Nick sleeping and no one else in the house.

She took the key and laid it on the kitchen windowsill behind the sink. Tomorrow, I'll find a better place for it, she thought.

This time, when she went back to bed, it was quite some time before sleep would come. Every now and then, she thought she heard noises coming from the attic, but she consoled herself with the "old wood" theory.

At last, she drifted off.

"Mom!" Nick shook Ella's shoulder.

Her eyes popped open instantly, but she couldn't quite get her bearings. The moonlight illuminated the ivory curtains in a comforting glow. But the bedroom furniture was all out of place. She hadn't finished putting things right, yet.

"Mo-om!" Nick shook her again.

Ella forced her drowsy mind to focus. It seemed as if she'd just fallen asleep a moment ago.

Nick leaned over her face, shaking her and willing her to look at him. "Mom!" he hissed, finally losing his cool.

"Nicky?" She folded back the comforter like she'd done when he was a toddler needing a cuddle in the middle of the night. "C'mon." She patted the bed; all thoughts of making him sleep in his own room just a foggy memory.

Nick hesitated.

"What's wrong?" Ella asked. "Bad dream?"

"No. This time, someone's *definitely* in the attic."

Ella's heart lurched into her throat. She'd never heard him so adamant. She struggled to a sitting position. "What does it sound like?"

"Like something being dragged across the floor." Nick's voice trembled. "It was so loud it woke me up."

She placed her finger to her lips and then to Nick's lips so he would know not to say anymore.

The sound came again.

In the stillness of the moonlit room, it did sound like someone dragging, or pushing, something across the attic floor.

Without hesitating, she reached under the bed and pulled out the hammer she'd been using to hang pictures. She clutched it tightly in one hand. It gave her a feeling of comfort as she moved toward the bedroom door.

"I'm coming with you," Nick whispered.

Ella nodded. Now she wanted him to stay there, but she couldn't contradict her earlier plea. She didn't have time.

She put her finger to her lips again and motioned for him to get behind her. *I'd feel better with a gun*, she thought. The hammer felt almost ridiculously light.

When they crossed in front of the window, the moonlight snagged on the silver hammer head and Ella had a moment to envision how they must look, creeping past the window in their nightclothes, outlined by the moon. Nick's ninja jammies were black. He could disappear if he wanted.

Her feet froze when the sound came again. This time, it was further away, as if the intruder had moved to the other end of the attic.

Her purse was hanging on the bedroom doorknob, her cell phone inside. She plucked it from its little pocket and swiped the screen. No signal.

The landline was on its base in the kitchen.

Such an old house.

Everything was quiet.

She peeked out the bedroom door into the hallway. What courage Nick had shown getting out of bed and coming to her room.

"I ran," Nick said as if he'd read her thoughts. "I'm surprised you didn't hear me."

Ella smiled and they started down the hall like a little human train.

When they reached the door leading to the attic stairs, Ella stopped. Should have gone up earlier, she chided herself. She reached out to turn the knob, but of course, she'd locked it earlier. "Key's in the kitchen," she whispered.

"Let's call the police," Nick said. "Let them come and check it out."

Ella led the way to the kitchen. She fumbled around for a moment, trying to locate the unfamiliar light switch. Nick reached around her and flipped it on.

The room was flooded with soft yellow light.

She glanced at the windowsill behind the sink to make certain the attic key was still there.

The phone was on the opposite wall, but since it was a cordless model, she could carry it anywhere in the house. *Should I call the police?* She'd never been one of those people who panicked at every little noise, but then she'd never really been on her own, just her and Nick, before.

A large *thunk* came from overhead. Both she and Nick ducked and looked upward. It sounded like something had fallen over.

That decided her.

She dashed across the room, grabbed the receiver off the cradle and punched in 9-1-1.

Nick was right beside her, his eyes glued to the ceiling. "I think it really is haunted," he muttered.

Ella shivered. She didn't believe in ghosts, but she did believe in human intruders. *Should we get out of the house?* In a flash of inspiration, she wrestled one of the stout kitchen chairs—red vinyl seats on thick, chrome frames—and shoved it under the attic doorknob. Nothing was coming through that door.

"9-1-1, what's your emergency?" The dispatcher sounded sleepy, as if the call had woke her.

"I think someone's walking around in my attic," Ella whispered loudly.

"Mrs. Benefield?" The dispatcher's voice was monotone. "You know there are no boys in your attic. Chief Brown checked it out himself."

Ella pulled the phone away from her ear and looked at it to see if she was actually talking—or still asleep and dreaming.

"Umm, this is Ella Webb. My son and I just moved into the old rental house on Lilac Lane. 1701?" She hated the way her voice went up at the end of the sentence as if she wasn't sure, or was asking a question.

The dispatcher inhaled and plopped her coffee cup down—hard. "Ella Webb? I'm sorry ma'am, long story with Mrs. B. She actually lives near you on Lilac. I should have looked at the address closer when the call came in. What makes you think someone is in your house?"

Ella told her what was going on and the dispatcher instructed her to hold on. Ella could hear her calling "Unit Six" on the police radio.

"Unit Six. 10-65, please."

"I assume 10-65 means intruder?" Ella asked when the woman came back on the line.

"Nah," the dispatcher replied. "It means switch to a private channel."

The officer clicked his mic. "Headquarters?"

"Unit Six, we have a new resident at 1701 Lilac Lane. Noises in the attic woke her. Sounds like someone walking around."

Ella heard the officer respond. "10-4, en route. ETA five minutes."

"ETA?" Ella asked.

"Estimated time of arrival," the dispatcher replied.

"Oh. What should we do?" Ella asked. "Until he gets here, I mean?"

The dispatcher sounded fully awake now. "First, are all your doors and windows locked from the inside?"

When Ella assured her they were, the dispatcher seemed to relax a bit. "Is there any other outside access to the house? A cellar door, anything like that?"

"No," Ella replied. "No cellar, but there is an attic." She nibbled at her thumbnail. "Don't see how anyone could get in there, though. The access door is right here by the kitchen. I'm looking at it. Locked it myself just a while ago."

"Great," the woman replied. "Sounds like everything is as it should be. Just make sure the porch light is on. It will be easier for the officer to find – there are so few houses on your road. But don't worry, I'll stay on the line with you until he gets there." She sipped her coffee. "Tell me about the noises."

Ella walked into the living room, turning on lamps as she went. Nick was right behind her, still clutching his pillow.

"The porch light is on," she said. It illuminated the sheers and drapes at the big picture window. "In fact, almost every light is on." She chuckled self-consciously and then sat on the corner of the sofa. Nick pulled the afghan off the back of the couch and snuggled in beside his mom, listening intently as she told the dispatcher about the thunks and scrapes.

"But you said you checked all your doors and windows, correct?"

"Ye-e-s," Ella admitted, trying not to feel foolish.

"And there's *no* outside access to the attic?"

"No. Not at all." She pictured the outside of the house in her mind. "Well, there is a trellis attached to the house underneath the attic window, but that's all." She tucked Nick's afghan around him a little tighter. "I doubt anyone could climb that old thing."

"I doubt it, too," the dispatcher said. "But I'll bet a raccoon could. In a heartbeat."

Ella looked at Nick and mouthed. "Raccoons."

"Tell me about you and your boy while we wait." The dispatcher's voice was calm, conversational.

Ella began to feel better. There were no more sounds while they waited. She began to think it had been a mistake to call. She told the dispatcher so. "I feel kind of silly for calling. Maybe it *was* a raccoon, or the old house creaking or something. I've always heard that old houses settle."

"Sure," the dispatcher said. "But Unit Six needs a diversion. He was just making rounds, checking doors on businesses and stuff. Why not let him come on out and make certain?"

Of course, she *wanted* him to come and make certain. What if the noises started up again? But she didn't want to seem like *that* woman, the one who called for help every time a gust of wind blew a shutter loose. "Okay," she agreed. "I really would feel better. I just hate to be a bother. I'm sure it's nothing." But even as she said it, she saw her normally independent son glance upward again.

"No bother. It's what we're here for. My name's Marissa, by the way. Lived in Stutter Creek all my life. Husband's a deputy for the county, we can't work together for the city PD, nepotism rules and all that, but we're both in law enforcement, so to speak."

The dispatcher had rambled on and on and before Ella knew it, she heard the crunch of tires on the leafy drive.

She rushed to the front door with Nick clinging to her like a shadow. A police car sat in front of the house with its lights off.

"That's Officer Rodriguez," Marissa said when Ella asked why his lights were off. "He's running dark so as not to alert anyone who might be in the house or in the area."

She spoke into her microphone. "10-4, Unit Six. I'll tell her."

"He says to open the door when he gets there, but don't make any other noise. Just show him the access to the attic."

Ella's heart began to pound again. "Okay, do I – do you – have to hang up?"

"Not at all," the dispatcher replied.

"Thank you." Ella's voice trembled the way Nick's had done earlier. "I feel better with you on the line. If you don't mind."

Marissa made a *pfft* noise. "'Course not. Now, go open that door."

Ella peeked out the window just in time to see the officer stepping onto the porch. She opened the door and smiled timidly.

"Officer Rodriguez," the man said. "Are you Ella Webb?"

Ella nodded.

He smiled and stepped inside. "Show me to the attic."

Nick turned right around and led the way to the stairs. His fright had vanished as soon as Officer Rodriguez walked in with his heavily loaded utility belt. He held a large flashlight in his hand, but it was the gun on his hip that Nick's eyes kept straying toward. Ella had never seen the boy's eyes pop out the way they had when the tall, burly officer entered the room.

Chapter Four

"Right here," Nick said, removing the chair from beneath the doorknob. "I'm the one who woke up first. It sounded like someone walking around up there, or moving furniture or something."

Officer Rodriguez tried to hide a smile, almost succeeded, and then laid his beefy hand on Nick's shoulder. "You wait here, with your mom, so she won't be scared." He winked at Ella and stood aside as she went to the kitchen, got the key, and unlocked the door. "Remain quiet so I can hear, okay?"

Nick nodded vigorously. "Okay," he whispered.

The officer opened the door and mounted the steps. His megawatt flashlight lit up the entire stairwell. "Is there a light switch at the top, to illuminate the attic?"

Ella had to admit that she didn't know. She'd only been in the attic once, and that was the day the realtor had shown her the house. *I won't be coming up here much*, she remembered thinking. It had been dusty and full of cobwebs.

Officer Rodriguez continued up the steps until he reached the top. His wide form filled the narrow staircase. When he stepped off the stairs onto the attic floor, the old boards moaned in protest. Dust motes floated down.

Nick reached over and took her hand.

"Everything all right?"

Ella almost dropped the phone. She'd forgotten all about Marissa on the other end of the line.

"It's fine," she whispered. "Everything's fine so far. The officer just went into the attic. We can hear him walking around."

"Okay," the dispatcher replied. "I'll give him five minutes, and if he doesn't give me the all-clear, I'll send a backup unit."

They take this stuff very seriously, Ella thought. She wasn't sure if that made her feel more secure, or even more frightened. It seemed to validate the possibility that someone really could be up there. Then she thought of the woman called Mrs. Benefield. *Have to find out more about that. Tomorrow, though, not tonight.*

After a minute or two, Ella heard laughter coming from the attic. The sound gave her chills.

Nick moved closer to her, rubbing his corkscrew hair out of his wide eyes. They both leaned over and looked up the stairs. The laughter was accompanied by the sound of boxes being shoved around.

"Marissa, do you hear that?" Ella whispered into the phone.

Before the dispatcher could respond, they saw a tiny flash—as if from a cell phone—and Officer Rodriguez appeared at the top of the stairs wearing a crooked smile.

"Looks like you've got a nest of raccoons—or maybe I should say *had* a nest—I think they're all gone now." He held his phone out when he got to the bottom of the stairs.

Ella and Nick looked closely, but they couldn't see any raccoons.

"Headquarters?" he spoke into his mike.

"Go ahead."

Ella could hear Marissa on the phone and on his radio. It gave her an odd, disjointed feeling.

"I'm going to check the rest of the premises to make sure everything is clear. Go ahead and alert wildlife control to come out in the morning. Need to set some 'coon traps."

"10-4," Marissa replied. "Going back to the regular channel now." She clicked the mic and then spoke into the phone. "Glad it was just a critter or two." Her voice really did sound relieved.

"Thank you," Ella said. "I appreciate you staying with us that way."

"No problem," the dispatcher responded. "Hope we get to meet in person soon. Welcome to Stutter Creek."

Ella laughed and clicked the off button.

Officer Rodriguez was showing Nick the picture on his cell phone. "Not the 'coon, just the spoor," he was saying. "Apparently the critter was shoving boxes around, looking for food or nesting material. Might've been trying to catch a bug for dinner."

"Gross!" Nick's face mirrored his disgust. "I hope they catch them all – I don't think I want to share a house with something like that."

"City boy, huh?" the officer teased. "Just wait till you meet an old raccoon in the wild—do you like to fish?"

Nick shrugged. "I don't really know."

"Well, we'll get you into the PAL program—Police Athletic League—and you'll get to fish, camp, play basketball and more." He looked at Ella. "If it's all right with mom, of course."

"Sure," Ella agreed. "Sounds like fun."

"Great. And trust me, Nick."

The boy looked up at him.

"When you do meet a raccoon in the wild, you'll be amazed at how clean and neat they are." He winked at Ella again. "They like to fish almost as much as me and my daughter, Benita. Even my wife goes—if I'm on duty and can't make it."

He pulled a card from his wallet and gave it to Ella. "Here's the info. No rush, but if you think the boy would be interested. Feel free to contact the station and attend a meeting."

Ella nodded. "Thank you, thanks for everything Officer—"

"Rodriguez. Just call me Rod."

"Okay, Rod." Ella hesitated. "There's one thing I don't understand, though."

He locked the attic door and handed her the key.

"I just don't, I mean I haven't ever..." her voice began to falter. Finally, she blurted out. "Where are they now? Will they keep making noise? Are they going to come down and—"

"—get in the bed with us?" Nick finished.

Officer Rod pushed his hands down on his utility belt as if it had a tendency to ride up. Then he grinned. "I'm sorry. I didn't explain that very well, did I?" He motioned toward the attic door. "The critters apparently go in and out through a broken vent that leads onto the roof. I found a hole and pushed an old trunk up against it." He swiped at a line of gray dust on his uniform pants. "They won't be back tonight. Then tomorrow, Chet Boone from wildlife control will set some humane traps to catch them, when, and if they return." He looked at Nick. "Then he'll take them off to the woods where they belong."

Ella pulled Nick to her side. "We're so grateful for all this." Not knowing what else to do, she held out her hand.

The officer took it, and they shook formally. She couldn't quite meet his eye. In the back of her mind she was thinking, it's too good to be true. People don't act like this—don't care about strangers this way—I must still be dreaming.

But Officer Rodriguez wasn't finished. He went on through the house checking every window and door to make sure they were still locked. He even let Nick use his flashlight as they checked under the beds and in the closets.

Before he left, he told them to call if they heard anything else.

"Oh," he said as he prepared to leave, "one more thing."

Ella looked up at him. *What else could he possibly do that hadn't been done already?* "Yes?"

"Be sure to contact your landlord to see about getting that broken vent replaced."

Ella nodded and assured him she would.

After they watched Officer Rod climb back into his car and flash his emergency lights—for Nick's benefit, Ella suspected—she closed and bolted the front door and looked at her son. "Hungry?"

Nick nodded.

It was three a.m. Ella knew they should go straight back to bed, but she was too keyed up. She was certain Nick felt the same way.

She poured cold milk and they sat together at the kitchen table sharing another brownie. "It's been an exciting day," she said. "But I think I can go back to sleep now, don't you?"

Nick shrugged. "Maybe. I'm sure glad tomorrow's Saturday so we don't have to get up."

Ella laughed. "Me, too, kiddo. Me, too."

She rinsed their glasses in the sink and set them in the red plastic drain board to dry. "I'm going to brush my teeth." She gave him a look that said he should do the same. "Then I'll come and tuck you in again."

Nick nodded, but made no move to go.

The little attic staircase was just off the kitchen in the hallway.

Ella placed the attic door key back on the kitchen windowsill so she wouldn't lose it, and then turned out the kitchen light. On second thought, she walked over to the old fashioned stove and turned on the appliance light under the vent-a-hood. It gave the room a soft, cheery glow.

Without a word, Nick dragged the same red kitchen chair over and propped it under the attic doorknob like before. Then he turned and headed for the bathroom with Ella right behind.

They both gave their teeth a cursory going over and then she accompanied him to his room—again.

"There," she said, patting the comforter around his neck after she'd tucked him back into his cozy bed. His room wasn't completely unpacked either, but the first thing he'd done was taped up his poster of Drew Brees, the quarterback. Then he'd placed his football trophy on the tall chest of drawers opposite his bed. He'd been so proud when his team won the championship. It had been his first—and only—season to play.

Ella looked at the snug room. A blue hooked rug and plaid curtains added a masculine touch, and the moonlight still managed to peek inside as if to see what all the fuss was about.

"Could you sit for a while?" he asked. "Like before?"

It had really unnerved him, she thought. It was hard to keep in mind that he was still a little boy—he tried to appear so independent.

"Sure," she said. "Mind if I just lie down here beside you?" She yawned unexpectedly. "Guess it's catching up with me, too."

Nick scooted over. "Thanks, Mom." He folded back the comforter just the way she'd done earlier when he'd appeared at her bed.

She was thankful he was still her little boy. They'd always been close, her being a single parent, but the last couple of years with Anson had almost been their undoing. Their relationship had suffered—temporarily.

"I'm glad it was just a raccoon," Nick murmured.

"Me, too," Ella replied. "I guess I need to buy some dust masks so I can get up there and clean out the mess."

Nick didn't reply. He was already drifting away again.

Her mood lightened. *Maybe it will be okay. Maybe this town can heal us.* She recalled how kind everyone had been, and she was grateful. *Have to call Mom tomorrow and tell her all about it.*

She was nearly asleep when the sounds began again.

Are you kidding me?

Her eyes popped open and she lay staring at the ceiling.

Clunk.

Swish.

She glanced sideways at Nick to see if he'd awakened. He was still sleeping.

Did I imagine it? Maybe I dozed and was beginning to drea—

Clunk.

Swi-i-sh.

The cardboard boxes seemed to be moving around again.

She pushed aside the comforter and sat up. Swinging her legs over the edge of the bed, she prepared to stand when something *THUNKED* on the ceiling.

"Mom?" Nick's voice was muffled.

She looked over and saw only the top of his head sticking out of the bedclothes. "It's okay, baby," she soothed. "Go back to sleep."

"They're back, aren't they?"

Ella sighed. "I think they are. That last one sounded like the Big Mamou, didn't it?"

Nick giggled at their old joke—a hand-me-down from his Nana's Cajun family—and pulled his head out from under the covers. "At least they aren't ghosts. Right?"

"Right." Ella gritted her teeth and glanced up at the ceiling. *Raccoons. That loud? Surely the officer knew what he was talking about. Maybe I should have gone up and looked around with him. Inspected it for myself. Now, I either call them back, or put up with it until daylight.*

She crept to the bedroom door, closed it, and stuck Nick's desk chair beneath the knob.

Clunk.

Swi-i-sh.

Ridiculous, she thought. *A whole nest of raccoons.* Officer Rod must not have seen all of them. And then another, darker thought struck her. *What if it isn't raccoons? What if it is some kind of haunting? What if this is the reason the house was so affordable?*

She rechecked the lock on the one bedroom window—it was secure—then she twisted it and raised the window an inch or two, to make certain it wasn't painted shut in case they had to have an exit. Satisfied that they weren't trapped, she closed it, relocked it, and pulled the curtain back into place.

There was nothing more she could do without making another phone call or going into the attic herself, so she grabbed a pillow, crushed it into a new shape, and lay back on the bed beside her dozing son.

Ella knew she would never go back to sleep now.

Clunk.

And she really wished she hadn't left her hammer in the kitchen.

She turned on the ceiling fan and was eventually lulled back into an uneasy slumber by the hum of the blades slicing through the bedroom air.

Raccoons. Who would have thought?

Chapter Five

"Hello, Viola." Anson's voice was curt as he stepped past her into the house.

Her face registered shock. "You're not supposed to be here. I thought you were in jail."

He walked right on through the foyer into the living room. "Yeah, well, I got out. Good time and all that. Overcrowding, the judge released a bunch of us non-violent offenders."

"Non-violent my ass," Viola Webb said. "I saw what you did to little Nicky, and to Ella." Her eyes flashed with anger. "And just because some judge or politician let you out, that doesn't mean you can come in here, trespassing."

She walked casually toward the end table where her cell phone rested in its charger.

Anson saw where she was headed and placed himself between her and the table. He appeared even brawnier and harder than he did before. The glint in his eye was unmistakable; it matched his new physique. Viola had testified at his hearing. Apparently, he held a grudge.

"So where are they?" he asked. "Where are my wife and child?"

Viola walked right up to him. The top of her white-haired head barely reached his chin. "Nicky isn't yours, never has been. Everyone knows you never liked him—resented him, I'd say—and Ella is no longer tied to you, legally or otherwise." She got as close to him as she dared. If he hit her, perhaps that would be enough to put him back in jail. She thought it might. No matter what he said, she had a feeling he was probably on parole or probation. "Now, get out of my house. You're not welcome here." She tried to keep the tremble out of her voice, but the fact that he was here in the middle of the afternoon, so unafraid, made her even more nervous than if he'd snuck inside in the middle of the night.

Anson reached behind him and scooped the little cell phone up and flipped it open.

"Give me that!" Viola cried. "You have no business—" She reached for it and he dropped it into his other hand.

His face showed his enjoyment at his little game of keep-away.

But Viola didn't grab for it the way he expected. Instead, she turned and headed for the front door. She was outmatched and she knew it.

She heard his boots on the linoleum and glanced back to find that he'd strode off into the kitchen, probably checking to see if Ella or Nick were hiding there.

Viola hesitated, and then decided she wasn't going to play *any* games.

She hurried out the front door and dashed across the street to her friend's house where she dialed nine-one-one and told them there was an intruder in her home. She was pretty sure the restraining order against him was still valid. At least, she hoped it was. If so, that might be enough to violate his parole or whatever. Hard to believe he was already out. The order had said he couldn't come within five hundred feet of her house because that's where Ella and Nicky had wound up after he had slapped them around.

She watched anxiously from behind Laura's locked front door.

She never saw him leave, but when the cops arrived, Anson was long gone. The officer took a brief statement and then he and his backup officer went straight across and into Viola's house.

No one was there, but the back door, which Viola always kept locked, was wide open.

"And you didn't see him leave?" the officer asked after coming back across the street.

"Most certainly not." Viola looked at her friend. "And we didn't leave our post for a second." She looked down at the floor. "I was half afraid he was going to come over here after me."

The officer shook his head. "Do you want to stay here tonight? Or shall I accompany you back to your house?"

Viola looked at her friend.

"You know you're welcome to stay with me," Laura said. "I don't think I'd feel comfortable you staying over there alone after that monster walked right in."

Viola made her mouth into a thin line. "Be damned if I'll let him scare me! Did he take my cell phone?"

The officer looked at his partner. "Think I saw one on the kitchen table, did you?"

The pretty blonde nodded. "Sure did," she agreed. "He must have gone right past the table, out the back door and down the alley. Probably had his car waiting at the end of the block." She looked at Viola carefully. "Any chance you recall what sort of car he used to drive—when he was married to your daughter?"

Viola made a sound of disgust. "Drove her Jeep mostly. Had an old beater pickup, Dodge I think, blue and white. But it didn't run half the time. What my girl ever saw in him, I'll never know." She left Laura's house still tsking and shaking her head. At the bottom of the porch, she turned back. "Thanks for helping me out, gal." She winked. "I'll be calling you later if I get scared."

"I'll have the Smirnoff ready," Laura promised. They laughed together the way only old friends can.

When she picked up her cell phone, she was surprised to find it all in one piece. "Guess he didn't find what he was looking for," she told the female officer. Both officers had accompanied her back to her house. They patiently went through every room with her to make sure he wasn't hiding under a bed or in a closet. They even pulled down the stairs and went into the attic, though how he could possibly have gone there and then pulled the fold-outs up after him was beyond anyone's guess.

All in all, they did a very thorough search.

"I'm just glad I don't keep Ella's name in my cell phone contacts list. I was proud of myself for actually remembering to add the new numbers at all."

"What do you mean?" the first officer asked, surprised.

"Oh, her numbers are in there," Viola explained. "But not under her name. I simply listed both numbers in Business Contacts under Floral Shop, because Ella lives on Lilac Lane." She laughed at their bemused expressions. "Well, I have to have some clue to remind me where it is. I'm no spring chicken, you know."

They all shared another laugh, and then one of the officers got a call on the radio telling him the search had come back and Viola was right. Anson was out on probation.

"Well, he came in my house uninvited," she said. "Isn't that against the law? Doesn't that violate probation? I know it violates that restraining order Ella had."

The female officer nodded. "He had no right coming into your home. Soon as we find him, he's going right back to jail. Probation violation. We can't use the old restraining order since your daughter doesn't live here anymore."

Viola nodded and the officers prepared to leave. They promised her they would make extra tours through her neighborhood throughout the night as well as checking through the DMV files to see if they could determine what kind of vehicle he might own now.

"Much appreciated," she said. "I wish you could have seen him. The big bully!"

"We'll keep our eyes open," the blonde officer promised again. "And don't hesitate to call if you need us."

Viola said she would, and then she thanked them again. She made certain to lock the deadbolt behind them.

"Big old bully," she muttered again. She turned on the TV and drew the shades. "Just glad he didn't find out where Ella and Nicky have gone."

Guess I'd better call and tell her he's out. She picked up the phone and started to press the number listed under Floral Shop. Then she hesitated. There's no way he can find them in Stutter Creek. She left here without telling anyone, but me, just the way the attorney told her to do.

She put the cell phone down without pressing the number.

Let them live in peace awhile longer. He can't find them. He has no idea where to look.

Chapter Six

"'Morning." The man stepping out of his truck was tall and lanky. His black hair curved over the edge of his collar as if in need of a trim.

Ella carefully placed her mug of coffee on the wide porch rail. "G'morning," she replied. "You must be the wildlife wrangler."

In less than half a dozen long strides, he covered the distance from his truck to the place where she sat admiring the cool, fall morning.

"That's me," he said. "Chet Boone, critter wrangler." The patch on his khaki sleeve read Wildlife Biologist. His eyes were deep-ocean blue.

When he grinned, Ella felt something in her chest loosen up. It was like rounding the last curve on a roller coaster, knowing the ride was almost over. Or touching down on the runway after a bumpy flight. Or nearing the last turn before coming home from a long, arduous journey.

"Pleased to meet you." She held out her coffee-warmed palm. "Thanks for coming out on a Saturday."

He laughed. "Wildlife doesn't recognize weekends." He held up a pair of wire cages he had plucked from the bed of his truck. "I'll place a couple of these in the attic, bait them with dried fish—less smelly than fresh—and then we'll relocate this little family so you can rest easy."

"Sounds good." Ella opened the front door. "I'll show you where to go." She stepped inside. "My son is still sleeping. They came back, you know. After Officer Rodriguez was here last night. He thought he had them blocked out with a trunk, but somehow, they got back in."

Chet shook his head. "Officer Rod might have blocked one of them *in* the attic while blocking the others out. Raccoons are very active at night, and once they claim a place, it's really difficult to get them to move on."

They'd arrived at the attic door.

Ella went into the kitchen to get the key off the window ledge, then she unlocked the door. She'd removed the chair earlier. It seemed silly in the daylight. And she didn't want to make that kind of impression on the wildlife officer.

Now that she'd met him, she was very glad she'd removed it.

"There's a light switch at the top of the stairs," she said. "Do you want a flashlight, too?"

Chet smiled and produced a small one from his breast pocket. "Just like the Boy Scouts, always prepared. But thanks." He picked up the traps and started up the stairs. "Might think about installing a light switch down here at the bottom, too," he said. "These old houses don't always have all the conveniences, but that's more like a necessity if you ask me."

Ella nodded. "That would make sense, wouldn't it? I'll ask the landlord about it when I call to tell her about the broken vent."

"Is it Charlie Long? She owns quite a few rentals on this side of Copper Lake. If it's Charlie, tell her I'll do the repairs. If that's okay." He glanced down at her from the middle of the stairs. "I do home remodeling and repair on my off-days." His blue gaze was electric. It illuminated the narrow stairway more than any flashlight could have.

"Sure. Sounds great," Ella mumbled, running a hand through her choppy morning hair. "I'll do that." She dashed toward the bathroom and gave herself a once over. *No makeup. Sleep-scrubbed hair. Shadows under her eyes. In other words—normal.* She headed back to the kitchen for another cup of coffee. *Oh well, he's probably married anyhow. And what do I care? Just got out of one sorry relationship.* She was actually surprised that her thoughts even went down that road. After she'd made her escape from Anson, she was pretty certain she'd never want to get close to a man again. Or let a man get close to Nick, either. *But those eyes. And that wide-open grin. As if he had nothing to hide, and never would.*

Nick strolled into the kitchen in his pajamas. "I heard you talking to someone."

Ella nodded and poured him a small glass of orange juice, the pulpy kind. He was a strange kid. "The wildlife guy is here. He's up in the attic already."

Nick's eyes widened. "And you didn't even wake me?" He gulped his juice, handed the glass back to his mom, and then dashed to his room.

Ella heard him rummaging through his hastily arranged dresser drawers. Next, she heard the clink of wire hangers as he pulled jeans from his closet. In moments, he was back, completely dressed.

"Breakfast?" she asked.

He shook his head. "Okay if I go up?" His right foot was on the bottom stair.

Ella shrugged. "I guess so. Just ask Mr. Boone if it's all right. I don't want you in the way. Who *knows* how raccoons act if they feel cornered?"

Nick nodded and proceeded slowly up the stairs. "Mr. Boone," he called. "It's me, Nick. I'm coming up if that's okay."

Ella couldn't hear his exact reply, but it must have been affirmative because Nick continued up the stairs.

Every now and then, she could hear them talking in a low voice. Ella hoped it was really okay for Nick to be up there. She knew from experience that some men did not like to be interrupted when they were working. A slice of memory from her past breached the surface of her mind. Anson was sanding down an interior door that kept dragging on the carpet. Nick was seven. He wanted to help his new stepfather do everything. He was so delighted to have a man in the house. His grandfather's recent death had hit him very hard.

She had been in the kitchen, making lunch when, out of the blue, he had run back to his bedroom in tears. When she followed, to find out what was wrong, Nicky wouldn't say. It wasn't until several days later that she learned Anson had scolded him and told him to "get the hell out of the way."

That had been one of the first red flags.

She'd tried and tried to recall if there had been any beer drinking that day. Anson didn't always drink, but when he did, he didn't seem to have a brake.

The boy had avoided his stepdad for weeks after that.

When she finally told her mother about it, the older woman had tried to be positive. She hadn't wanted Ella to marry Anson. She felt they hadn't known each other long enough, but since they'd gone ahead, she tried to see the best in him.

"It's hard to regain the trust of someone who falls off the pedestal," her mom had said about the incident and the way Nick avoided Anson.

"I hope that's all it is," Ella said.

But even then, she had suspected there was more to it.

Unfortunately, she'd been right.

"Well," Chet spoke, coming down the stairs. "We've got evidence of a couple of critters that have been living the highlife in your attic." He glanced back at Nick, who was coming down behind him. "They've got a pretty good sized hole around two vents. Officer Rodriguez covered one, but he probably didn't see the other."

"I've got some plywood and mesh screens in my truck." He walked past Ella to the front door. "I can repair them temporarily, but I'll need to get the landlord's permission to repair the drywall and replace the vents. Nick is going to help me if that's all right with you?"

"I know right where Mom keeps the hammer." Nick grinned.

Ella whacked him lightly on the shoulder. "Of course, he can help," she said. "I'll whip up some pancakes for you men when you're through."

Nick practically glowed when she said "you men." He was just at the age where he was beginning to test his mettle—and her borders.

"Neighbor! Oh, neighbor!" The shrill voice cut into the soft morning like a rusty saw into a sapling.

"Hey, there," Chet replied, setting the plywood and screens on the ground near his truck.

The elderly woman in a pink bathrobe climbed out of her ancient Pontiac and approached them gingerly.

"I noticed a new family moving in." She stopped right in front of Chet and peered up into his face. "But I couldn't tell who was who, with all the comings and goings. Are you the man of the house?"

Chet smiled and shook his head. "Sorry, just the visiting repairman." He held out his hand apologetically.

The old woman looked at him suspiciously. "Thought I saw the cops here last night. Wanted to come by and talk about that."

Ella had exited the house by then. She stood on the porch, unsure if she wanted to engage this person or not. There was something decidedly off about anyone who would drive up to a new neighbor's house wearing a robe and fuzzy slippers, not to mention two or three pink foam curlers at the edge of her hairline.

Didn't know they still made those things, she thought.

"Well," the older woman continued. "I see that you are doing some work and I just wondered since you seem to be so handy, if you would stop by my place." She turned and pointed at the two story barely visible through the trees. "Boys," she said. "In my attic."

Ella flinched. *Did I hear that correctly?* She hopped down off the porch and strode toward the woman. "Mrs…?" She held out her hand.

The elderly woman simply looked at her for a moment. Then she seemed to understand. She grasped Ella's hand. "Benefield," she said. "Barbara Benefield. You the lady of the house?"

Ella gave the hand a brief shake and then released it. She fought the urge to wipe her palm against the leg of her jeans. The woman's hand was dusty—or perhaps it was powder. "Yes," she admitted. "I'm your new neighbor." She looked around for Nick. "And this is my son, Nick. Now, what were you saying about your attic?" The dispatcher's comment from the night before played through her mind.

Mrs. Benefield looked her up and down. "Well, I saw you had the police here last night, and I wondered…" She craned her head around and glanced over her shoulder toward her own house.

Ella saw Nick following her glance, his eyes wide as cupcakes.

The woman lowered her voice. "Was it boys?" She spared a quick glance at Nick. "Were those boys in your attic, too?"

Ella shook her head. "No, no, no. There *were* noises in our attic, but it turns out a family of raccoons has been living there. That's why Mr. Boone is here." She stopped and examined the older woman's face to make sure she understood. "Mr. Boone is the wildlife biologist for the wildlife refuge in the state park."

Mrs. Benefield sniffed and patted her curlers. "Oh, I see." She turned her nose up. "Well, I just hope you get them all out, because if your house is like mine," she glared up at the obviously much lower roofline of Ella and Nick's rental, "and I happen to know that it is, then you probably have boys in your attic, too."

She spun on her fluffy heels and stalked back to her Pontiac where she immediately lit up a cigarette and stomped down on the gas pedal.

She'd left the car running, so when she tromped the gas and slipped the gearshift into drive, the car fishtailed in the loose dirt until the balding tires grabbed hold and she shot across the road in a wide U-turn.

Ella, Nick, and Chet Boone were left coughing and waving away the fine red rooster-tail of dust her tires had sprayed into the air.

"What the—" Nick began.

Ella just looked stunned.

"Don't worry about her," Chet said. "Everyone in Stutter Creek knows Mrs. Benefield lost her only son forty years ago. Tragic drowning. Now, she has a touch of dementia, and every so often she is convinced Benny and his friends are in the old attic playroom, playing marbles."

"Oh my God," Ella breathed. She wished Nick hadn't heard all that. "But she didn't seem to recognize you at all."

Chet shrugged sadly. "Part of the dementia, I suppose. Sometimes she does, sometimes she doesn't." He picked up the plywood and squares of wire mesh and started back to the front door. Ella caught herself staring at the way his dark hair barely kissed the collar of his khaki uniform shirt.

She closed her eyes and took a breath. "But, do you suppose she just has raccoons, too? Could that be the problem?"

"Could be," he said. "I'm sure it's been checked, but even so. It wouldn't hurt to check again, would it?" He continued on into the house, leaving her and Nick in the front yard.

Nick was standing by the truck, looking toward the old woman's house in disbelief. All that was visible from their front yard was the very tip of the roof.

To Ella's knowledge, Nick had never known anyone with dementia or Alzheimer's. Her mom and dad were his only grandparents, since his biological father had wanted nothing to do with him—and his Granddad, Ella's father, had died of heart failure when Nick was just about to turn seven.

Not surprisingly, Anson had not had a good relationship with his parents. In fact, she and Nicky had never even met them.

Have to have a talk with him about senile dementia later. She squeezed his shoulder and enticed him to follow her to the house. *Boys in the attic,* she thought. *That's just creepy.*

From the stairway, they could both hear Chet Boone whistling a tune. "Where's my helper?" he called as if on cue. "I could sure use some assistance up here."

Nick broke from his mom's gentle grasp and hurried toward the stairs. "Be right there," he called.

Ella headed straight into the kitchen. She was determined to find out more about Mrs. Benefield. If the poor woman was that far gone, shouldn't someone be staying with her?

Chet and Nick came clomping down the stairs a half hour later.

"That didn't take long," Ella said. She'd taken the opportunity to brush her hair and teeth and put on a dab of blush. She hoped Nick wouldn't notice. He was apt to say anything. Never knew what might come out of that boy's mouth.

"Hey, Mom," he began.

Ella thought his tone sounded questioning, so she quickly changed the track—she could just imagine him saying *Hey, Mom, why'd you go put on makeup, you never wear makeup?*

"Hey, Nick," she called right back. "How many pancakes, three, four, five?" She smiled when she said it, but she hoped it was enough to steer him away from whatever he'd been about to ask.

"Yeah, four sounds good," he replied. "Hey, Mom?"

She quirked an eyebrow at him.

"Mind if I go over to Mrs. Benefield's with Mr. Boone? He's gonna go ahead and check her attic while he's here."

That wasn't what she expected to hear. "Oh, I don't know," she answered, uncertainty clouding her face. "I'm not sure a little boy should actually go up into her attic since she already thinks they're up there, playing."

Chet Boone nodded. "Your mom's right," he agreed. "I never thought of that. Tell you what." He sat down in one of the red kitchen chairs and looked Nick in the eye. "I'll stop back by when I leave there, tell you what I find. Okay?"

Nick's face fell, but he nodded.

Such a good boy, Ella thought. *Always has been such a good boy.*

"Stay for breakfast?" She pointed the spatula at the skillet where the first of the pancakes were bubbling.

He inhaled deeply. "Don't mind if I do. Four sounds good to me, too."

Ella laughed and took down another coffee cup. She had seen the way he looked at Nick, and she wondered if he was staying just to make him feel better.

She walked over and ruffled her son's hair. "Proud of you," she whispered. "I've seen so many kids pout and throw a fit when they don't get their way. But not my Nicky."

He looked up at his mom and smiled a tiny smile. "Thanks," he said. His self-esteem had taken quite a hit when they'd lived with Anson. But it had been a month or two after they had him arrested before Ella found out the full extent of the verbal abuse that had been going on. She didn't learn about most of it until after Anson actually went to jail. Then Nick felt safe enough to tell her about the name-calling and verbal threats.

She felt tears building behind her eyes. Not for her. Anger had cured her years ago. These tears were for her boy. He'd lost part of his childhood, possibly part of himself, too. And there was no getting it back. What's worse, I let it happen, she thought. That's what always brought on the tears—the knowledge that not only had she not stopped it, she'd actually caused it, in a roundabout way, by marrying that piece of human garbage.

Now Nicky seems to latch on to every man that comes along, searching for a real father figure, or something. She thought of the way he'd tried to please Officer Rodriguez, and now, Chet Boone. He tried so hard to get into their good graces, because he never could with Anson, no matter what he did or how well he behaved.

"Be a man," Anson always said when Nicky got hurt, or cried because he was sick with fever or throwing up. "Oh,

for God's sake, just try to be a man. Not a crybaby." Even
the time Nick had fallen off the fence and broke his finger,
Anson had insisted it wasn't broken. "It's only a four-foot
fence," he'd bellowed. "He's just a mama's boy. You've
spoiled him and turned him into a little crybaby." Ella had
taken Nick to the ER herself.

When they'd returned with his finger splinted and his
pupils big as moons from the painkillers, Anson had simply
laughed and started drinking. He never said a word about
how wrong he'd been or how sorry he was. He just went on
a three-day binge and didn't come home.

Ella stood at the stove; the heat from the gas burners
almost as hot as the guilt that engulfed her like a forest fire.

Flipping the pancakes, she tried to clear her mind of all
the ugly, threatening emails, text messages, and phone calls
she'd received from Anson when he was out on bail,
awaiting trial. She'd had the restraining order, of course, but
every now and then, she'd get up in the morning and see
him sitting in his truck down the street, staring at the house,
just out of reach of the law.

A bout of boyish laughter brought her back to the
present. She turned just in time to see a folded triangle of
paper—corner of a napkin, no doubt—go flying over the
"goal post" hands of Chet Boone.

"Score!" Chet crowed. He looked up at her as if to say,
"*sorry for the noise, but we're having a game here.*"

Ella smiled and turned back to the stove. She slid the
first batch of pancakes onto a plate and stuck it in the "low
heat" oven to stay warm. Soon, she had a second batch
ready, along with a couple for her, too.

"Ta-dah." She set the plates on the table with a flourish.
"I assume you boys have washed up, right?"

Chet made the silliest face. "Race you to the can," he said.

Nick was momentarily flummoxed. No one they knew called the bathroom the can. When it dawned on him what the can was, he leapt from his chair and rushed down the hall, Chet right on his heels.

Ella scooped pats of butter onto the pancakes and tried to turn off the suspicious nature of her mind, but it was too late. The rat was out of its cage and now it was going to run the labyrinth whether she wanted it to, or not.

Too good to be true, her mind insisted. *No one bonds with a kid that quickly. Why would a grown man take up with her son so quickly? Should I put a stop to it now? Is he a God-forbid, child predator? Wouldn't that be the icing on the friggin' cake?* And last but not least, *I won't let him get hurt again. Not by anyone!*

Nick arrived back at the table, out of breath, hands slightly drippy. Ella couldn't help herself; she smiled as she poured his milk into his favorite jelly glass. It had come from Nana's house and was about fifty years old, but her mom had insisted he bring it. "He needs roots," she'd said. "Needs to know I'm always here, too."

Ella wasn't sure how an old jelly jar helped one put down roots, but her mom had been right, Nick cherished the glass. He would hardly drink out of anything else. Ella felt bad that her mom was right, again. But that was also part of the problem. One of them was just as stubborn as the other. She was definitely her mother's daughter.

Right then and there, she decided that no matter how attractive Chet Boone was—and boy, was he *ever*—she was going to keep him away from her little Nick. She couldn't take a chance on some other guy screwing up his self-esteem the way Anson had done. Not when they were just getting back to normal.

"Okay, children," she said, eliciting a look of pure chagrin from Chet, "it's time to sit down at the table and have our breakfast like grownups."

"Yes, ma'am," Nick replied.

"Yes, ma'am," Chet echoed, a note of comedy in his tone.

Ella could barely keep her face straight as she said Grace. "Dear Lord, thank you for these thy gifts, and for all our many blessings." Before she could say Amen, Nick tacked on: "And for our new friends in our new home."

"Amen," they all said together.

Ella looked at him in awe. If only it were that simple. If only everyone really was what they appeared to be.

The guys dug in and polished off the pancakes in record time. Ella examined Chet's hands as he ate. No wedding ring. Not even a lighter place where one might have resided. She saw nothing but strong brown fingers and wiry black hairs peeking out from the edge of his long sleeved shirt.

I was certain he would be married like Officer Rodriguez. That would make everything so much easier.

When they were done, Nick scraped his plate and placed it in the sink. He ran hot water and added a few drops of fragrant, Dawn dish detergent. He'd always been her best dishwasher. It was something they'd enjoyed doing together. One more thing Anson had chided him about, women's work he called it, pretending he was only teasing.

Chet Boone stood and copied Nick's movements, easing his scraped plate into the hot water, too. Then he opened the top drawer and took out a fresh dishtowel—*how did he know they were in there?*—and began to rinse and dry while Nicky washed.

Ella cleaned off the table and swept the floor. Surreal, she thought. This is just surreal.

In moments, the critter catcher was headed toward the front door. "I'll stop back by after I've checked on Mrs. Benefield." His voice was as warm as his personality.

Why isn't he married? Ella wondered. What's wrong with him?

"That's great." She walked out onto the porch with him. "So kind of you."

"Least I can do." He had one long leg already in the Park Department truck. "Thanks for the best breakfast I've had in months." He grinned. "But don't tell Martha down at The Drugstore I said that. She's been my cook for years."

They all laughed. She could hear the confusion in Nick's laugh, but he was too polite to ask about it now. Ella knew she'd get the third degree later, though.

Ella and Nick were getting ready to go into town when the Park Department truck pulled up again.

She could have gone out to meet him, but she sort of enjoyed just watching him. *Admit it, girl. You're intrigued.* She didn't think they made nice guys like him anymore. Besides, she liked the way he climbed out of the truck and took the porch steps two at a time. He had the longest legs.

"Mom!" Nick's voice was petulant.

She dropped the curtain and stepped away from the window guiltily. "Sorry, honey. Were you saying something?"

"I was just asking if we were going to leave before Mr. Boo—"

Bing bong

Nick looked at the front door. "Never mind." He ran to open it.

Ella wanted to yank him back, ask him why he'd suddenly forgotten the rule about never opening the door unless she said it was okay, but it was too late. He already had it open and Chet Boone was stepping inside.

"Ma'am," he said, hat in hand. "Just wanted to let you know that I did check Mrs. Benefield's attic and it's as tight as a drum. No sign of critters anywhere." He chuckled. "Now she claims she never even had any children, much less any boys in the attic."

Ella shook her head. "That's just sad, doesn't she have any family who could stay with her?"

He shrugged. "Her neighbor on the other side, Floyd Jenkins, checks on her every day. He's an old bachelor, never married. She usually calls him if anything goes wrong."

Nick was looking back and forth from one to the other as if they were speaking Greek. Then he said, "I'll bet she's lonely."

From the mouths of babes, Ella thought. She noticed how he smoothed his screwy hair down self-consciously. "You're probably right, kiddo. But you know, not everyone likes to have people around all the time—"

"That's true," Chet Boone agreed. "Probably why Floyd Jenkins never married."

Ella peered at his face. She wanted to ask him if that's why he wasn't married, but, of course, that was none of her business. She brushed a wisp of her own hair off her cheek and felt her face redden at the very thought of questioning him about his personal life.

"Well, I've got a few more errands to run." He looked at Ella. "Just tell Charlie to give me a call if she wants me to go ahead and repair the vents." Then he seemed to have second thoughts. He reached into his breast pocket, pulled out a business card and handed it to her. "Or you can call me after you talk to her."

Ella examined the card. It was cream colored with the black silhouettes of deer, bear, raccoons, and other wildlife scattered across the top. Below the images, his home and cell numbers were listed.

She tucked the card into her pants pocket and nodded.

He smiled and stepped off the porch. "See ya soon, Nicky-boy." He gave them both a little wave before climbing up into the truck.

In moments, he was gone and the two of them were left standing on the porch with their mouths open. No one had ever called him Nicky-boy before.

Except for her.

Chapter Seven

"Hello, dears," Martha called out when they walked through the door of The Drugstore. She immediately found snowy white aprons for both of them. Nick didn't even grimace when she looped the strings around his middle and tied it in front like a real waiter. It hung almost to the tops of his shoes.

"Ever waited tables?" she asked.

He shook his head, eyes big. "But I've watched Mom do it plenty of times." He smiled at Ella. "And now that we're the owners, I will help out so she doesn't have to do that anymore."

Ella chuckled sheepishly. He'd really taken their little chat to heart.

Martha just smiled. "Right now is our slow time, between breakfast and lunch, but later, there'll be plenty for you to do even if you don't wind up waiting on customers. There's always stocking and prep work and cleaning—always so much cleaning—and taking out the garbage—"

Nick's eyes grew larger and larger as she ticked off the chores that had to be done on a daily basis. "But I have to go to school sometime."

Both women laughed and Nick realized she was only speaking in general terms.

His mom patted his shoulder. "How about an old fashioned soda? That's something I need to learn how to do right away." She looked at Martha. "I understand it's a big draw for tourists."

Martha nodded as she waddled back behind the counter. "Come around and get started. No time like the present to learn something new."

"Me too?" Nick asked. He'd hesitated to go behind the counter because even though he'd often sat at a booth doing his homework at the Kettle Restaurant where his mom waited tables back home, he'd never been allowed to go behind the counter or in the kitchen.

"Oh, my yes," Martha answered. "You and your mom own this place now. Not only are you allowed behind the counter, I think it's sort of a requirement."

Ella hugged the older woman in a little side hug. It was just so wonderful the way everyone seemed to treat Nick like an equal even though he was only ten years old. Back home (*there you go again, there is no back home, this is home*) he was ignored or tolerated, except for Nana. She often went overboard to make up for the way he was treated by his stepfather.

After an hour of pulling handles and measuring syrups—Martha kept all the soda recipes in a flip book with laminated pages—Ella thought she was getting the hang of making the drinks. Even Nick enjoyed trying his hand at the foamy concoctions.

"Now," Martha instructed, drawing a glass for herself. "Let's have ourselves a little snack and a drink while we go over some housekeeping chores."

"Housekeeping?" Nick moaned.

Martha waved her hand at him. "Not *real* housekeeping, that's just my word for the bare bones of running this place."

"I have so much to learn," Ella said, drawing a root beer for Nick and one for herself.

Martha brought homemade rolls and butter to the table. "Seems fall is the time for homemade bread," she alleged. "And cookies. But for cookies we'd need milk and we've already got our soft drinks."

Ella laughed. "I can see we think alike in that respect. Our sweet neighbor, Norma, came by with homemade brownies yesterday. She even helped us with some boxes and things. But I couldn't eat one until I bought some milk."

Martha nodded, buttering a roll as she spoke. "Oh, yes, Norma is a good one. When her man is out of town on one of his runs—which is three weeks out of the month—she often pops in for a sandwich or bowl of chili." She passed the roll to Nick and took another for Ella. "You'll find yourself getting acquainted with pretty much everyone here in Stutter Creek. At one point or another, everyone stops by for a soda or cup of coffee in the winter."

"I can't wait to take over," Ella said, biting into the warm, buttery bread. "But I am so grateful to you for staying on and helping us learn the ropes."

Martha smiled. "Oh, it's a blessing to me. As soon as you get Nick enrolled and started in school, you can start opening up in the mornings." She rolled her expressive eyes heavenward. "I can't *tell* you how much I'm looking forward to that."

Ella giggled. "I'm enrolling him Monday. What time should I be here to open?"

Martha shook her head. "Why not get him settled in first, then on Tuesday you can meet me here at six-thirty. We open at seven-thirty for breakfast, but it takes that long to get everything ready."

"I can help," Nick piped up. "I can come in with you and have my breakfast here. Help you guys get everything ready. Right, Mom?" His expression was a bit worried. "I mean. You won't leave me home alone, will you?"

Ella shook her head. "Of course I won't. But maybe we should tell Martha why you don't feel comfortable staying at the house alone."

"I'm all ears," Martha said. "I hope it's nothing bad."

Ella looked across the table at her son. "Not too bad, but there for a bit, we were certain we'd inherited a ghost."

"Oh, my." She put her roll down and raised her glass. "Raccoons, right?"

Nick and Ella just looked at each other.

"How'd you know?" he asked bluntly.

Martha grinned. "I've lived here a long time. I know that the wooded area where you live is a haven for those little bandits. I hope you got someone to come out and set some traps."

Ella saw her opening. "Actually, yes. Officer Rodriguez came out in the middle of the night when we were certain someone was walking around in the attic—"

"And then he turned around and called Chet Boone, our local critter catcher, right?"

Ella and Nick looked at each other again. She shook her head. This small town life was going to take some getting used to. "That's exactly right," Ella said. "And he's even going to do some home repair up in the attic. Seems like they had a couple of holes up there. Which reminds me. I've got to call Charlie, the realtor, and make sure this is all okay."

"Oh, she'll be okay with it," Martha said. "Anything Chet wants, Charlie does. Been that way for years, since they were in high school together."

Ella bit her lip. She'd been wishing for an opening to ask about the attractive wildlife biologist, but hearing this, she wasn't sure she wanted to know anymore.

"She left him at the altar, you see. Back when they graduated."

"Oh, that sounds really bad."

Martha took another bite of the roll, so Ella did the same. For a moment, the older woman was silent. But she could see that Nick was all ears. He loved grownup talk.

"Not *too* bad," Martha said at last. "Everyone knew it was for the best. Chet had always had his heart set on college, his mother waited tables for me for years, and of course, she wanted more for him."

Just like us, Ella thought.

"She really didn't want him to get married so young, but Charlie said she was expecting—" here, she raised her eyebrows and glanced toward Nick as if to ask permission to continue, but he'd heard enough.

"Can I make another root beer?" he asked.

Ella looked at Martha who nodded. "If your mom thinks it's okay."

"Just this once." She smiled. "And be careful not to make a mess."

He slid out of the booth and walked around the end of the counter. He was still wearing his long apron. Ella was surprised he didn't want to take it off.

Martha smiled. "Such a darling boy."

"He certainly is." Ella tried to keep the melancholy out of her voice. "Now, what were you saying about Charlie?"

Martha wiped root beer foam from her upper lip. "She took off the night before the wedding, left him a note saying she'd made a mistake, there was no baby after all."

"How awful."

"Oh, no," Martha swept crumbs from the red and white checkered tablecloth into her hand. "Like I said, everyone knew it was a blessing. Even Chet. He was just trying to do the right thing. Let me tell you that boy couldn't get out of town fast enough." She chuckled and it was clear whose side she was on. "He went right on up to

Colorado State University, got himself a degree, and never looked back."

"But you said Charlie would do anything for him. That sounds like she still carries a torch."

"Oh, yeah," she chuckled again. "Didn't take long for her to realize she'd lost out on the best thing she'd ever had."

"Oh, my." Ella didn't want to be too nosy, she was just so curious she pushed ahead anyhow. "But isn't she married, now?"

Martha nodded. "Richest man in two counties. They own half of everything around here."

Ella shook her head sadly. "And him, Chet Boone? Surely he hasn't been alone all these years."

Martha stood and dusted the crumbs off her hands into the dustbin just inside the storeroom. "Married a girl from college. Head over heels they were. Brought her home, built a beautiful cabin on his parent's old place, his mom had moved on to the city with her new husband by this time, and then his Lily got sick. Turns out she had ovarian cancer." The older woman dabbed at the corner of her eye with the tip of her apron. "She's been gone five years now."

Ella was stunned. "So young. Has he never remarried?"

Martha shook her head. "I don't think he even goes out. Though I think Charlie would dump that rich husband of hers in a heartbeat if Chet gave her so much as a second glance."

"Ewww." Ella shuddered. "That's just wrong."

Martha laughed. "Don't worry, I don't think he ever would. Give her a second glance, I mean."

Nick came back to the table and cocked an eyebrow. "Get you ladies anything else?" He held a pad and pencil he'd picked up from behind the counter.

The two women looked at each other and cracked up.

As early lunch customers began to trickle in, Martha took the opportunity to let Ella and Nick practice running the digital cash register. It was very simple once they figured out the shorthand codes for all the menu items.

After several hours of practicing everything from waiting on customers to making sodas and sandwiches, Ella and Nick were beginning to feel at ease. Martha introduced them to everyone who came through the door. There were only a couple of people she didn't know. They were tourists who had heard about The Drugstore while visiting the lake or one of the campsites in the national forest.

When Ella and Nick finally headed for home, they couldn't stop talking about how awesome it was to be the new owners of such a wonderful establishment.

That evening, they dined on the box dinners Martha had sent home with them, club sandwiches with chips and pickles.

"This is one of the meals we'll be serving, isn't it?" Nick asked. He was really getting excited about being a restaurant owner.

"Yes, it is." Ella blotted her mouth with a napkin. "I sort of wish Martha would just stay. She makes everything so easy."

Nick agreed. He'd taken a shine to the grandmotherly woman, too.

"Oh," Ella exclaimed. "In all the excitement, I completely forgot to call Charlie, the realtor." She took out her cell phone and scrolled down to the realtor's number in her contact list. But when she tapped the CALL button, it said No Service.

Frowning, Ella went to the landline. Guess I have to get used to this, she thought. She looked at her contact list and punched in the numbers on the old-fashioned cordless phone. *Wow. It really is like Mayberry, in more ways than one.*

When Charlie answered, Ella identified herself and told the realtor about the raccoons and the need for attic repairs.

"I'll call the wildlife biologist over at the park headquarters," she said. "He takes care of all wild animal complaints in this county."

Ella bit her lip. She sensed that Charlie really wanted to make that call, but she didn't want to be dishonest. "Oh, he's already been called." She caught her breath and hurried on. "You see, us being such city slickers, we didn't know what was causing all the ruckus, so I called the police to come out and check. It was the middle of the night, you know."

Charlie made a noise of affirmation.

"Anyhow, long story short, they called Mr. Boone and he came out and set some traps. That's how I found out about the needed repairs."

"I see." The realtor's voice was cool. "Well, it sounds like you've got things under control. I trust Chet—we go way back—so just tell him to do what needs to be done and send me the bill."

Ella exhaled. That was easy. "Great. Thank you. I will."

"Wonderful," Charlie responded. "And I'm sorry for the inconvenience."

"Thank you," Ella replied. She didn't think the other woman sounded very sorry at all. Before she could sever the connection, the realtor was already gone.

Ella looked at the phone. Then she went to her purse and pulled out the card Chet Boone had given her. She'd been careful to transfer it from her pocket to her purse so she wouldn't lose it.

He answered on the first ring. "Hello."

"Mr. Boone?" Ella stood with the phone in her hand. She hadn't meant to be so formal; it just came out that way after she talked to Charlie.

"Ms. Webb?"

She laughed. "Yes, it's me. The raccoon lady. But, please, call me Ella."

"Only if you promise not to call me by my dad's name anymore."

"That's a deal." She stood dumbly, momentarily forgetting why she had called.

"Critters?" he finally prodded.

"What? Oh, yes, I called the landlord about the critters."

He laughed.

Ella thought he had the nicest laugh. She wished she could think of something to say so she could hear that laugh again. Then she scolded herself for being such an idiot. *Giddy as a teenager. And I certainly don't need to go down that particular road again—even if it were possible.* She was remembering another boy's laugh, a lifetime ago. She'd fallen in love with his laugh and wound up pregnant at the tender age of seventeen.

"Ella?"

Chet Boone's voice glided out of the phone and into her ear.

"Oh, I'm so sorry. I was just standing here, gathering wool as my mom would say."

He chuckled gently. "No harm in daydreaming. Where would we be if we didn't have dreams?"

She looked around the large, cozy kitchen. "I certainly wouldn't be embarking on my new career as a business owner," she admitted. "But back to reality. Yes. I called Charlie. She said to tell you to do whatever was necessary to fix the attic, then send her the bill." Ella wiped her brow. She felt as if she'd just run a race.

"All righty then," he replied. "Tomorrow's Sunday. I hope you don't mind if I come out in the afternoon and check those traps I set. I really don't like to leave them more than a day or so. Animals need water, and besides, they can really make a mess when they're caged up."

Ella had forgotten all about the traps. "Oh, yes. Please do. I wouldn't want anything to be caged longer than necessary. In fact, should I go up and check them now?"

"No—if you haven't heard anything, I'm sure there aren't any in there. They'd be making an awful racket if they were."

Ella's eye strayed toward the staircase door. "Well, actually, we've just now come home. I don't know if there's been any racket or not."

"You can check if you'd like." His voice was soothing. "And if there happens to be anything, just call me and I'll drop what I'm doing and come right over."

"Oh. Okay."

"If I don't hear from you, I'll assume everything is all right, and I'll just come out tomorrow."

"That's a deal," Ella replied. She hung up and took the key from its place on the window ledge. *I'll just run up and look. Won't take but a sec.*

And that's exactly what she did.

When she was certain both traps were empty, she turned and fled back to the kitchen. Something about the attic gave her the creeps. She knew it had only been the raccoon making the noise earlier, but still, she didn't breathe properly until she'd closed and locked the attic door.

She laid the key back on the window ledge and vowed to find a better place for it later.

Chapter Eight

She awoke with a strip of daylight soaking into her quilt. Apparently, the curtains had a slight gap.

It felt so good to sleep in for a change. For a moment, she wondered what day it was. *Oh yeah, Sunday. No church. Not yet.* She thought there was something on the agenda for today, she just couldn't remember what.

Stretching like an oversized cat, Ella debated simply rolling over and going back to sleep, but the idea that something was planned for later bugged her.

She sighed and sat up.

No noises in the night. That's why she'd slept so well.

Then a sudden thought hit her and she leapt from the bed and dashed down the hall to Nick's room, certain he would be gone, the bed empty.

But of course he was there, a caterpillar in his dinosaur-comforter-cocoon.

She breathed a sigh of relief. Anson hadn't broken out of jail during the night and stolen him away. It was just a crazy thought, a burst of paranoia, that's all. New house, new noises, new worries. *The fun never ends.*

Heart slowing after its irrational rush of adrenalin, Ella went back to her room, donned her jeans and sweatshirt, and then wandered into the sun splashed kitchen to put the coffee on.

While it was brewing in the old-fashioned Mr. Coffee, she strolled from room to room, casually peering out each window, her eyes sipping at the view as she waited for the coffee.

Delighted with the look of the day, she opened the kitchen window and allowed the damp scent of autumn to waft through the room.

Finally, she smiled. *This is good.*

When she heard the last gurgle, Ella poured herself a cup of Folgers and moved around the house admiring her new life from every window. Only the front porch looked out over the road and a single rooftop—Mrs. Benefield's—otherwise it would appear they were smack dab in the middle of the wilderness.

Standing at the front door, admiring the turning leaves of autumn, Ella was more than surprised when the phone trilled.

She set her coffee on the window ledge and dashed to the kitchen to answer it before it could wake Nick.

"Hello?" Who would have thought a dash from one room to the other could leave one so breathless?

"Hey, there. Hope I didn't wake you."

She recognized Chet Boone's voice immediately.

"Oh, no. Not at all. Well, actually, Nick is still sleeping but I've been up for awhile." *Am I rambling?*

"Good," he replied. "I thought I'd come over and check those traps—might bring a box of doughnuts if that's all right. Repay the breakfast you made me last time. Though I know, doughnuts are a poor substitute for home cooking."

Ella didn't want to feel so pleased, but she did. No, that's all right she was going to say. I checked the traps myself. They were empty. Instead, she heard her voice say, "That would be wonderful. Nick loves doughnuts and I can't recall the last time we had them." She automatically brushed one hand over her morning hair. "I'll supply the coffee."

Half an hour later he was knocking on the front door, doughnut box in hand.

"I didn't know we had a doughnut shop in Stutter Creek," Ella exclaimed, drinking in his scruffy chin and disheveled hair as surely as she'd drunk in the morning view only moments earlier.

"It's not *what* you know but *who* you know," he replied.

Then he grinned and her heart flip-flopped in her chest like a toy monkey on a string.

"Seriously," he continued, "we do have a small bakery just up the mountain on the way to the Timberline Ski Lodge." He handed her the box and scraped his damp shoes on the sisal mat. "It's only open part time in the off season, but give it a few more weeks and that place will be packed every day." He stepped inside, still smiling. "Skiing burns a lot of calories."

Ella led the way to the kitchen. "I've never been skiing," she admitted. "Is the lodge near your house?"

He slid into the same chair he'd sat in before. "Yup, my cabin is actually on the lodge road—gets pretty congested when we get fresh snow."

Ella set a mug of black coffee in front of him. She could easily imagine him on the slopes, hair curling over the collar of a royal blue ski suit that matched his eyes.

"Thank you." He picked up the coffee and sipped. "Any noises last night?"

Ella shook her head. "Not one. It was wonderful."

"Probably nothing in the traps then." He plucked a glazed doughnut from the box and dipped it in his coffee before devouring half of it in one bite. "Maybe I can go ahead and get started on the repairs—if it's all right with you, that is?"

"Of course," she agreed. "The sooner, the better." She nibbled a chocolate doughnut. "And I did check the traps after we spoke on the phone last night. Nothing was in them. Thank goodness."

He laughed. "Good girl."

Ella liked his teasing manner. Maybe that's what makes me feel like a teenager, she thought. *He seems young, and makes me feel young, too. As if the last few years hadn't happened at all.*

Together, they shared the doughnuts, though nerves would only allow Ella to nibble around the top while drinking her third cup of coffee.

Chet may have been somewhat nervous, too. But he covered his with questions and jokes.

He: "So, what made you decide to move to Stutter Creek?"

She: "The Drugstore was for sale, and I have some experience with restaurant work."

He: "Oh, of course. I knew that." He bonked his forehead with the heel of his hand. "Actually, Martha told me about you and Nick after you interviewed with her. She said she'd finally found the right folks to take it over." His blue eyes were fathomless. The sunlight played hide and seek in the waves of his hair. "I always thought a member of the family would step in and take it over—you know? But I guess after what happened to Allie, their niece, none of them were that keen on it anymore."

Ella set her cup down and coffee sloshed over the rim. "What did happen—if you don't mind me asking?"

Chet opened his mouth to reply, but Nick walked in rubbing his eyes. "Well, good morning sleeping beauty." Chet's voice was jolly.

It was apparent to Ella that whatever happened to Martha and Joe's niece wasn't a story for little ears. I'll have to remind him to tell me another time, she thought.

She held up the green and white doughnut box. "Look what Mr. Boone brought."

Nick's eyes lit up and he immediately took his seat and pulled a paper towel off the roll on the table.

Ella poured a glass of milk to go with it. Nick wolfed down the first chocolate doughnut and gulped half the milk while reaching for a second one.

"Slow down, son," she admonished jokingly. "No one's going to take them away from you."

Chet stood and took his mug to the sink. "At least I know how to win friends here." He glanced back at Nick. "I'll get my tools and meet you in the attic."

Nick shoved the remains of the second doughnut in his mouth and nodded vigorously.

Ella leaned back and crossed her arms. She was delighted the two seemed to hit it off, but what was that old saying about if it seems to good to be true, it probably is? Anson had seemed near-perfect too, back in the day. *Or was it just because I was so desperate to get away from Mom's house and all her "advice" about how I should raise Nicky? Weren't there red flags with Anson from the very beginning?* She rose and carried her cup and Nick's glass to the sink.

Nick leapt to his feet and charged down the hall to his room to get dressed. Ella poured herself another half-cup of coffee. At first, Anson had been very attentive to both her and Nicky. The three of them had played catch in the yard, attended the latest kid movies on Saturday afternoons, he even took them to Disneyworld once. But when the new wore off, and he began to spend all his time with "the boys," she and Nicky had discovered their real worth.

It's a guy thing, he'd said after an afternoon of basketball with his buds. But Nicky's a guy, she had murmured. And he's your stepson. Besides, Ted and Jimmy Ray bring their sons to the basketball court. You told me so.

He'd just looked at her as if she'd suddenly developed brain damage. And she'd let it slide because he was still a good husband, then. No more discount-store, unheard-of-brand food, no more reduced-price lunches at school, no more begging her mom for forty bucks for school pictures or twenty for over-the-counter kid's medicine that wasn't covered by Medicaid.

Life had been better—in some respects.

And if he wasn't exactly the stepfather she'd assumed he would be after they were married, well, nothing was perfect. She would just have to pick up the slack. Together, she and Nicky attended the movies he once took them to. But she was the one who went to Doughnuts with Dad at school—Anson suddenly being called out of town at the last moment—and it was she who signed him up for his first season of football. She even watched the games with him on TV when Anson decided Sundays were suddenly his golf days.

It was a gradual thing; the feeling that she and Nick had begun to seem more like unwanted baggage rather than loved ones.

She reached up and wiped a drop of moisture from her cheek as Nicky dashed around the corner and headed for the attic stairs. *Darn it. Thought I'd washed that mood away last night. But every time Chet comes around, I start reliving the past. Maybe it's my subconscious trying to remind me what happened the last time I let a man get too close, too fast.*

Nick started up the stairs.

"He's still outside, I think." She had just unlocked the attic door.

Nick changed course and headed for the front porch just as Chet rang the bell.

Bing bong

Such manners. Anyone else would've come right back inside—especially after just eating breakfast together.

Nick grabbed the doorknob and flung it open. "I'm ready!" The excitement in his voice hinted that he was certain Chet was here simply to allow him to assist in a building project.

Has he been that deprived, that he takes up with any stranger who comes along? She thought about her own actions, practically falling all over herself the first time she'd met Chet. It made her wonder, *have I been that deprived, am I that desperate?*

Chet seemed to read her mind. He looked up and caught her eye as Nick dashed past. "You don't mind if he helps me, do you?"

Ella sniffled and laughed self-consciously. "I was about to ask you the same thing."

He stopped for a second. She was sure he was going to ask her what was wrong, but she didn't give him a chance. Instead, she headed straight on out the front door as if that had been her intention all along.

Once she was outside, she felt ridiculous. *I've just let my ten-year-old son go into the attic with some guy I barely know—again. Yesterday, I wondered about him getting so close so fast. What if his name is really Chester as in Chester the Molester?* She sighed and turned back to go inside. *Just have to go up with them, I guess. Hope Chet doesn't think I'm hanging around just to get his attention because I am seriously coming to the conclusion that attention is the last thing I need.*

She headed for the stairs just as Nick called out in a strange, loud whisper, "Mom, Mom! Hurry. Ya gotta see this."

All thoughts left her mind at the sound of her son's voice.

She hit the stairs running.

When she reached the top, she was relieved to see Nick standing near the attic window looking at something in the corner.

"What is it?" she asked.

He was standing near one of the wire traps.

Inside, cowered into the corner in a small ball of black and gray fur, was a young raccoon. It was obviously terrified.

"Ohhh," she breathed. "It's just a baby. It wasn't there last night. I swear it wasn't."

"Hasn't been here long at all—just long enough to eat the fish. But it isn't really a baby. More like a teenager," Chet said. "Babies stay with their moms. This one is probably just learning to live on its own."

She looked at his face. "What will we do with it?"

He was donning heavy leather gloves.

She didn't like the look of those. They looked official.

He picked up a dark canvas cover that was the same shape as the rectangular trap. "We'll take the little guy out into the woods, look for spoor, and release it. Maybe we'll get lucky and actually put it where the rest of its family lives."

He slipped the cover down over the cage. The handle on top of the cage poked up through a slit in the canvas so that he could pick it up without fear of getting scratched or bitten.

"Could it have rabies?" Ella asked. "I've always heard raccoons carry rabies."

"Not this one," he said. "Clear eyes, good appetite, a healthy fear of humans. Nah, it's just a little scavenger."

"Whew," Ella breathed a sigh of relief.

"Can we go with you out in the forest?" Nick's eyes were almost as bright as the raccoon's.

"Sure," Chet said. "But remember, this is a wild animal. We won't try to touch it or pet it. We'll simply open the cage and let it come out on its own." He looked down at the cover. "Hopefully it isn't too traumatized."

Nick nodded, his little boy face thoughtful. "Okay, let's go let him out before he has a heart attack in there or something. He must be so scared."

Ella agreed with her son. He was such a kind boy. Thank God she'd got him away from Anson before he lost that sense of compassion.

She was surprised when Chet handed her the second, empty cage. "Will you carry this one down for me?" He held the one with the raccoon in it far out from his side so it wouldn't bump into his leg as he walked.

"You bet." She tried not to let herself feel like a favored kid being asked to help the teacher, but that's exactly the ridiculous way she felt. She was certain he would've asked Nick to carry it if the boy had been just a little bigger.

Down the stairs and out the back door they went. "Just set that one beside my truck if you don't mind," he instructed her.

She did, and then they followed Chet down Norma's narrow bunny trail into the forest behind the house. They hadn't gone very far when she realized how the tall pines obscured the sunlight. In moments, she was downright shivery.

"This should do it," Chet said, pointing to a scattering of raccoon spoor at the base of an oak tree.

"We didn't go very far from the house," Nick said. "Won't it come back?"

"Good point," Chet agreed. "It probably will try to come back, but we're going to fix those vents so nothing can get in, besides, if we take it very far away, it might die trying to find its way back." He looked at Ella as if to ask how much he should divulge. "An animal needs to stay in the territory it has grown up in. Otherwise, it would be encroaching on another animal's territory. And that doesn't usually end well."

Nick nodded. "We studied animal habitats in school last year."

Chet set the cage down and slipped off the cover. The raccoon still cowered in the corner. "It's all right now, little one," Chet murmured. "We aren't going to hurt you." While he was talking, he was carefully pulling up on the door at the end of the cage. When he had it secured, so that it wouldn't fall back down, he motioned for the two of them to back away.

They weren't more than five steps back when the little creature found its nerve and shot out of the opening and up a tree.

The leaves of the oak were still plentiful and mostly green, but some orange and gold colors were beginning to peek through. Try as she might, Ella could not see the little raccoon at all.

"Wow, he sure took off, didn't he?"

Chet laughed and picked up the cage and cover. "That's a good sign. I think he feels safe in the tree. Now, back to work."

On the way to the house, Chet stopped and placed both cages into the bed of his truck.

"Wow," Nick said, looking into the bed of the truck. "What are those things?"

Chet picked up a couple of traps. One was big enough to catch a bear. It had nasty looking serrated teeth and rusty hinges. The other appeared to be a smaller version, for coyotes or foxes, perhaps. It was smooth, not serrated. Both appeared to be very old, and extremely wicked. "Picked these up at an auction over in Yellow Bend," he said. "I collect anything having to do with wildlife. Even the cruel aspects."

"But. You don't use them, right?" Nick's voice held a note of concern. "Those things would *crush* an animal's foot."

"They sure would." Chet shook his head. "I could never harm an animal that way. These are antiques. They're going up on the wall of my workshop strictly for decoration." He grinned sheepishly. "As soon as I finish building the workshop, that is."

Ella laughed. "A man with a plan."

Nick looked a little confused, but he climbed into the truck bed and helped Chet rearrange the traps. He had several more humane traps like the two that had been in their attic. Some were smaller and one was quite a bit larger.

"I really shouldn't have bought these," Chet muttered. "I don't have a place to put them yet, but the guy was just giving them away. I couldn't pass 'em up." He took a can of WD-40 lubricant and gave all the traps—modern and antique—a quick spray.

"Shoot," Nick said. "We've got a whole empty store room under the carport. I bet you could put them in there. Right, Mom?"

Ella loved it when her darling son put her on the spot. "Oh, sure," she agreed. "If they aren't dangerous." She eyed the huge serrated teeth on the larger trap. "That thing looks evil."

Chet laughed. "It is evil. I want it to show how bad things can be. I'm—well," his voice faltered. "I'm sort of planning a small museum dedicated to the conservation of our local wildlife." He ran a hand over the dull and rusted teeth. "I just call it my workshop to keep folks from asking too many questions."

"Well, okay. But I'll have to keep that storehouse door locked. I just don't like the looks of them. Understand, Nicky?"

He nodded, but still looked slightly uncertain.

"Do you have the key handy?" Chet asked when Nick wasn't listening.

"I'll get it." Ella dashed into the house and retrieved the key. When she took it back outside, Chet had found a small finishing nail protruding from just above the doorframe.

She watched as he placed the traps in the room, locked the door, and hung the key upon the nail. "Now I can retrieve them without having to bother you." He smiled. "But, of course, if you'd rather keep the key in the house, that's okay, too."

Ella looked at the key. It was impossible to see unless you knew to look for it. "No, I like it there," she said. "Nicky will never need it. And if he ever got the bright idea to look for it, I don't think he'd look out here."

"Where is he, anyhow?" Chet asked.

"I think the other chocolate doughnut was calling his name."

They turned back toward the house, laughing together.

Ella thought she heard a vehicle accelerate somewhere down the road, but when she looked, there was nothing to be seen, but a fine film of dust hanging in the air. Probably Mrs. Benefield again, she thought. *That woman drives like a maniac.*

Chapter Nine

Back in the house, the three of them headed upstairs to the attic.

"I'm surprised you want to be involved in the actual repair process," Chet mentioned, looking at Ella as he pulled out the broken vent slats.

Ella was saved from trying to cover up the real reason she was hanging around when Nick pointed at several clumps of black and gray fur clinging to the jagged wooden slats. "Mr. Boone thinks we might have had a few of them living up here at one time," he said. "Look at all this fur."

Nick began to pull at the fur, rolling it into a ball in his palms.

"Oooh, I don't know if you should be doing that." Ella looked at Chet. "Don't they have fleas or lice or something?"

He laughed, his blue eyes twinkling. "They could have fleas, but I don't think they would be in that little clump." He measured the broken slats so he could replace them with the new ones he had brought. "Besides, if they had fleas, the whole attic would likely be infested."

"Yuck!" Ella said. "Do we need to call an exterminator?"

"Nah." Chet's voice was nonchalant. "Not unless you start itching." His mouth twitched at the corners. "No use looking for trouble."

Ella nodded, not really convinced. "Okay, if you say so." She rubbed her palms up and down her arms willing herself not to scratch.

"Anyhow," he continued. "I'm sure they're gone now. And with this," he held up a rectangle of heavy wire mesh, "there's no way they can get back in."

"Thank you," she responded. "I didn't know what a wimp I was."

"Uh, Mom?"

Ella turned to Nick. "What is it?"

He was pointing at something in the corner behind a large cardboard box. "You might not want to see this, but I have a feeling you'll want to sweep it up."

Ella's heart sank. "Is it something dead?" She was envisioning the skeletal remains of a raccoon, or even a rat.

"Oh, no." Nick's voice was light. "It's just a pile of poop."

"Oh, thank goodness." Ella laughed shakily. She peered over the large box. "Ewww, you're right kiddo. I'm going downstairs for my broom and dust mask. Double yuck!"

Nick laughed, too. "At least it's just those little round pellet things like we saw out in the woods."

Ella waved her hand in the air as she started back down the stairs. "I'll bring you a mask, too," she said.

He groaned.

The repairs and clean up took two more hours. By then, everyone was getting hungry and thirsty.

"I'll go down and make some iced tea and sandwiches." Ella slipped off a glove to wipe a hand across her brow.

She was proud of Nick. He had been quite a trouper, holding boards and wire while Chet nailed or sawed. He'd even swept up poop with his own dust mask on. "I can't wimp out if Mom doesn't," he'd said. "Besides, I might want to work with wildlife someday, too."

He'd thrown the idea out so casually, like a hook into the middle of a lake, that Ella didn't even know how to respond. Last she'd heard he was going to play pro football like his idol, Drew Brees. *Is he that vulnerable that any half-way decent man can make such an imprint on him in one or two days?*

She shook her head to clear away the doubt and to clear away the next thought that came: *or is it possible Chet really is an exceptional man?* She glanced toward the area where he was working.

He was bent over, picking up pieces of wire and wood, cleaning up his tools and putting everything back in its proper place. His wavy hair shadowed one eye and his blue work shirt stretched taut in all the right places.

He looked up and caught her examining him.

Her face flamed and she was glad for her dust mask.

"Anyone here like pizza?" he asked.

"Yeah," Nick said. "My favorite is pepperoni."

Ella chuckled. "I feel so filthy." She dumped the last bit of dust from the pan into the plastic trash bag.

"There's a Pizza Hut in Pine River." Chet looked down at his dusty clothing. "I'd need to run home and grab a shower though."

Nick's face was so comical Ella couldn't help herself. She burst out laughing.

"You mean we don't even have a Pizza Hut in this town?" Her son's tone of voice said he was certain someone was pulling his leg.

"It's only a half hour away," Chet said. "Especially if you know the back roads."

That gave Ella a bit of a start. Once again, the idea that they didn't really know this man forced her to rethink her first inclination, which was to say yes.

"Do we at least serve pizza at The Drugstore?" Nick asked, still disappointed.

Ella shook her head. "Soup and sandwiches only, kiddo. And breakfast of course."

"But I like pizza for breakfast," he said.

Chet smiled and mouthed, "Me, too."

Nick sighed. "Well, all right. I can always take my Nintendo."

"Sure," Ella agreed, fighting back an eye roll. The handheld game had cost almost as much as the regular version. She'd put it on her credit card after she'd made the decision to move to Stutter Creek. It wasn't a bribe. Not exactly. It was just a tool to help him pass the time on the trip—and to keep the grumbling at bay. And it had worked.

"But you know what?" she said to Chet, her voice carefully neutral. "Nick and I could just meet you there." She was leery of getting into a man's car and driving out on some back roads, even if he had been working in her attic for the past two hours.

Chet raised an eyebrow questioningly.

Ella hurried to explain. "I think I need to get the lay of the land. Find my way around, you know? I'm sure we'll be making a few trips to the nearest Pizza Hut on our own later."

He nodded. "That's a deal, then. It's on 4th and Cuthbert right there in Pine River. The highway you go in on actually intersects Cuthbert. Just hang a right and go north until you hit 4th Street."

"Got it," Ella replied. "We'll meet you there in about an hour." She looked at her watch. "Let's say three o'clock. That'll give me an extra half hour to clean up."

"Mo-o-m," Nick whined. "It won't take that long to shower. I'm starving."

Chet laughed and pulled out his wallet, pretending to check his finances. "I hope we make it in time for the buffet then."

Ella turned and looked around the small attic. It was clean and well secured. Chet had done a marvelous job repairing the vents, and she and Nick had swept and dusted the entire area. Not a bad days work, she thought. Even all the empty boxes were flattened and ready for recycling.

They followed Nick down the stairs and she automatically turned and locked the attic door. If Chet thought it odd, he didn't comment.

She laid the key on the windowsill and then walked with him to the front porch. "If you'll give me the bill, I'll send it to the landlord."

Chet smiled. "I'll give her a call," he said. "No worries." Then he turned. "I'll see you guys at three o'clock."

Ella nodded. "I think Nicky's already in the shower."

Chet laughed and started to his truck, tool box in hand. Then he stopped. "And don't worry," he said softly. "You can trust me."

Ella opened her mouth to protest. To tell him she knew that, or something just as mundane, but then she closed it again. "Is it that apparent?"

He shrugged and smiled. "No worries," he repeated. "Just wanted you to know."

She didn't know what to say. Telling someone you're trustworthy isn't the same as proving it. But oddly enough, it did make her feel better. That's ludicrous, her rational mind whispered. He could say anything, just like Anson always did. But it didn't necessarily make it true.

She might have gone on scolding herself as he climbed in and started the truck, but once again, the sound of another vehicle caught her attention.

This time she saw it. A light colored sedan had been parked beside the road and was now pulling away, headed back the other direction, toward town. *Maybe they were lost and pulled over to make a U-turn or something.* She could well imagine the car's GPS unit saying "re-cal-cu-lating." The thought made her grin. She watched the car drive away. The windows were so darkly tinted, there was no way to see who was driving. *Not that I'd know them anyway,* she thought.

Ella stepped back inside the house and locked both the screen door and the wooden door behind her. Something about the car worried her. She'd heard a vehicle when they were coming out of the woods. *Two lost tourists in one morning?* They hadn't seen that much activity on Lilac Lane since the day they'd moved in. *I'll have to ask Norma if that's normal.* She laughed at herself for the play on words.

"Mom, come on," Nick called. "I'm already out of the shower and you haven't even started yet."

"Coming," she trilled. "I'm coming." She walked into Nick's room. "But hey, don't forget, you don't open the door for anyone while I'm in the shower, okay?"

"Sure," he agreed. He was sitting on the edge of his bed, pulling on his shoes.

"Not even if you know the person," she said.

"You mean like if Mr. Boone comes back or something?"

Ella swallowed. "Yeah, or like...anyone. Okay? Promise?"

"Geez," he grumbled. "I promise." He finished tying his shoes and plucked his game off the nightstand. "Think they have a Game Store in Pine River?"

"I wouldn't be surprised," Ella replied, silently envisioning the high prices of new games. "I wouldn't be at all surprised."

She turned on the water and let it warm up while she pulled off her dirty clothes and dropped them in the hamper. When she caught a glimpse of herself in the mirror, she was dismayed to see the vertical line of worry back on her face, right between her eyes. That line had softened after Anson had gone to jail. He'd only been sentenced to eight months for assault, barely even a slap on the wrist in her opinion. But what mother wouldn't feel that way after seeing the ugly red hand mark on her boy's face? She knew if she hadn't taken pictures and gone to the hospital for x-rays of her own cheek, he wouldn't have received any time at all.

Now, she was beginning to wonder if he'd got out. Was that him lurking about Lilac Lane, watching her, looking for a chance to—

Bam! Bam! Bam!

The bathroom door rattled under the onslaught of someone's fist.

Ella's heart leapt into her throat and she grabbed for the nearest towel, her nakedness lending an even deeper layer to her feelings of vulnerability.

"Mom!" Nicky yelled, pounding on the door again.

Ella yanked open the door, clutching the towel around her body. "*Nicky!*" she demanded. "What's wrong?" She couldn't stifle the panic, not completely.

He was standing outside the door, video game in hand, barely even paying attention to what he had just done.

"Why are you pounding on the door? You scared the life out of me."

"Sorry." He shrugged. "I didn't think you could hear me over the water."

Ella sagged against the doorjamb. "What is it?"

He finally looked up. "Can I make a ham sandwich to hold me until Pizza Hut?"

She exhaled and laughed shakily. She could have joyfully throttled him. She'd been envisioning someone—okay, Anson—breaking in the front door, murder in his eyes. "Yes, yes," she said. "But just one. We'll be eating soon."

"Okay, thanks." He wandered away, oblivious to the heart attack he'd just caused.

After a quick shower—even the warm water couldn't make her relax now—Ella got out and toweled off roughly. She dragged the brush through her shoulder-length hair and called it good. She put on mascara, lipstick, and a dusting of blush before she gave up and stepped into her most comfortable jeans. She topped the jeans with a turquoise tank and a super-soft flannel shirt. Her well-worn boots completed the ensemble.

She didn't even bother looking in the mirror after dressing. No one I need to impress, she told herself. *Just going as friends. Just going to be nice. Certainly don't need any entanglements. Barely got out of the last one semi-unscathed.* Her fingers went to her cheekbone subconsciously.

In the kitchen, she took a deep breath and picked up her car keys and purse. For the first time since they'd arrived, she wished the place had a garage. But it's just a rental, she reminded herself. Later, if The Drugstore works out, we can search for a house—with a garage. Give it six months to a year. It'll fly by in no time, in fact, by the time Nicky starts sixth grade, we should know if we're cut out to be business owners. *What am I saying? It's all or nothing here, no going home, no looking back.*

Pep talk in place, she called Nick and started toward the door.

"I'm really starving," he said as he joined her. "If not for that ham sandwich, I'd probably be dead by now."

Ella sighed and herded him toward the door. "Did you put everything away when you were finished, the mayonnaise, the cheese, the ham?"

"Yes, ma'am," he said. Then he stopped, peeled out from under her hand, and darted back to the kitchen. "Except for the bread."

Ella laughed and opened the front door. "I'll meet you outside."

She stood aside as he rushed past her and hurried on to the Jeep. "Got your game?" she called.

He held it up.

Ella locked the deadbolt and gave the handle a jiggle to make sure it was engaged. She had checked the back door when she picked up her keys and her purse. Even the attic door was locked. All secure, she thought. *Everything is fine.*

They climbed into the Jeep and she typed Pizza Hut, Pine River, NM into the Garmin GPS. When they hit the outskirts of town, they finally got a signal.

"You don't need that," Nick said. "Mr. Boone told us where it is, remember?"

Ella nodded. "I know. I'm just practicing. If this is going to be our home, I want to make sure I know all about it. I don't want to have to rely on other people, know what I mean?"

Nick's face clouded. "Sort of. But you always tell me not to be afraid to ask for help in class and stuff."

Ella chuckled. "You're right, kiddo. I guess I'm just getting used to being on my own again." She sensed Nick was about to question her use of the word "again" (he had no memory of the short time it was just the two of them—when she was a single mother trying to make it on her own with a baby—back in the days before she went crawling back to Nana's house in what she felt was defeat), so she punched the power button for the radio and started scanning channels. "Here," she said, pretending to give up, changing the conversation. "Find us a good station."

Nick gladly took over.

Neither of them noticed the tan or cream-colored sedan parked off the road on Jasmine. It was pulled in behind the bank of mailboxes that served the entire area. If they had noticed, they might've assumed it was simply a neighbor getting his mail.

Or Ella might have recognized it as the same vehicle she'd seen earlier.

*

Chet was right.

The drive was exactly thirty minutes through some of the most beautiful country Nick and Ella had ever seen. "I like the white trees," Nicky said in awe. "What are they, Mom?"

"I think those are birch trees," she replied. "They're sort of eerie, aren't they, standing so straight and tall, like a platoon of sentries?"

"If you say so," Nick said. "I just thought they were cool."

Ella glanced in the mirror. The trees had made up a small, pocket forest. Driving through it, Nick may have been in awe, but Ella had been delighted. It's like a planting of virtue, she thought, so pure and white. An ode to someone. *The Taj Mahal* of Stutter Creek, New Mexico. A labor of love.

Yep, she decided, it's definitely time for some rational, adult conversation.

They finished the drive in comfortable silence. Nick playing his Ninja Warrior game, Ella vacillating between wishing she'd said no to this little outing, and hoping—just a little bit—that she'd found a true friend. But as for the latter, she'd never been graced with one yet. Neither male nor female. Having left high school to give birth to Nick, she'd taken her mother's advice and simply acquired her GED rather than graduate with her class. Not that she'd really wanted to walk across the stage seven months pregnant, anyway. She knew it didn't bother some girls, but the fact that Tag would be there, looking up at her, turned her stomach almost as badly as the morning sickness.

When she'd told him she was pregnant—after the one and only time they'd had sex—he had laughed, saying it was a good joke. And then, when she'd convinced him she was serious, he'd refused to look at her. "I'll pay for an abortion," he'd said. "But I can't be a father. I'm going to Texas Tech to play football. You know I've got a full ride." And still, he hadn't looked at her.

She'd turned around and walked out, backbone straight.

Ella hadn't thought of him in a long time. Her latest problems had finally exorcised him from her mind. Heck of a way to get over someone, she thought. Replace him with someone worse.

She turned up the radio and took note of the lovely scenery. I'm over them, she told herself. Both of them. The only man in my life now is Nick. He's the only one I need to worry about. There isn't room for anyone else.

Not even Chet Boone.

Chapter Ten

There were quite a few vehicles in the parking lot of the Pizza Hut, but Chet's work truck was nowhere to be seen. "Looks like we're early," she told Nick. "Let's go on inside and get a booth."

The Pizza Hut was just like countless others they'd visited over the years.

"Hope they didn't run out of buffet pizza," Nick said. "Mr. Boone said that's what we had to order." His face looked seriously worried.

So literal, Ella thought. "If they do, I think we can order straight off the menu if need be." She clasped his shoulder briefly. At his age, parental affection in public was a strict no-no. Together they stood just inside the warm, fragrant restaurant.

"I love that smell," she said. "Yeasty bread—"

"Topped with meat. Yum!"

Ella turned to see who had spoken and Chet was standing directly behind them, grinning and rubbing his stomach.

"There's a booth." Nick pointed across the room.

"Go get it, buddy," Chet replied. Then he leaned in toward Ella. "Sorry I was late—"

"You weren't late at all," she interrupted. "We were actually a few minutes early. And I warn you, Nicky is starving."

He smiled and touched her back, guiding her across the busy dining room to the booth Nick had picked out.

Ella tried not to flinch when she felt the gentle pressure of his fingertips, but suspicious was her middle name these days.

What a dweeb I am, she thought. *Such a nice man and I can't even appreciate it.*

She slid into the seat beside Nick and Chet took the one across from them. A waiter came for their drink order and instructed them to visit the buffet if they desired.

Nick was filling his plate with several slices—pepperoni, hamburger, Canadian bacon, and a mixture of all three—until he caught Ella giving him "the look."

He stopped, smiled sweetly, and headed back to the table. He knew his mom couldn't stand to see food wasted. He didn't know it was another holdover from the days of single (desperate) parenthood. But he knew he was expected to eat whatever he voluntarily put on his plate.

Chet had as much on his plate, or more, and Ella took only a couple of small slices—one of veggie, one of pepperoni—and they all met back at the table where their drinks and salads were waiting.

When Nick had eaten four slices and was eyeing the fifth as if it had suddenly sprouted a coat of mold, Chet grinned and said, "I wish I'd picked up one more slice of that Canadian bacon and hamburger. I'll bet it's all gone by now."

Nick saw his opening. "Here," he said, holding out his plate, "have mine, I don't mind."

"Are you sure?" Chet appeared worried. "I don't want to deprive you."

"Oh, no. I don't mind at all. Really."

Ella couldn't believe it. Was he doing that just to spare Nicky a scolding?

Chet popped the point of the pizza slice into his mouth and devoured the whole thing in three bites. "Thanks, Nicky-boy. Now I won't need dessert."

"You must have a hollow leg," Ella said. She couldn't resist checking out his lean physique.

"Yep," Chet replied. "It's wooden, I hollowed it out to hold extra food. Never know when I might need a snack out in the woods."

Ella giggled and Nick looked down under the table. He might've asked to see the leg if Chet hadn't pulled out his wallet and selected a handful of singles.

"There's a juke box in the corner," he told Nick. "You know how to play it?"

Nick nodded. "I sure do. Pizza Huts almost always have one." He glanced at his mom. "Is it okay?"

She studied Chet. *So generous. First getting Nick off the hook for taking more pizza than he could possibly eat, now this.*

"Sure," she answered. "I suppose it's all right."

"Play B-17 for me," Chet said.

Nick nodded.

"You're spoiling him," Ella chided. "Actually, you're spoiling both of us." She brushed her bangs to the side and tried not to look into his eyes. Inside, she felt a hollowness of her own. It threatened to overtake her good mood. *It's just too soon. Too much, too soon.* She remembered how Anson would quibble over every dime and nickel she spent on Nicky. How he called for an accounting of every penny she gave her son while he thought nothing of blowing an entire paycheck on a weekend with "the boys."

After a few moments of silence, Ella realized she'd been woolgathering again. She let her eyes find Nick standing at the jukebox near the front of the restaurant. He appeared to be examining every song.

She allowed her gaze to travel back to her dinner partner.

Chet appeared to be watching the other diners.

To break the silence she asked, "What is B-17, is it your favorite song?"

He smiled slowly. "Something like that. It's an oldie but a goodie. I hope you like it."

A song came on. "This is B-17?"

He nodded. "It just came to mind, sitting here across the table from you."

Ella sat back and listened to the old Van Morrison song, *Brown Eyed Girl*.

Then she raised her own brown eyes to his blue ones.

He was still smiling, but it was a gentle smile, not a teasing grin at all.

She liked that smile, but it still made her uneasy. When something seems too good to be true, her mom always said, it usually is. How many times had she been forced to admit when her mother was right? It was the bane of her existence. And it was always in hindsight, after the mistake had been made.

But that smile, and the look in those deep blue eyes did something to her insides that hadn't been done in a long time.

"It's nice," she murmured. "I actually love this song."

Chet nodded. "Me, too."

Then Nicky was back, chattering a mile a minute. "They've got all kinds of stuff on there, Mom. You shoulda came up with me, they've got a bunch of country songs like you listen to, and some of that old stuff, too."

She started to say, "I can't wait to hear what else you chose," but the spell was blown away when *Gangnam Style* came on.

Nick grinned. "Just for you, Mom. I know how much you love this song."

Ella swatted him playfully. They'd laughed about this song when it first became popular. She was so glad Nicky was there to break the tension that had been building at the small table.

She gave up and let herself enjoy the moment. Everything was nice. It was as if the sun had come out on a cloudy picnic. There was no more awkwardness, no more tension, and no more holding back. She made a conscious decision to live in the present, not in the past. If this man wanted to treat them to a bit of fun, what was the harm in that? After all, he was well known in town. Everyone liked him, even Martha said so. Ella finally relaxed.

They no longer had to answer to anyone.

After all Nick's songs were finished, it was getting late.

"I guess we'd better be going," she said. "Nicky starts school tomorrow."

Chet looked at Nick. "Big day, huh?"

Nick shrugged.

"You nervous?" he asked.

Nick started to shrug again, and then he nodded. "I've never been the new kid."

"You'll be fine," Chet assured him. "I grew up in Stutter Creek. It's a great place to go to school."

Ella thought she could see Nick visibly relax, too.

"You really went to school there when you were my age?"

It was obvious Nick was having trouble picturing Chet as a boy his age.

"Yep," Chet replied. "My folks live on the other side of Copper Lake. Got a sis who became an attorney. Lots of kids go right on to college from Stutter Creek High. We've got very good teachers."

"Do you have any kids? I mean, you and my mom are the same age, right?"

That took them both by surprise. Then Ella realized Nick was simply hoping Chet would have a child his age so he would know someone already.

"Sorry, buddy," Chet shook his head. "I wish I did have one or two. I'll bet they would really like you."

Nick smiled and ducked his head. "That's okay. I didn't think you had any. You're too much fun."

Ella opened her mouth to protest, but then she closed it again. Anson had been the total opposite of fun. Nick was certainly entitled to his feelings—she only wished she'd paid closer attention to them years earlier.

Outside in the parking lot, Chet escorted them to the Jeep. "I'll just follow along behind you if it's all right. I'm in no hurry."

Ella nodded. "Thank you for a lovely time. It was great to take a break from the house for a while."

He stood outside her door, leaning down, one hand on the top of the door frame, smiling. "It was my pleasure, Brown-eyed-girl."

Ella blushed and glanced at Nick to see if he was listening. But he was already absorbed in ninjas again.

"Well," she said. "I'm sure we'll see you soon."

"You bet," he said. "I hope we can do this again."

Ella threw caution to the wind. "Me, too."

He slapped the top of the Jeep before stepping away.

For a moment, she could almost picture him coming back, leaning down into the window, blue eyes staring into hers, lips nearing—

She closed her eyes at such a preposterous notion. *Barely divorced. Ex-husband now an ex-con. Yeah. I really need to get involved with a new man. Need it like I need another hole in my head. 'Course they do say the third time's a charm.*

She opened her eyes just in time to see Chet climb into his work truck. He gave her a funny little salute and she pulled out onto the main road that led back toward Stutter Creek.

Chapter Eleven

He honked and waved when they reached the turn off for Lilac Lane. Ella couldn't help wondering what he thought about the birch forest as they drove through it on the way back. This time, the trees wore shimmering mantles of gold. It was late afternoon. They'd shared a very late lunch, or very early dinner, she wasn't sure which. Nevertheless, she and Nick would have plenty of time to sort out his clothes and fill his backpack for tomorrow's first day. Plus, she wanted a little alone time with her boy. Find out what he was really thinking about their big move.

"That was fun, wasn't it?" she asked as they drove up the lane.

Nick nodded. He was deep in ninja warfare.

"I like the way our little house looks when we pull into the drive." She hummed a bit and that got Nick's attention.

"You're humming that *Brown Eyed Girl* song aren't you?"

"Hmm. So I was. It's an old song from way back. I've always liked it." She pulled into the carport and engaged the Jeep's parking brake. The pine trees were fragrant. Several branches touched the metal roof of the carport. They made a shushing sound when the wind blew. It also sent their tangy green fragrance into the Jeep's open windows. "We may regret not having a garage when it snows this winter," she said.

"I think he likes you," Nick replied.

Ella stopped with her finger on the automatic window button. The windows stopped halfway up. "Chet Boone?"

Nick rolled his eyes. "No. *The Incredible Hulk.*"

Ella ignored the sarcasm. Choose your battles, her mom always said. "He seems like a very nice man," she replied.

"Just a friend, though." She pushed the button to roll up the windows again. "It's nice to have a friend."

Nick stepped out of the Jeep and looked at her through the rising passenger window. "It's okay, Mom. I'm not a baby. I know you aren't married anymore." He started around the vehicle toward the front door. "Besides, it seems like he actually likes me, too."

Ella felt her heart break. Felt it crack into a million pieces. Felt one tiny shard pierce her breastbone, as if it would live there from now on, shrapnel from a failed relationship. *Seems like he actually likes me, too. He'd known how Anson felt about him all along. Why didn't I leave that heartless bastard years ago? What was I so afraid of?*

She unlocked the front door and gave Nick a little hug as they entered together. "You are some kid, you know that?"

Nick shrugged out of her grasp. "Yuck. What's that smell?"

Ella stopped in the living room, heart suddenly pattering against her ribs like hailstones on a metal roof. *What is that smell? You know what it is. It's Aramis cologne. You smelled it for years. Lay next to it, tried to wash it out of the sheets and his shirts and off your skin when he came in drunk and demanding things he had no right to demand.*

Aramis. The only cologne he'd ever used. He never seemed to run out. She'd even gifted him with different kinds for his birthdays, and Christmas, but they always wound up in the trash or shoved to the back of the bathroom cabinet, unopened. The bad thing was, she actually liked the scent of Aramis—it was clean and spicy— but he used so much it was overwhelming.

Eventually, she was pretty certain it had seeped right into his pores.

"Smells like Anson," Nick said. "But he's in jail, so I know it isn't."

He trotted off toward his bedroom.

"Nicky," she called. "Wait."

He turned a question in his eyes.

"I – I don't know what that smell is, but would you help me find out before you go to your room?" She wanted him near her. She didn't want him out of her sight until they discovered the source of the odd scent. *Should I call Chet? Or Officer Rodriguez?*

"Sure," Nick said.

And just like that, it was decided. They'd handle this one on their own. *Where's my damn hammer? Am I going to have to get a gun? Why am I such a wimp, is every single woman this frightened?* She thought about Mrs. Benefield and the "boys in the attic," and she almost fainted. *Get a grip, for God's sake.*

The living room was easy. There was nothing for anyone to hide in or behind. The sofa was against the wall, the recliner right there, on one end. The kitchen wasn't bad either, and the back door was securely locked just the way they'd left it. No one could have gotten in without a key, she thought, but she didn't say it out loud, she didn't want Nick to know how frightened she really was.

As they passed by the attic door, Ella jiggled the knob. Still locked. Nick didn't even notice. He was headed to his room.

"Everything's fine in here," he said as he peeked into his closet and under his bed.

Why is he suddenly so brave she wondered, remembering how frightened they'd both been when they'd heard the raccoons.

"Great." She forced her voice to sound normal. She didn't smell the cologne as strongly here, but the scent was still there. *Maybe it's just soaked into my nose hairs and now I'll never be rid of it.*

She left him in his room and continued on to the bathroom. The shower door was clear but frosted. It was apparent no one was hiding there.

Ella stepped into her bedroom, just a few steps down from the bathroom. The smell completely overwhelmed her. She felt the pepperoni pizza rise to the back of her throat. *What the hell?*

She searched every inch of the bedroom, but found nothing that could account for the scent. I'm losing my mind, she thought. And then she spied the partially opened nightstand drawer. She glanced inside and saw a small bottle of Aramis. The pull top was slightly askew and the amber liquid had been leaking out into the drawer. *How'd that get there?*

Chills gripped her as surely as if she'd come down with a severe case of the flu.

"Nicky? Would you come here for a moment?" Could he have packed it without her knowing about it?

Nick walked in holding his nose. "Pee-yew!"

"I know," she said. "Look." She pointed at the drawer.

"That's Anson's," he said.

"Yes." She picked the bottle up and pushed the little stopper all the way in. Then she took it and dropped it into the bathroom trash. "Did you pack it, do you remember?"

Nick shook his head. "I can't stand that stuff."

"Yeah," Ella said. "I hear you." She shrugged. "I guess it got mixed up with some of my stuff and I just didn't see it. Must have been leaking out all this time."

Nick looked at the drawer. "I think it's probably in the wood now. How will you get the smell out?"

Ella thought for a moment. "Maybe baking soda will absorb it. First, I'll give it a little cold-water scrub, then the baking soda."

Nick nodded and headed back to his room. "I'm putting stuff in my backpack. Can I take my lunch tomorrow?"

"Sure," Ella said. "I'll get it ready." She was so relieved to find the cause of the smell; she wanted to jump for joy. *For a moment, I really thought he'd been here, but that's impossible. There's no way for him to know where we are.*

After scrubbing the spot and dumping half a box of baking soda on it, Ella walked around in a daze for several moments, taking things out of the fridge and cabinet and then standing there, looking at them, unsure why she'd taken out the peanut butter with the ham and cheese. *Surely he hasn't learned where we are. Surely he wouldn't even bother with us if he did.* But that glare across the courtroom when she'd testified against him had been frightening. And the way he mouthed something at her as they were leading him away after his sentencing. She never knew what he'd said, her lawyer had been turning her away as he was led past. What had it been? *I'll get you? You'll pay for this...*something along those lines?

Ella didn't know. She'd lost a lot of sleep over it, wondering what sort of threat he'd made this time, until she'd finally made the decision to leave Albuquerque completely. That's when she'd made peace with herself and her past. *I screwed up, she'd finally admitted. First with Tag, and later, when Anson had come along, I screwed up again. But I hadn't been a teen the second time. I'd just been alone, with little to no self-esteem, an over-bearing mother, and a low paying job. The worst combination in the world for a single mother trying to make ends meet. And then I met him. Anson. And it had seemed so good—almost too good to be true. If only I hadn't stayed with him so long. If only I'd admitted how awful he was right away. If only I'd never met him at all.*

When Nick came out of his room, she was still going over all the "if only" in her mind while making his lunch. "Hey baby," she said, putting her thoughts to rest at last. "You want a juice box or bottle of water?"

"Water. And some Oreos." He picked up a snack bag of the black and white cookies and dropped them into his lunch box.

"I have a feeling you're going to love your new school," Ella said. "Especially after what Chet said."

Nick raised his shoulders. "We'll see. I just hope their PE isn't lame. I hate when they make you go out and walk around the playground and call it Physical Education."

Ella stifled a smile. "Me too, my little athlete. I hope they make you do a full hour of calisthenics or ninja training or something."

Nick pretended to ignore her, but when he turned toward the living room, she saw him flexing his biceps, checking to see if he'd lost anything since football ended last year.

How could any man not be proud of that boy? She tossed her head to get her bangs off her brow. *It's amazing he has any self-confidence at all, though, the way Anson nagged and belittled him.*

"All right." She finished his lunch and placed it in the fridge. "Time for a little TV or a good book. You got anything on tap there, kiddo?"

Nick was in front of the television, but he had a book on his lap. "Just looking through *Diary of a Wimpy Kid*," he said.

Ella sat beside him. "How about if I read some?"

Nick snuggled in under her arm like a chick under the hen's wing.

That was answer enough for her. They read for half an hour, then she reluctantly shooed him to bed and tucked him in.

"At least we don't have to worry about raccoons tonight," he mumbled after they'd said a quick *Now I Lay Me Down to Sleep*.

"Thank goodness for that," she agreed. "Want me to stay until you fall asleep?" She pushed the thick fringe of hair off his forehead. He was the spitting image of his father. The one he'd never met.

"Maybe," he said. "Just tonight."

She lay down beside him and crossed one arm lightly over his chest.

"Thanks, Mom."

Ella kissed his temple in response.

When she woke twenty minutes later, he was snoring softly.

She carefully sat up and got her bearings. *Guess I was tired, too.* She crept from the room making certain to leave his football nightlight burning.

The phone rang as she walked through the kitchen in search of a glass of wine to end the day.

Gotta be Mom, she thought, reaching for the receiver with one hand and her favorite wine glass with the other.

"This Ms. Webb?" Chet's voice was jovial.

She was pleasantly surprised, but tried not to show it. "Well, hi," she replied. "Would this be Mr. Boone?"

"No, it's his son. Hope I'm not disturbing you." He sounded sincere. "I know Nicky has to get up early, but I just wanted to tell you how much I enjoyed the company this evening."

"I enjoyed it, too." She smiled and poured a dollop of wine. "Actually, I should say *we* enjoyed it. I haven't seen Nick so relaxed and happy since we moved."

"He's a great kid," Chet replied. "You're very lucky."

Ella was completely taken aback. "Yes, I am. But, unfortunately, not every man feels that way. About a woman with kids, I mean."

"Idiots," Chet said. "Some people just don't know what they are missing out on."

Ella took the cordless phone and headed back to the couch to relax and watch the evening news. She set her wineglass on the end table where the coaster should have been. She didn't see it anywhere. Have to ask Nicky about it tomorrow, she thought, getting another from the other end table. The coasters had been a birthday gift from her mom. It had been a special gift, sort of a peace offering. They were clear, heavy Lucite with pictures of her and Nick embedded in the core. She loved them. There were only two, but she'd unpacked them herself when they moved in.

She was certain both had been in their accustomed places yesterday, one on each end table flanking the couch. She looked around again, but the missing one was nowhere to be seen. It wasn't on the coffee table or under the coffee table or even under the couch.

Ella finally gave up and plopped down, moving the southwest-inspired throw pillow at the last second.

The missing coaster hit the floor with a solid *plonk*.

How odd, she thought. Nick must've stuck it under there for some reason. Thank goodness it didn't break.

She put the cork-backed coaster in its place and sipped her wine.

Chet was telling her how much fun he'd had over the summer when he'd volunteered as an assistant coach for the Little League Baseball team.

"That's amazing," she said. She hadn't meant for the thought to slip out into conversation, but there it was. Now she had to justify it. "I mean, you being a single man without any children of your own." Oh, God, that didn't sound right, either. "I just thought those coaches were usually parents of the kids or something. But I wouldn't really know."

Chet was silent for a moment. "You mean Nicky has never played baseball?"

He didn't seem the least bit perturbed about her assumptions. He was just surprised that a ten year old had never played baseball.

Ella bit back the first ugly thought that came to her mind. "No," she said. "He played football—and loved it—but he never got to try baseball."

"Maybe we can change that this summer."

She sipped her wine and sighed. "I guess you've gathered that Nicky hasn't had the best when it comes to father figures. I didn't even know all the things he was missing. I'm so glad we came to Stutter Creek."

"I'm glad, too," Chet murmured. "I think it may have been fate."

Ella pictured his dark blue eyes as they had looked when he was leaning against her Jeep in the Pizza Hut parking lot. Are the lids half-closed now, she wondered. The black lashes fringed out against his cheek? Is he lying on his own sofa, phone in hand like me? Or is he in bed already, lights out, talking to me in the dark the way I always wanted Tag to do when we were dating?

His next question brought her out of her reverie. "Am I moving too fast, calling and inviting you out again when we've just barely gotten home?"

Uh oh. What did I miss? "Umm, come again?" she asked.

He laughed an indulgent ripple of sound that tickled her eardrums and gladdened her heart.

"I *thought* I'd lost you there for a moment." His words were low and slow. "I said we should get together again, soon."

Ella laughed, too. Hers was a bit more self-conscious. "Sorry," she admitted. "Woolgathering—told you it was one of my worst habits."

"If that's your worst habit, I think we're okay. It's that hair in the shower drain that really gets me going. Well, that and leaving the lid off the toothpaste."

Ella snorted. "Well, I guess we might as well give it up, then. Those are my other bad habits."

He chuckled softly. "Seriously, that new movie starts at The Quadriplex in Pine River. I believe it's called *The Time Bandits*. I've heard it's a fantasy, sort of like Harry Potter."

"Oh yes," she replied. "Nicky made me watch the trailer when it came on TV. He was really excited about it." She chewed the tip of her thumbnail. "It's just that I, well, I'm not sure if I should—"

"What? Get involved with another man who might leave like Nicky's father?"

How did he know about Tag? "No, that's not it at all."

"Oh. Sorry," he said. "When you said he hadn't had much of a father figure I just assumed the guy had pulled the old disappearing act."

Ella realized he didn't even know that Anson wasn't Nick's father. "It's a long story, and complicated," she said. "Just suffice it to say that Nicky's *stepfather* wasn't much of a dad, even if he was the one paying the bills and laying down the rules."

"Oh—"

"And I'm just afraid of letting him get attached to another man who might not be what he appears to be." She had a sudden memory of Anson, as he'd been when they first got together. He was so handsome, his rusty hair reminding her of *Erik the Red* or some other famous Viking. She'd felt so good in his arms then, his broad chest like a safe house she could run to when thunder threatened. And if he hadn't been as warm and loving with Nick as she hoped, at least he hadn't been cruel. Not then. She'd told herself it would simply take time. That he just had to *learn* how to be a parent. She'd had Nicky for five years at that point—she'd had lots of time to learn how to love. Except it hadn't taken any learning. It had been automatic since the day he was born. That was the thing. That's what she'd pushed to the back of her mind. She'd even convinced herself it would be the same for Anson. That he would fall in love with her boy just like she had.

But it hadn't been that simple.

Not at all.

But I can't keep dwelling on that. It's poison. And it's over now.

Chet was quiet.

"Sorry to be so blunt." She gulped the remainder of her wine. "But from now on that's how I'm going to live my life. Honestly. With eyes wide open. And Nicky comes first. Above all else."

Still, he was quiet.

Guess that's that. I've alienated him completely. Oh well. Better now rather than later. Save us all a lot of heartache.

"That's something you just don't have to worry about with me," he said at last. "I've been sitting here trying to think of a way to say that without it sounding false and ridiculous. But I can't. So I'll just have to show you. If you will let me. It doesn't have to be all at once—I was afraid I was moving too fast—but I've got all the time in the world. There's no rush."

"But if it doesn't work out, Nicky still gets hurt." Her voice was tiny. She felt as if she was speaking a new language for the first time. *The language of independence, perhaps.*

"No. It doesn't have to be that way," Chet replied. "If it doesn't work out—though I can't see why it wouldn't—then I'll still be his coach and his buddy. Just like Officer Rod and the Police Athletic League." He cleared his throat. "Not everyone just talks the talk. Some of us actually know how to walk the walk, too."

Ella was dumbfounded. *Too good to be true,* her Mom's voice whispered in the back of her mind. *Don't be so cynical, Mom,* her own voice whispered back. But she knew it wasn't that easy. He *did* seem too good to be true.

"Let's see how school goes tomorrow," she said. "That will probably set the tone for the rest of our year." She tried to make it sound lighthearted, like a joke, but in reality, she was afraid it was the absolute truth.

"That's a deal," he agreed. "On one condition."

Ella hesitated. "Condition?"

He laughed softly, teasingly. "You have to promise to call me if any more critters get in."

She exhaled. *What did I think he was going to say? Wow. Anson really has made me gun shy.* "Sure, she replied. I really appreciate all you did for us in the way of repairs and relocating the little thing."

"That's what I'm here for. And El?"

No one had called her El since she was a little girl. It made her feel young. "Yes?"

"Even if we never go out again. Don't ever hesitate to call me, anytime. Even if there aren't any critters. Deal?"

Ella clutched the receiver tighter. "That's a deal."

"All right. I'll talk to you soon then."

They both hung up at the same time.

What have I just done? Have I cut the thread of something that was just getting started? That would be about par for me. I sew up the bad guys and cut the good ones loose without a second thought.

Maybe I didn't offend him. He said call him anytime. I just didn't agree to go out again. Not yet. And that's only common sense coming through, for a change.

She wandered through the quiet house turning off lights and checking doors one last time. *He said call him anytime, even just to chat. But could I do that? Would I ever have the nerve to just pick up the phone?*

In the bathroom, she washed her face, brushed her teeth, and checked on Nick one last time. He was sleeping so soundly she was impressed. If she had been the one who was about to embark on being the "new kid," she would have been a bundle of nerves.

Dropping a gentle kiss near his hairline, Ella tiptoed from the room. Her own bedroom was cozy in the light of the bedside lamp. She grabbed her Kindle and slid beneath the covers. There were several books on her to-be-read list and now seemed the perfect time to dive in. She loved having a choice of reading material and a little time to herself.

Chapter Twelve

Propping a second pillow behind her head, Ella touched the menu icon and began to scan her library.

She awoke some time later, Kindle face down on her chest and bedside lamp still burning. *Guess I need more sleep,* she thought, remembering how she had fallen asleep with Nick earlier.

Scrape.

Thunk.

She looked up at the ceiling. *Really? Again?*

Her heart sped up as she lay, waiting.

Is that what woke me? Sounds from the attic? She pinched the inside of her elbow. *Yep. I'm awake.* Her eyes slowly tracked around the room, taking in all the nuances of her new bedroom, making mental adjustments here and there for future reference. *Could use a coat of paint, maybe a milk chocolate with some floral window treatments. Of course, that will be a while down the road after we get into the groove with the restaurant.*

Her eyes continued to take in the room while her mind continued to wonder when the next sound would come. In truth, she was simply putting off having to deal with the noises. She was certain they would come again, but if they didn't, she wouldn't have to leave her cozy little nest.

Growing drowsy, she decided she must have dreamed the sounds for a change. Ella began to drift away. At the last second, she raised her head and placed her Kindle on the nightstand. That's when her gaze fell on the closed bedroom door.

Closed?

Her entire body went cold.

She *never* closed her bedroom door. Nick might need her in the night. If the door was closed, she might not hear him call out.

Did I close it?

No, definitely not.

Does the floor slope? It's hasn't closed on its own before. Would Nick have done it?

She looked up at the ceiling again, but all was quiet. The curtains were pulled tight so she couldn't see outside, but she knew it was near midnight or even later.

Could it just be the wind blowing?

While these questions were circulating through her mind, Ella was carefully climbing from beneath the blankets, slipping into her house shoes—the faux leopard pair Nick (with Nana's help) had bought for her birthday last year—and reaching for her trusty hammer again. Getting to be a habit, she thought, hefting its comforting weight.

Good thing I put it back after last time.

First, I'll check on Nick. Then I'll worry about the sound—if there was indeed a sound. She took a deep breath and pulled on the doorknob. She half-expected it to be locked or stuck or something. But it opened as easily as ever.

Hammer gripped in her right hand, she peered into the dark hallway. Nicky's nightlight spread a minute glow through his open bedroom door. Ella headed toward it as if toward a lighthouse beacon.

Two steps from the door, she turned, certain her own door would be slowly closing behind her, but everything was still. Nevertheless, her skin crimped into gooseflesh.

Why am I so cold? Is the house haunted by more than raccoons?

She rubbed her right arm with her left palm to smooth away the prickles, but she wasn't letting go of the hammer.

At Nicky's doorway, she hesitated and looked behind her once more. Nerves, she assured herself. Just nerves.

She stuck her head into Nick's room.

Her son was sound asleep, just as she'd left him.

Ella let out a sigh of relief.

Idiot, her subconscious scolded. You must have dreamed—or imagined—the whole thing. *Except for that pesky bedroom door being closed. Didn't exactly imagine that, did I?*

She crept away from the doorway and headed back toward her own room.

No way I'll get back to sleep now. Might as well make another door-check.

Hammer still in hand, she pushed her hair back and began her check with the attic door. It was still locked. Front and back doors, too.

A quick stop in the bathroom told her all was fine there, as well.

She began to relax.

Only a dream and a coincidence about the bedroom door. I'll just have to use a doorstop from now on. Old houses and all that.

In the kitchen, she flipped the switch and the overhead light winked off the rim of the wineglass she'd left on the counter.

One more glass might help me go back to sleep.

She poured a generous amount, and stood, sipping.

Her hand barely shook.

She laid the hammer on the counter and rubbed the back of her neck. The air had grown chilly again as if she were standing in a draft. She clasped her arms around herself. *Must be the cold wine.* She downed the remainder of it quickly, determined to fall back into her warm blankets and grab a little shuteye before the first day of school.

She reached for the switch, but the lights went out before her hand could get there.

Chapter Thirteen

The kitchen was plunged into darkness.

Ella drew her hand away from the switch as if it were a snake. The chills she'd experienced while sipping the cold wine intensified until she was literally shivering with fear and adrenalin.

Her first thought was no thought at all.

It was pure gut-grabbing panic.

Where's the flashlight?

She couldn't remember unpacking it.

Once her eyes adjusted, there was just enough moonlight to see across the kitchen. She found the doorway and made a beeline for Nick's room to check on him. Though why he would have even wakened was beyond her—there hadn't been a clap of thunder or bolt of lighting—nothing. But as always when anything happened, her first thought was of Nicky.

As she passed the attic door she automatically reached out and gave the knob another twist to make sure it was still locked.

In Nick's room, all was quiet. He had turned onto his side, but was still sleeping peacefully. Her panic began to abate—her boy was okay, that was the main thing.

Ella peeked out his window. The wind was gusty, but not loud. The pine trees swayed back and forth as if to a silent melody.

That's the problem, she told herself, the wind. A tree limb fell on a power line somewhere, that's all. Funny, though. It didn't seem *that* windy.

She made her way to her own bedroom to check the breakers. The breaker box was in her bedroom closet. *But how will I be able to see them without a flashlight?*

Back to the kitchen she went, in the dark, in search of matches and candles. Now that the fear had begun to abate, she was beginning to get mad. *I'll be a total wreck tomorrow to meet Nicky's teacher, not to mention working at The Drugstore.*

Then it dawned on her. She had a flashlight app on her cell phone. She'd just gotten so used to not using the phone that it was getting to the point where she sometimes forgot she even owned one.

She grabbed her purse off the table and dug it out. The flashlight app was nice and bright. Still need to buy a real flashlight, she told herself. Especially with winter coming. *I should make a list of things I need in case of emergency.* It occurred to her she'd never been on her own in a crisis situation. She'd always had her mom or Anson. *At least he had been good in situations like these. But that doesn't matter now—seeing Nick smiling and happy the way he was at the Pizza Hut—that's what matters. I wouldn't go back to the way it was for anything.*

Holding the phone-light toward the floor so she wouldn't trip over anything, Ella made her way to her bedroom.

She stood in front of the closed closet door.

It would be as black as death inside.

She would have to push aside all the clothes she'd just unpacked and hung up yesterday. *What if someone is hiding in there? What if someone has been in the house all along and they've just been toying with me? Idiot—get real. You've read too many scary books. Seen too many horror movies. This is real life and it's just a power outage, nothing more.*

Irrational or not, Ella did not want to open that door. She would rather have poured cold water on a bad tooth. But there was no other way—she had to know if a breaker had been tripped.

Steeling herself in case someone—or some*thing*—leapt out at her, Ella reached for the knob. In her mind she could actually see the thing crouched on the other side of the flimsy door, something human-like and raccoon-like at the same time, or worse yet, Anson himself, wearing his prison orange, standing there, reaching for her from out of the past. *You owe me*, he would say. *You owe me, now you're going to pay.*

Scrape

THUNK!

Ella flung her arm over her head and ducked.

The sound had been directly overhead.

Boys in the attic?

Mrs. Benefield's words floated to the surface of her mind like dead fish in an aquarium. The wind gusted at the windows, eddied around the locks, searched diligently for a way inside.

Ella slowly straightened up. *It's not boys in the attic, it's not toys in the attic, if anything it's the wind, or those pesky little rodents back again.* She didn't know if raccoons were really rodents, but in her mind they were now on the same par with them. Besides, if raccoons were living up there, maybe rats and mice were, too. Maybe Chet had only gotten rid of part of the problem.

Nightshirt sticking to a sudden moisture in the center of her back, Ella dragged in a shaky breath, reached forward one more time and yanked open the door.

Nothing leapt out at her.

Nothing floated out on a sea of green mist.

No red rimmed eyes glared at her above an orange jumpsuit.

She shined a light inside.

There was nothing in the closet except for the clothes she'd unpacked and hung up yesterday. And a couple of empty wire hangers clinking together from the draft created when she pulled the door open with such force.

Ella looked at those barely moving hangers and it was all she could do not to slam the door shut again.

I have to do it. I have to check the breakers. There's no one but me.

She shoved the clothes aside with the same hand that was holding the light. Crazy shadows flitted around the small closet like trapped moths, but she didn't stop until she'd uncovered the gray rectangular breaker box set into the back wall. The thin metal door was fastened with a sturdy latch.

Ella reached forward in slow motion and twisted the butterfly latch.

All the breaker switches were pointing the same direction. Nothing was out of place.

Quietly, she closed the box.

Scrape

She raised her eyes to the ceiling, heart fluttering like the mothy shadows.

It has to be raccoons. Somehow they've gotten back in, or they're trying to. Or squirrels, I didn't even think of squirrels. They're much smaller than 'coons, they could get in through the smallest opening.

She began to doubt her decision to rent the old house.

Then a brilliant idea occurred to her. The critters—whatever species they were—might have chewed through the wiring somewhere in the walls.

That's why the power went out!

She felt so much better when that idea occurred to her. It made more sense than the wind—although she supposed it was *possible* a branch or tree had blown over onto a line somewhere.

Should I call someone? I'd feel like an idiot calling Chet. I just told him we needed to be nothing more than friends. Hate to call nine-one-one again, they're going to get the idea I'm as loony as poor Mrs. Bene—

Something caressed the back of her neck.

Ella screamed and whirled around.

The phone flew from her hand.

It struck the floor and slid across the hardwood into oblivion.

The flashlight app disappeared.

She fell to the floor in an attempt to locate it in the thick darkness; terrified that whatever had caressed her was now reaching toward her, slithering out of the blackness under her bed.

On her knees in a blind panic, Ella swept her hands from side to side. Someone was making a sound like uh-uh-uh. She was pretty sure it was her, but she didn't know how to stop.

Crunch.

The phone cracked beneath her knee.

Shit!

She grabbed it up and tried to swipe the screen with her forefinger. She found only a series of cracks. The screen wouldn't come on. She shoved the useless thing into her pocket and scrambled toward the door, toward the hammer she'd left on the kitchen counter. The back of her neck felt so vulnerable, *so* exposed.

She heard Nick moan as she passed his room again. His sleep had finally been disturbed—no doubt—by her scream.

Ella lunged through the kitchen door. Miscalculating its width, she banged her shoulder on the edge of the jamb. The terrific blow knocked her back a step, but she recovered and kept going, hand already reaching for the hammer she'd left beside the wine bottle.

It was not there.

But she knew it should be.

She grabbed the half-empty wine bottle instead, prepared to battle whatever might come her way as she rushed back toward the barely-sleeping Nick.

The lights popped on.

In her bedroom, the clock radio beeped to let her know it was back in operation.

Ella's breath was hot and harsh in her throat.

She rushed back to Nick's door and gazed in at him as if she were one of the ghosts of Christmas past waiting to take him on a horrifying adventure.

Scrape

Thunk!

She squeezed her eyes shut and clutched the sides of her head as if it might explode. The wine bottle was cool against her fevered cheek.

I know what that sound is, she felt like screaming. That's nothing but a tree branch on the roof. Somehow it caused the lights to go off. That's all it is. That's all. There's nothing here. Nothing but me and Nick and maybe a mouse or a squirrel or—

What about the touch on the back of your neck, and your bedroom door being closed, and where oh where, has your little hammer gone? The voice in her head was part her, part Anson. Even though he wasn't here, she still blamed him for putting her and Nick in this position.

Ella staggered to Nick's window, wine bottle in hand like an old drunk on a Bourbon Street bender, and looked out at the windy night.

I can't do this. Tears rolled down her cheeks. *This place is haunted. It is. Something is in here with us. We have to go, have to move—I've traded one monster for another.* She wiped her eyes and crept back to the kitchen where she picked up the receiver of the landline to call someone.

But at the last moment, she couldn't make herself dial the numbers.

She replaced the receiver—thankful, in the back of her mind that the landline still worked—and sank to the floor, hand still gripping the neck of the heavy blue bottle.

When the sun came up, she had moved to the living room, positioning the old recliner so that she could see the front door, the kitchen door, and the hallway all at the same time.

She'd dozed fitfully, kitchen and living room lights still burning, jerking awake every time real sleep threatened to overcome her, certain that some barely heard noise had wakened her, or certain that something was hovering over her, or behind her, or even just outside the field of her peripheral vision. But there was never anything there.

Ella finally gave up and sat up.

Her neck was bent and so sore she could barely move her head.

Great way to start the week, she thought.

Great way to start our new lives.

Forcing herself from her chair, Ella went in search of the hammer. She was sure she'd simply laid it somewhere else in her panic. But she couldn't find it.

Her cell phone, when she put it on the charger, came on, but it was useless, the cracked screen made it impossible to swipe anything, even if she had been able to get a signal.

She spied the wine bottle on the floor beside her recliner. *Anyone would think a wino lived here.* She uncorked it and poured the remaining bit of wine down the drain. But she couldn't bring herself to part with the heavy bottle. It had felt just right in her grip. *Call me Goldilocks, it felt just right.*

Ella took the bottle and placed it in the kitchen window, knocking the attic door key into the old sink. In the early morning stillness, the key made a distinct metal *clink* against the porcelain.

Ella recalled how they'd hidden the storehouse key on a nail behind the doorjamb. She looked for a similar nail near the attic door. Sure enough, just to the right of the upper corner, she spied one. Perfect, she thought. She tied a short loop of string through the hole in the top of the key. Then she hung it on the nail. One less thing to worry about.

When she reached into the cupboard for her coffee mug, she noticed that the sunlight through the bright blue wine bottle created an interesting fog-colored cylinder on the white counter.

Very artsy, Ella thought.

Too bad I'm too exhausted to care.

Chapter Fourteen

Bleary eyed, Ella went on autopilot, filling the little basket on her ancient Mr. Coffee with Folgers Select, determined to search every inch of the house before she woke Nick. After splashing water on her face at the kitchen sink, she gulped a cup of hot coffee, scalding her tongue in the process.

Then she carried her cup, room to room, and examined every closet, every nook and cranny, looked under every bed. She even forced herself to take the key back off the nail and check the attic. The screens were still in place behind the new vents Chet had installed. She could see nothing out of place.

The flattened boxes didn't appear to have been chewed or moved. The thick pink insulation that lined the walls and ceiling seemed undisturbed.

She actually tugged at the new slatted vents to make sure they were secure. They didn't even wiggle.

Ella sighed and headed back downstairs.

Ghosts. It has to be ghosts. Something touched me. I did not imagine that.

On instinct, she went back to her closet and opened the little door to the breaker box. Once again, all the switches were pointing the same direction.

Ella reached out and laid her palm flat against them to make certain each one was pushed in firmly. Once, she had called a repairman when the electric range wouldn't come on. It had cost them a seventy-five dollar service call to find out Anson simply hadn't reset the breaker properly after he'd replaced the stove element.

Unfortunately, that wasn't the case this time. All the little switches were pushed over as far as they would go.

Closing the metal door, she was about to twist the butterfly latch back into place when something occurred to her. Ella yanked the door open again. *Weren't the switches all pointed the other way last night?* She couldn't be certain, she couldn't be certain at all.

Going to her purse, she pulled out an ink pen and drew an arrow on the metal door. The arrow pointed the same direction as the breaker switches. *Now, if it happens again, I'll know. I'll know for sure.*

That tiny bit of knowledge empowered her, made her feel as if she'd done something proactive. *Now, if I could only find where I left the hammer.*

Shaking her head, Ella went to Nick's room and woke him gently. She was still amazed that he'd slept through everything until she remembered how he seldom awoke when Anson had come staggering in, drunk and disorderly. Maybe sleep is simply a naturally occurring defense mechanism of young boys, she thought.

She went to the kitchen to stir up a batch of chocolate chip pancakes, his favorite.

Am I going nuts, she wondered as she stacked the pancakes on Nick's plate. For a moment, she seriously wished a certain blue-eyed critter-catcher was sitting down with them as he had before, but she quickly pushed that wish away. *Too soon. Too many unknowns. Best to play it safe. Got more to worry about anyhow, with all the sounds and things that went bump in the night. But maybe that's why I should call him. There must be more critters in the attic, maybe they're in the walls and that's why I can't find evidence of them upstairs. But what about those breaker switches?*

Yawning, she poured herself another cup of coffee before calling Nick to hurry before the pancakes got cold.

By the time she and Nick were out the door, the events of the night were already growing dim. There was too much to look forward to for both of them.

The touch on the back of her neck seemed ridiculous in the light of day. And the closed door and missing hammer just seemed to be evidence of her tortured, woolgathering mind. *Too many things to remember. Too many details to keep track of. That's all.*

*

Beth Stockton opened her fifth grade classroom and flipped on the lights. Today was book fair, so she had a lot of prepping to do. As a class, they would go to the school library to shop. The book catalogs had been sent home the previous week so the students could go over them with their parents. And so the parents would have an idea of how much money to send on shopping day—today.

It was a great fundraiser for the library. The kids always got so excited about books. Of course, there were a few of the students who would spend their money on posters and fancy pencils, but most would buy at least one book. And that was always a plus.

Beth was lucky she was still around to teach. She'd gone through an awful period just after her father passed away and her first husband left her for a younger woman. She'd been so depressed she could have been a walking advertisement for Zoloft. Then she'd returned to Stutter Creek and crossed paths with Danny's father, a serial killer.

What could have been Beth's demise turned out to be one of the best things that had ever happened to her. Not only had she rediscovered John, her very first crush from her teenage years, but she'd also found Danny, the new love of her life.

Turk's silly doggy grin came to her mind and she thought, *Yes, I found you, too, you big galoot!* She laughed to herself and began to write the day's instructions on the whiteboard.

"Ahem."

Beth spun around, marker held aloft like a weapon. She was still a bit jumpy, even after four years.

"Sorry," Ella said. "We didn't mean to startle you."

Ella and Nick had turned his paperwork into the school office and the Assistant Principal had walked them to the fifth grade wing before being called back to the office for a minor crisis.

Beth grinned self-consciously. "It's all right, I was just deep in thought." Her eyes fastened on Nick. "New student?" she asked with a smile.

Ella nodded. "We just moved here from Albuquerque." She walked forward, holding out her hand. "I'm Ella Webb, new owner of The Drugstore Café, and this is my son, Nicholas."

"Nick," the boy said, holding out his own hand.

Beth shook hands with both of them. "Pleased to meet you both. My name is Mrs. Stockton." She looked at Ella. "Call me Beth. Martha is such a dear friend, we're all still in mourning about Joe." She took a deep breath. The man's death had hit the small community hard—even though it was completely expected due to his emphysema and heart ailments. "I heard The Drugstore had been sold—and I'm very pleased to meet the new owners." She looked directly at Nick. "You are going to love Stutter Creek. And you picked a great day to start school. We're going to shop at the book fair today."

Nick's mouth opened in an O and he looked at his mother.

"Do you like to read?" Beth asked.

Nick nodded vigorously. "I love to read."

Beth walked to her desk and found one of the catalogs that showed all the books available for purchase. "Take a few minutes to look over this flyer while I dig out your textbooks."

Nick and Ella moved to the side counter where they were able to spread the colorful catalog pages out for faster perusal. "Look, Mom, they've got the whole entire Harry Potter set in paperback, and there's one about ghosts in the White House and, ooh, look at this. I want this one about Drew Brees, and—"

Ella laughed. "Hold up there, kiddo. How much allowance money have you saved up?"

Nick looked at the floor. "I've got ten dollars Nana gave me for my birthday, and I think I still have a couple of bucks in change."

"Okay, then." Ella pulled out her wallet. "Twelve bucks it is." She looked at his crestfallen face. "And another ten for helping me carry in all those boxes yesterday."

Nick let out a *whoop* and went back to studying the catalog. In a few moments, he tallied up the books he wanted.

Beth stacked his fifth grade textbooks on an empty desk and then affixed a bright yellow nametag to a locker at the back of the room. With a Sharpie marker, she wrote NICK on it in bold black letters. "You're all set," she told him. "Go ahead and put your things in your locker. Just keep out the catalog, your money, and your notebook and pencils." She patted a desk. "This will be yours, right here by Seth Garza. I think you two will get along—he loves Harry Potter, too."

While Nick was checking out his books and money situation, Beth took Ella by the arm and walked her to a corner of the room. "Let me invite you to come in and volunteer any time you have a free moment, which I'm sure you won't have since you're a new business owner." She looked at Ella closely. "But just know our classroom door is always open to parents. We have Muffins With Mom coming up next week. All the kids love it when their parents can come and eat breakfast with them."

Ella touched Beth's arm. "Sounds great," she said. "I think we are really going to like it here." She refused to let the events of last night spill over into this moment. Instead, she glanced over at Nick, still engrossed in the book catalog. "At least I'm certain we picked the perfect day to enroll."

*

After seeing that her son was in goods hands in his new school, Ella felt both relieved and terrified. What if Nick loved his new school, but they couldn't live in their new house? What if he adjusted, but she couldn't? She had no one in Stutter Creek to fall back on. At least in Albuquerque she'd had her mom in case of emergencies—overbearing, perhaps, but always there in a pinch.

Ella put the worrisome thoughts out of her mind and headed to The Drugstore. Like a shark, she couldn't stop moving or she'd drown in the memories of the horrific night she'd endured. Or in pure exhaustion.

On the way to the cafe, she passed a Hometown Hardware store. Hammer, she thought. Flashlight.

She pulled into the parking lot, walked straight inside and found both items without too much problem—she wasn't a frequent hardware store shopper—paid with her credit card, and took her purchases back to the car. It made her feel like a real adult. As if she were taking even more steps to alleviate the fears from last night.

Her hand fell to the hammer as she drove. It was shiny silver with a light blue rubber grip. *What happened to the one with the red rubber grip?* She pushed the thought away. *I'm not going to obsess about it. I misplaced it, that's all. It'll turn up. Things always turn up when you least expect them to.*

When she walked into The Drugstore, Martha was behind the counter with her bright white apron wrapped around her stout frame, the long, thin strings double tied in front.

"Ella!" She greeted her as if she were a cherished friend rather than the woman who would soon take over the business that had been her life for so many years.

Ella smiled and moved behind the counter. She hugged the older woman gently. "How's everything going?"

Almost every table and booth had at least one diner, and several of the swivel stools at the old-fashioned bar were occupied as well.

"It's a great morning," Martha said. She flipped an egg on the griddle without pausing. "Sunny side up." She slid her spatula under the egg and then let it slide onto a heavy ceramic plate waiting on the stove-warmer. She added a generous helping of home fries, four slices of thick, pepper bacon, and a side of griddle-fried toast.

Ella's belly rumbled.

"Skip breakfast?" Martha asked.

Ella laughed and shook her head. "Not if you call three cups of coffee breakfast."

"That's not breakfast," Martha replied. "I'll make you a quick omelet."

Officer Rodriguez stopped by the bar. He had a toothpick riding in the corner of his bottom lip. "I heard that." His voice was jovial. "I hope you're teaching Ms. Webb all your tricks, Martha." He patted his uniformed midsection expansively. "Best breakfast in town."

Martha waved her hand in his direction dismissively. "Oh, you."

Ella could tell his compliment meant a lot to the older woman. "I promise, I won't let her move off to Florida until she teaches me everything she knows." She took the proffered bill from the officer and looked at the amount listed there. She hoped she could manage the place well enough so her prices would always remain that low.

"Everything get straightened out at your place?" he asked.

She nodded. *Should I tell him about last night? Will they all think I'm nuts? Am I nuts?*

He handed her a twenty and told her to keep the change.

Ella stuck the paper receipt onto the sharp metal spike standing beside the register. *Missed my chance. Should have spoken up. Didn't want everyone in the place to know all my problems.* She bit her lip and resisted the urge to run after him, ask him if he could...*Could what? That's the problem. What could he do? I checked the entire house from top to bottom. There was nothing there.*

A tension headache had settled on her head like a tight cap. She rubbed at a tender spot directly above her right eye. She was so tired she had to force herself to focus on the dining room.

"Here, eat this." Martha sat a plate before her. It contained a small omelet and a slice of toast. "It will help that headache, too."

Ella thanked her and took a few bites. It was as delicious as she'd known it would be. As she ate, she observed Martha as she took a steaming plate of food to booth four, the last one on the far side.

The woman was the epitome of efficiency. She never made a trip across the dining room that didn't include bringing something to a guest or taking something back to the kitchen. No wasted steps, Martha had told her. She recalled the same advice from her manager at The Kettle Restaurant.

She finished off the omelet, drank a small glass of orange juice, and hurried to the restroom to wash her hands with disinfectant soap so that she could begin helping Martha cook and serve.

Will I have someone else clean the restrooms? Or is that a chore I have to do myself? As the warm water cascaded over her soapy hands, Ella was once again reminded of just how many things she had yet to learn. *Have I bitten off more than I can chew? No, that's just last night's lack of sleep talking. Have to rein in that attitude if I'm going to make a go of this.*

She took a deep breath and pushed through the ancient batwing doors that separated the restrooms from the dining area.

The dark wooden counter ran the length of the small dining room. In the center, the six old-fashioned spouts of the soda fountain stuck up above the glossy surface like the graceful necks of beautiful brass swans.

Booths ran along the two longest walls and down the center. And in the front windows were two small tables covered with the same heavy, red and white-checkered oilcloth. Every surface was highly polished wood or metal. Even the ceiling was antique punched tin right up to the loft-like storage area that ran around the room on three sides.

Each time she walked through the door, Ella fell in love with the historic little diner all over again. It really had served as the town's drugstore back in its heyday. In fact, the historic plaque out front verified that the building had been in continuous use since it was first built over a century earlier.

Woolgathering, she scolded herself. Then she rushed to put on her own snowy apron.

Martha grinned when Ella appeared at the table next to the one she was serving. A new couple had just sat down and Ella had their menus and ice water. "I'll be back in a moment to get your order. How about a cup of coffee while you wait?"

They both nodded and Ella filled two steaming mugs from the restaurant grade Braun coffee maker. She placed them on a round tray and added tiny barrels of cream and an old-time sugar shaker. *Wonder if it would be more cost effective to buy the tiny packets of sugar? Have to talk to Martha about that—wait, would that play havoc with the ambience?* She decided it probably would. *So much to keep in mind, she thought. So much to do.*

Working side-by-side, Ella and Martha handled the breakfast crowd with ease. "You're really good at this," Martha said when they both found themselves at the grill.

"Years of experience," Ella replied. "I've been a waitress since I first found myself pregnant with Nicky way back in high school."

Martha nodded. "Single parenthood is tough." She patted Ella's shoulder. "You've done very well with the boy, though. He's an absolute doll."

Ella smiled and loaded another plate with eggs and home fries. "He is, isn't he?"

The two of them laughed companionably.

After another hour of non-stop customers, with Ella carefully observing everything Martha did on the griddle and with the regular customers, the place finally emptied and the women took their coffee cups to a back booth while Jan, the only other morning employee, loaded the dishwasher.

Martha fanned her face with a napkin folded accordion style. "I tell ya," she began, "as much as I love this place, I'm beginning to feel the strain on my old body." She sipped her coffee and dabbed at her eyes. "Joe, he's the one who really loved this old building."

Ella reached across the table and patted Martha's hand. "You must miss him so much."

"That's the truth." Martha's voice wobbled. "He was my man. For fifty-two years." She closed her eyes. "You should have seen him when we met—a strapping young man. Logger, he was. Strong as an ox, but gentle as a lamb." She looked at Ella. "I'm sorry. Don't know why I'm so morose this morning. Just get that way when I'm tired— guess it really is time for me to retire. Florida, here I come."

"You deserve a rest, but I'm serious when I say that if you decided to stay in Stutter Creek, I would be delighted to keep you on in whatever position you chose. Part-time, full-time, even just as a come-and-go consultant." She smiled sincerely. "You and Joe made this place into a real anchor business. If you want to keep your hand in, that is completely understandable." She watched the worry lines on Martha's old face soften as she talked. *Maybe this isn't the day to tell her about my problems at the Lilac Lane house. The dear old thing seems overwhelmed with her own problems—having to give up her entire way of life.*

She tried not to feel guilty about buying the diner, after all if she didn't buy the place someone else would, but even so, it broke her heart to see Martha so melancholy.

Chapter Fifteen

At 2:50, Ella left The Drugstore and headed back to school to pick up Nick. She couldn't wait to hear about his day. In the back of her mind, she was worried that something had gone wrong, that he hated it, and wanted to go home. *What would I do then?* She chewed a thumbnail and thought of calling her mom. Here in town, she had better service. She picked up her cell phone and looked at the cracked screen. *Damn. How could I have forgotten that? Because no one ever calls me, she thought sadly. But that's okay. New life. Things will be different, eventually.*

She stuffed the phone back into her purse and wondered where the nearest phone store was located. She hadn't seen one here in town so she assumed it would be in Pine River.

The school was only a few minutes from The Drugstore. *Dare I let Nicky walk over from school? Or should I get him on the school bus or just try to make certain I can pick him up every day?* Ella just couldn't make herself allow him to walk. Kidnapping was one of her worst fears—especially since they were basically alone now.

Do we need the school bus? Maybe not yet, maybe I'll just make it a point to pick him up everyday. Surely Jan can handle things for half an hour each day.

As she was debating the issue in her head, Nick emerged from the far door with a light haired boy about his own size. When he saw her waiting at the curb, he gave the boy a little wave and jogged toward the Jeep.

"Hey!" She made her voice as cheery as possible. "So, how was it?"

Nick removed his backpack and tossed it in the back seat. "Not bad," he said. "Mrs. Stockton didn't make me introduce myself or anything."

Ella smiled but didn't comment. Coming from Nick, that was high praise indeed. "Good deal. Who was the boy you were walking out with? He in your class?"

Nick looked back as if to remind himself who he'd been with. As if it hadn't been only thirty seconds earlier. "Oh, him? That was Seth. He likes football, too." He reached into the back seat and retrieved his backpack. "Look what I got at the book fair." He removed the boxed set of Harry Potter paperbacks he'd marked in the catalog that morning.

Ella held her hand out and they bumped fists. "Glad you got them before they sold out, kiddo."

"Thanks, Mom." He removed a holographic bookmark that featured a gryphon perched on a spire, and opened the first book. "Mrs. S. gave us twenty whole minutes to read after we got back from the fair." He held his place with his finger. "I'm going to start from the beginning and read my way straight through the whole series. Last time I had to read them out of order 'cause someone wouldn't turn in book three to the library."

"I remember," she said. "You sure won't have that trouble this time." She drove into a slanted parking space in front of The Drugstore. "You can read and do your homework at one of the booths while I work with Martha."

Nick pulled another bookmark from his bag. "Got you this," he said. "I had a couple bucks left over." He held out a glittery blue rectangle with a gold tassel on one end. "Follow Your Dreams" was written on it in curvy script.

"Oh, honey, it's beautiful." She leaned over to hug him. Unexpected gifts were rare and special.

"Don't freak out." He pulled back with a smile.

She thumped him on the knee and stuck the bookmark over her visor so it wouldn't get bent in her purse. "You just made my day, sweetie. Thank you."

Nick jumped out of the Jeep; backpack slung over one shoulder, and dashed toward the door. Like most boys, he wasn't a fan of **PDAs**—parental displays of affection—especially not in public.

Martha looked up with a wave. She was busy readying the grill and food prep area in anticipation of the supper run. "From five o'clock on," she said when Ella had put her apron back on, "we'll have a steady stream." She looked over at Nick who was seated at one of the tables in the window. "Around six, it will be almost packed. Jan only works breakfast and lunch, so that leaves the two of us plus Belinda Montoya for supper. I don't think you've met Belinda yet, she was away at a volleyball clinic the last time you were here."

Ella looked at her quizzically.

"Belinda's on the junior varsity at Stutter Creek High."

"Ahhh," Ella said. "Doesn't she miss a lot of weekends? Looks like that's when we'd need her the most."

Martha nodded emphatically. "Some. But not as much as you'd think. Our poor team doesn't usually advance very far after the regular season and most of those games are on Saturday afternoon."

Ella laughed. "I don't know whether to be pleased or sad."

"Both," Martha said. "I kept thinking I might hire another part-timer, but somehow it just continued to work out, you know?"

"I guess so." Ella's face was thoughtful. "I wonder if Nick can really help?" Her voice was low. She didn't expect Martha to answer, she was simply thinking out loud.

"Oh sure," the older woman answered. "He'd be great at prep." She indicated the way she was rolling silverware in napkins and filling the salt and pepper shakers. "I don't know if I'd want him slicing veggies." She pointed at the plastic containers of freshly sliced lettuce and tomatoes. "But I'll bet he could bus tables and run the dishwasher. That would be a tremendous help on the evening shift."

Ella bit her lip. He has to be here anyway, she thought, rather than simply joke about hiring him to wait tables, why not get him really involved? Especially since it was going to be their livelihood. "I'll talk to him," she said. "Heck, I'll bet he could even take drink orders and act as host if need be."

"Now you're talking," Martha said. "Up until a few years ago our niece, Allie, came and helped every summer." She didn't look at Ella when she said this. "The Drugstore employed almost all our young family members at one time or another." The way her voice fell off at the end of the sentence, Ella got the impression that she wished she hadn't spoken.

"Do you want to talk about it?" Ella asked.

Martha stopped what she was doing and shook her head. "Not really. Not right now. Maybe later, when there's a lull—tomorrow or the next day—and when Nicky isn't around." She smiled tiredly. "Or maybe not. I'm sorry. I shouldn't have even brought it up. I just forgot myself there for a moment."

Ella was completely perplexed. She knew something had happened, there had been another mention earlier. Now, she was determined to find out exactly what it was. But just then the little bell over the door tinkled.

First things first, she thought, pushing the question to the back of her mind.

"Well, hi there," she called when she realized it was Chet who had just walked in. She was so relieved to see him she couldn't believe it. She adjusted her apron and resisted the urge to pat at her hair.

He grinned and strolled to the bar. "Nice to see you." His twinkling eyes told her he wasn't just making conversation.

Ella felt her face grow warm. "You, too," she admitted. *If I get a chance, I'll tell him about last night. See what he thinks.* She picked up a menu. "Would you like a booth," she asked. "Or a table?"

Just then, Nick spied him. "Hey, Mr. Boone! Look what I got at the book fair." He held up *Harry Potter and the Sorcedrers' Stone*. His eyes twinkled, too. "I got all seven of them. Mom let me."

"Great series." Chet gave Nick a thumbs up as he made his way to a booth near the back.

Ella was a bit surprised he didn't go and sit down with Nick at the window table. They seemed to have developed such a connection over breakfast and pizza. *Then I went and told him we just needed to be friends. But didn't he say that* wouldn't *affect his relationship with Nick? Maybe he just didn't want to interrupt him while he was reading.* She got the answer when the bell over the door tinkled again and Charlie walked in.

She flipped her streaky blond hair over her shoulder and made a beeline for Chet's table.

Ella stopped in her trek to take water and the menu to Chet. She simply watched as Charlie slid into the seat opposite him.

Sensing a change in the atmosphere of the diner, she turned her head to see Martha peering at her oddly.

She smiled and turned back to the bar for a second glass of water.

Nick had gone back to his book when he saw that Chet wasn't alone. Smart boy, she thought. *It isn't any of our business what Mr. Boone does or who he has dinner with. Silly me for assuming he'd come in just because our Jeep was out front.*

"Hi, there!" She hoped her voice wasn't *too* bright. This was her landlady, after all.

Charlie looked up. She appeared to be surprised to see Ella in her role as waitress/owner. "Ms. Webb," she said.

"Please, call me Ella." She placed the water and menus in front of them. Chet seemed to be making it a point not to look at her.

Charlie nodded. "Ella. Nice to see you. I hope you're settling in now that Chet has taken care of the raccoon problem. So sorry about that, by the way."

"Yes, we're settling," Ella replied. She wanted to tell her about the strange noises. Wanted to ask if the house had a ghostly history, but the woman's porcelain complexion was blotchy, her eyes puffy. *Either she has a severe case of allergies, a real possibility this time of year, or she's been crying her eyes out for some reason.*

"Glad to hear it," Charlie replied.

Her voice sounded thick, phlegmy. Ella still couldn't decide if it was allergies or heartbreak. She gave Charlie a smile. She hoped it looked real. "I'll be back in a moment to take your order," she said.

Chet nodded, but Charlie said, "Just bring me a glass of tea. Please. I'm not the least bit hungry."

Ella quirked an eyebrow at the critter chaser.

Chet glanced at the menu. It was obvious he wanted to order, but being a gentleman, he appeared to be hesitant.

"Oh, go ahead and eat," Charlie commanded. "Just because my life is in turmoil doesn't mean you should starve."

"How about a turkey club, to go?" he asked politely. Then he added, "And bring one for Charlie, too."

"Of course, would you care for a drink to go with it?" Ella stuck the pencil behind her ear. This guy has baggage, too, she thought. Way more than I first realized.

"Tea for me, also," Chet replied.

Ella nodded and strode back to the counter keeping her back as straight as an iron rod to keep from turning around to see what they were saying now that she was gone.

I knew it was too soon last night on the phone, she thought. This just proves it. They're leaving and taking their dinner with them—obviously going somewhere private to share it. *Wonder where* Mr. *Charlie is tonight?* But even as she thought it, she realized the pair weren't hiding anything. Still, it rankled. She couldn't help it. The woman seemed to have him wrapped around her soggy little finger.

"That Charlie," Martha said. "Ain't she a one?"

Ella nodded. She was trying to appear nonchalant, but her insides were roiling. *Just have to play it cool. Didn't want a relationship anyway. Not now, maybe not ever. Just Nick and me for a change. From now on, I have to remember that.*

"She does seem to be very upset," Ella said.

Martha made a noise that sounded like *harrumph*. "She won't leave the boy alone—"

Ella laughed inwardly at Martha calling Chet a boy.

"—she's always got something she needs his help on. If it isn't one thing it's another. Sometimes I wonder why he puts up with it."

All the while she was talking, Martha was assembling the club sandwiches.

Ella poured the iced tea into paper cups and added lids and straws. Martha put chips and pickles into the white paper boxes containing the sandwiches, and Ella totaled the whole thing on one ticket. "Oh," she said. "Do they usually split the ticket? I didn't think to ask?"

Martha shook her head. "He pays. He always pays. In more ways than this, too. Or so I imagine."

Curiouser and curiouser, Ella thought. *Just one more reason to keep my distance.* But in the back of her mind she was recalling how he'd promised to teach Nick to play baseball next summer. *Not fair. Not fair at all. Maybe he will still help Nicky, someday, but we won't hold our breath. One more thing I'd better add to my list—learn to throw a baseball.*

The couple left as soon as Ella accepted Chet's money. She was amused to find he'd added a five-dollar tip even though their total was only sixteen bucks. *Good tipper or guilt tipper?* She smiled as she stuffed the cash into the tip jar on the counter. *Whatever. We'll take it.*

As Chet and Charlie left, Beth, John, and Danny Stockton came in.

Beth immediately took Danny to Nick's table and introduced them. Ella was proud when Nick put his bookmark in his book and gave the younger boy his full attention.

In moments, the two were laughing at something in a book Danny had in his back pocket.

Beth and John sat at the bar.

Martha introduced Ella and John. Then to Beth she said, "I was so glad to hear that Nicky was put into your class."

"Me, too," the teacher agreed. "He's a great kid. Look at the two of them."

Everyone turned to glance at Nick and Danny who had their heads together looking into the book. "I knew Nick would like that Knock-Knock Joke book. Danny adores those jokes."

Ella agreed. "You guys have no idea how relieved I am that Nicky loves your class and is making friends already." She ducked her head. "I was so worried he might not like it here—it's the first time we've ever had to change schools, you know."

John picked up a menu and examined it as though he'd never seen it before. "Stutter Creek is about the best place on earth to raise kids," he said. He didn't meet Ella's eyes, and she was a bit confused by that.

But in a moment, it was all made clear.

"We want to order sandwiches," Beth said, sparing a glance at her husband's tense shoulders. "But I have to admit I forced John to bring me here so I could ask you something ..."

John shook his head and drank deeply from the glass of ice water Ella set in front of him.

"Okay..." She waited for Beth to continue.

"Well," she looked at John again. "I've convinced some of the guys in town to volunteer to be Rent-a-Gents on Saturday in order to raise money for new school playground equipment. I thought if we auctioned off the men and their skills—you know, handy-man, painters, plumbers, mechanics, whatever—to the highest bidders, it would be a really fun and cost-effective way to raise some dough."

Ella burst out laughing as a red flush crept out of the top of John's shirt collar. He was obviously not too happy about the whole thing. "Sounds like fun," she said. "How can I help?"

"Easy," Beth began. "I know you just got here, but we were hoping The Drugstore would be able to cater the thing. You know, box lunches and iced tea?"

Ella looked at Martha who immediately broke into a big grin. That was all she needed. "Of course we can. We'll need an approximate head-count and a few days to order extra supplies."

"Yay!" Beth clapped her hands together. "I was going to have the cafeteria ladies do it, but it takes an act of Congress to get anything organized when the school district is involved. Especially at the last minute." She glanced up at Ella, her friendly face open and kind. "Besides, we thought it would be an excellent way to introduce you to the whole town."

Ella's hand went to her chest. "Wow, I'm really touched. Thank you for thinking of me." She felt tears spring to her eyes and she blinked hard and looked away.

Beth smiled. "Okay, I'm sending out RSVP letters tomorrow. They'll go home in the kids' folders. We should have our count in a couple of days."

"Sound's great, if we have the count by mid-week, we should be able to order the extra food and get it by Friday, right, Martha?"

"Exactly right. Now, I want to know which gents are going to be rented out. I've got some eaves that need repairing."

John raised one hand. He still didn't meet anyone's eye. "I'm your huckleberry," he joked, quoting Doc Holiday in the movie *Tombstone*.

"Wonderful," Martha said. "I'll make certain to get a front row seat, then." She dusted her hands on her apron and chuckled to herself. "Gotta get those eaves fixed before I put the place on the market."

The front door opened and a girl with curly black hair swept in as if in front of a storm.

"Ella Webb," Martha called over her shoulder, "meet Belinda Montoya, your other part-time employee.

While she was shaking hands with Belinda, Beth and John took their leave. From the front of the room, she heard Danny say, "Aww, do we have to go?"

Chapter Sixteen

When they finally closed The Drugstore, it was after seven.

I hope I can do this, Ella thought as she subconsciously cataloged all the things they still had to do before Nick had to be in bed at nine. Then she stopped. Supper was done; they'd made tuna melts and ate them together at the window table watching the few cars and passersby on the street outside.

"I like that wooden sidewalk," Nick had volunteered around a mouthful of food. "It seems really ancient."

Ella nodded. "I like it, too. Can you believe we actually own it? The plaque says Billy the Kid walked those very same boards. He probably visited The Drugstore, too."

Nick's eyes were wide. "I read part of it, but I must've stopped before I got to that part. Wow. I wonder who else might've come here?"

"Most likely every outlaw in this part of the country. You know, it also had a couple of rooms upstairs at one time—what we now use for storage—and the man who built it would rent them out like hotel rooms whenever he could."

Ella felt very lucky to be having supper with her boy. Martha even sat with them for a moment, when they had a lull.

He'd finished his homework, saving the harder story problems for Ella to help with when she stopped by his table now and then.

"Hey kiddo."

Nick looked at her, chip poised halfway to his mouth. "Yeah?"

"If you want to earn some extra cash, I could let you bus a few tables."

"Awesome!" Nick practically shouted. "And Mom..."

"Yes?"

Nick looked down, suddenly uncertain.

"What is it, Nicky? Another math problem or something?"

Her son shook his head. "I was just thinking...it might be a dumb idea, but what if we remodeled the upstairs area and rented out the rooms like in the old days? I'll bet we could even get Mr. Boone to help us."

Ella stood looking at him for such a long moment that he ducked his head and grabbed another chip. "I guess it's stupid."

"No, honey, no." She felt terrible. "It isn't stupid at all. In fact, it's a wonderful idea."

Nick's head came back up with a big old grin plastered across his face. "It is? You really mean it?"

"Yes, I really do." She was thinking about what Chet had said about the ski season. "I don't think we can do anything right away—maybe not even this year—but as soon as we have our feet under us, and we see that we can really make a go of this place, I think we should try it. Most definitely."

Nick pumped his fist into the air. "Yes!" he said. "And I will help with the work, just like I did in our attic." His face was beaming.

Ella bumped fists with him and went back to her work. *He's like a different kid. Happy. Relaxed. Helpful. No more sullen looks and slammed doors because he could never seem to do anything right—at least where Anson was concerned. Thank God that's behind us now. Like the old saying goes, better late than never.*

They finished up the closing routine, locked up the café, and headed to the Jeep.

The sky was cobalt, the sun having slipped behind the mountain over an hour ago. Ella tried not to compare it to the color of Chet's blue eyes.

She started the Jeep and checked the gas gauge. One thing about living on the outskirts of town, it took more fuel than she'd anticipated. *Better fill up while I'm thinking of it.*

They stopped at the Corner Grocery Store and filled up. Juanita, the owner, was already like an old friend. She waved as they drove away. Ella had paid at the pump with her Visa card.

"When we get home," she said. "Get your bath and get ready for bed then we will have some TV or book time." She glanced at her son in the passenger seat. His eyes were already heavy lidded. It had been a strenuous few days. She was really surprised he didn't have his video game out. He almost always played it when they were in the car.

Her phone beeped. She had a message, but no way to retrieve it. She couldn't swipe the screen. *Maybe I can see who sent it when we get home—in the light.* The screen light still came on, but it was very dim. She knew it was only a matter of time before the phone gave up and quit working altogether.

"Hey, maybe we can make a trip back to Pine River this Saturday. I have to get my phone replaced. Sound good to you? We could stop in for pizza again."

"Will Mr. Boone be there?" Nick's voice was sleepy.

Ella squeezed her lips together and focused on the dark ribbon road ahead. The moon was low in the sky, and the shadows of the pines were long and spiky. They reached across the road like bony fingers. "Not this time," she said. "I think he's busy."

"Okay." Nick buried his head into his jacket like a little turtle. "Maybe he can go with us next time."

"Maybe so." Ella kept her voice neutral. She didn't want to think about Chet Boone. Much less try to explain his actions to her son.

She was still getting used to the solitude of the small mountain town. It was sort of spooky, driving home at night, the only vehicle on the road.

She turned the radio on low and checked her rearview mirror. Way off in the distance she could see a pair of headlights that appeared and disappeared with each dip or curve.

Wonder who the text is from? Mom? Norma? Maybe even Beth Stockton. She'd given the cell number to Nick's teacher as a matter of habit. *Maybe she wants to tell me something else about the catering job.*

She was happily humming along with The Beatles on the oldies station when the far-off headlights suddenly grew much larger in her rearview.

Wow. They're really in a hurry.

In another moment, a tan colored car flew around her.

Maybe they have an emergency or something. She always gave folks the benefit of the doubt. *One of my shortcomings, Mom always said. See the best in everyone, too trusting, too gullible.*

She would have gone on and on listing her supposed shortcomings, Nicky snoring gently in his turtle shell, but the car that had flown around her suddenly reappeared in front of her, red tail lights flashing like hot lava as the driver slammed on his brakes.

Ella had to jam one foot down on the brake and the other down on the clutch before downshifting to third, then second, and all the way down to first before the driver of the other car sped up again.

"Dammit!" she muttered under her breath. "Must have been a deer or something." There were yellow, diamond-shaped Deer Crossing signs everywhere—the kind that sported the silhouette of a leaping deer—and they always made her think of Santa and Rudolph. "But I sure didn't see anything."

She slowly built her speed back up to fifty-five.

Her nerves were jangled now. She didn't want to go any faster than fifty-five. Nicky had jerked and mumbled when she threw on the brakes, but he hadn't fully roused.

Stupid drivers. Her good mood was now brittle, in danger of shattering. She half expected something to jump out in front of them at every turn.

Finally, the intersection that would take them to Lilac Lane loomed ahead. It was the only intersection with a stop sign between her house and the town of Stutter Creek.

There was no sign of the light colored car. She assumed it had turned the other direction. But when they were almost to their own driveway, the car careened out of the bar ditch where it had been idling behind a stand of juniper trees.

Ella's head whipped around as it blew past her again, this time headed in the opposite direction. *Was it following us?* Her mind immediately shied away from that prospect. *No. Probably just turned the wrong way at the intersection. It couldn't be Anson. He doesn't know where we are...we were so careful. Besides, if it had been him, wouldn't he have run us off the road back there?*

Completely rattled, Ella continued on to the rental house and started to pull into the drive.

At the last moment, she took her foot off the brake and continued down Lilac Lane until she was certain the other car was nowhere in sight.

Her hands were shaky on the wheel. Just the possibility of seeing Anson terrified her. His last text had been a threat. He insisted that everything that had gone wrong in their marriage had been her fault. She *made* him do everything—the "playful" slaps, the shoves, the hurtful words. According to him; everything was rosy until she and Nick started to "disrespect" him. And on top of that, there'd been that murderous look in the courtroom.

She inhaled deeply to still the shakes.

There were no lights in the rearview.

Ella looked for a place to turn around.

Nick mumbled something in his sleep as she pulled into a side road a couple of miles past their house. She executed a swift turnaround and then headed back. *Will I always be looking over my shoulder, afraid that he is coming to get revenge?*

She steeled her nerves and drove up to the house.

It took every ounce of courage she possessed to cross those few moonlit feet from the carport to the front door. The spit of lawn was crackly with autumn leaves. It gave her a shiver every time one crunched beneath the sole of her shoe.

Nick was really tired. It took quite a bit of gentle persuasion to wake him long enough to get him from the Jeep into the house. Finally, she practically dragged him from the vehicle, all the while thinking, *what if the car returns now, while we're out in the open? Anson said he would get me. What if it is him and he turns into the drive and sees us and just keeps on coming?*

But that didn't happen. She quickly she got them both inside and closed and locked the door behind them.

Nick stretched and started to lie down on the sofa.

"Oh no you don't, kiddo." Ella grabbed his arm and directed him on toward the bathroom. "Shower, brush teeth, you know the drill."

He groaned and mumbled something about doing it in the morning.

"Nope." She was stern. "Not gonna start *that* on the first day of school." She gave him a tiny push. "I want to hear the shower going in one minute."

"Ohh-kay," he said around a huge yawn.

She continued on to the kitchen where she placed her purse on the table and took out her cell phone. Through the cracked screen, she could barely make out the fact that the text was from Chet Boone.

"Well," she muttered. "Wonder what he wants?" She couldn't swipe the screen to bring up the actual text; she could only see the notification.

His business card was in her wallet.

Should I call him from the landline? See what he has to say? She couldn't decide. What if he was still with Charlie? What if she answered the phone?

She opened her wallet to retrieve his card.

The shower came on in the bathroom.

Ella smiled. Then her eye was drawn to the large window in the living room.

A car was driving slowly toward the house.

Chapter Seventeen

Ella grabbed the cordless phone and dashed to the window. She was formulating a plan in her mind. *If it's him, I'll call the cops, no hesitation.*

The drapes were open, but the sheers were still covering the big plate glass. The edges of the sheers glowed in the headlights.

"Drive by," she muttered. "Just keep on driving by." She crouched out of sight. She could hear the shower. It was still going in the bathroom.

The car approached the driveway to the house.

"Keep going," Ella breathed.

It turned in to the drive.

The headlights lit up the front yard, and the front window, for a brief instant. Then the driver shut them off.

Ella rubbed a hand across her face. The sudden flash of light made her blink and back away. *Dammit!* She looked down at the phone in her hand. Nine – one – she was about to press the one again when the car door opened and a man stepped out.

For a split second, the dome light showed him clearly.

Chet?

Her finger found the off button on the phone.

What is he doing here?

She stepped over and opened the front door before he could ring the bell. She was afraid the sound of the doorbell might cause Nick to jump out of the shower and come running.

"Chet?" she asked. "Is that you?"

He was just stepping up onto the porch. "Yes, ma'am. I hope I'm not intruding. I—I just went for a drive after Charlie left, and I wound up here."

Ella looked past him. She was relieved to see that the car he was driving was some shade of blue, not tan. It appeared to be a late model Mustang. "But where's your truck?" She was truly surprised.

He turned and looked at the vehicle in the driveway as if he, too, was surprised. "Oh," he said. "I just wanted to blast some tunes. Ride some back roads." He avoided her eyes. "Truck's no good for that. I—uh, sorta felt the need for—"

"Don't say speed," Ella said. "Do not say—"

"Speed." A brief grin touched his lips, but it didn't reach his eyes.

"I can't believe you just said that." Ella noticed he had a ball cap in his hands. He was turning it around and around. His gaze was on the green doormat. It showed a frog on a water lily. Underneath, it said Welcome to My Pad.

"Would you like to come in?" She felt as if a partition of ice had sprung up between them. Something in his demeanor was off. It felt as if they'd never shared a breakfast or a pizza, or even a dusty morning in her attic. And the joke about the need for speed had fallen into the dust.

He spoke softly, without looking at her. "I don't want to be a bother."

Ella was dumbfounded. She thought she had problems. Apparently she wasn't the only one. *Guess I need to stop focusing on myself so much.* "Of course you're no bother. Nicky's in the shower. We just got home a few minutes ago." She moved aside so that he could enter. She couldn't help but scan the road behind him—in case the tan car was coming back.

Chet stepped inside. He was careful not to bump against her. "I guess he has to get in bed soon."

"Oh, we've got some time. I'm sure he'll be delighted to see you."

Chet smiled, but again, it didn't reach his eyes. Ella thought he had aged in the short time since she'd seen him at the café. He seemed sad. The first day he showed up at her house, Ella recalled thinking he was the most positive person she'd ever met.

She pointed toward the sofa. Then she perched on the arm of the recliner. "I don't want to be too nosy," she couldn't believe she was saying this. "But, is something wrong?"

Chet sat on the sofa and ran a hand over his messy hair. He was still holding the ball cap in his other hand. On the front was a fierce looking eagle with the words Stutter Creek embroidered beneath the picture. "Brought this for Nick," he said.

"He should be out any moment now." Her words were barely out of her mouth when Nicky came strolling out. He was wearing Ninja Turtle pajama bottoms and rubbing his wet hair with a towel.

When he saw Chet, he came to a complete stop. "Uh, hi." The expression on his face was so comical; Ella had to stifle a laugh.

Chet grinned an honest to goodness grin and that made her feel much better.

She forgot about the tan car.

Nick crossed the room and sat on the opposite end of the sofa.

"Brought you this," Chet said. "I'm counting on you to wear it when we start practice in the spring."

Nick took the ball cap and tried it on. Took it off, adjusted the band, and put it back on. "How's it look?"

"Looks great," Ella said. "Stutter Creek Eagles, huh?"

Chet nodded. "Great bunch of kids. We've even got a couple of girls. But we lost our pitcher last year. Moved away." He glanced at Nick's bicep. "How's *your* arm?"

Nicky blushed and laughed. "I have no idea," he admitted.

"Saturday," Chet said. "Let's give it a try. I've got a ton of equipment. I'm sure we can find a glove you can use."

Nick's eyes lit up. "Yeah," he said. "S'it okay, Mom?"

Ella hesitated. "Sure. As long as I can tag along." She hated to risk having Chet think she was inviting herself on his account, but she wasn't going to let Nick go anywhere with anyone. Not alone.

"Of course," Chet said. "Wouldn't have it any other way—"

"Oh, wait!" She clapped a hand to her forehead. "This Saturday we have plans."

Chet's smile disappeared as Ella hurried to explain. "Beth Stockton, Nicky's teacher, asked us to cater a fundraiser for the elementary school. It's going to be this Saturday in the gym."

"We also have to go to Pine River and get your new phone," Nick chimed in.

"That's right," Ella said. "But we may have to do that on Sunday afternoon, instead. I'm sure it will take all morning to get the sandwiches made for the fundraiser."

Chet was oddly quiet. "Drop your phone or something?"

Ella nodded. "Cracked the screen." She thought of the text he'd sent. "I can tell when I get a text, but I can't read it, much less reply." There was no way she could tell him what had really happened, not with Nick sitting there. He had also assumed she had dropped it, so she didn't correct him. She was still amazed that Nick had slept through that horrific night.

"I was about to make a pot of decaf," she told Chet. "Would you care for a cup?"

He nodded and stood.

"Me, too," Nick said. He'd just grabbed the remote and was scanning the channels.

"Did I hear you say you'd like some hot cocoa, Nick?" She knew he really meant coffee. He always wanted coffee.

Nick capitulated without a fight. "Sure, Mom." He didn't bother to look up. He'd taken his Harry Potter book from his backpack and appeared to be reading and watching TV at the same time.

Ella went to the kitchen and rummaged around until she found the instant cocoa. She placed a cup of water in the microwave. While it heated, she filled the coffee pot with water and the basket with decaf. She also reached over and turned the counter-top radio on low. Waves of soft rock drifted into the silence.

Chet took his seat in the same red chair he always chose.

She stirred Nick's cocoa and watched as the tiny marshmallows began to melt. "Come and get it, kiddo," she called.

Nick laid his book aside and came to the table. "Can I take it in the living room," he asked. That was a no-no at his Nana's house, but his mom wasn't that strict.

"If you promise to pay attention and not spill it." Ella gave him "the look."

Nick crossed his heart with his index finger. "Promise."

She plucked his cap off as he walked by. "Don't want you to have hat head," she explained, fluffing his damp hair with her fingers.

"Aww, Mom, jeez." He glanced at Chet, embarrassed.

Chet just shrugged as if to say, *moms, what can you do?*

By the time Nicky was ensconced on the couch again, the Mr. Coffee was gurgling merrily. Ella thought there was nothing as comforting as the sound and smell of fresh coffee.

She took her favorite mug from the drain board and reached into the cupboard to retrieve one for Chet. She imagined she could feel his eyes on her back as she stretched to reach it. For the first time in a long time, she wondered what her rearview looked like.

When she set his cup on the counter, she was afraid to turn around, afraid the heat in her face would be all too apparent to the man who was causing it.

"Need a hand?" he asked.

Ella shook her head. "You take it black, right?"

"Yes, please."

"Everything okay with you tonight?" she asked. "I mean, blaring tunes and riding the back roads sounds like something I used to do when I needed to decompress."

She heard the scuff of chair legs on linoleum.

"What song do *you* blare?" He was standing directly behind her. Their reflections merged in the kitchen window. She couldn't tell where one began and the other ended. Everything was a blur. As he spoke, his breath feathered the side of her neck.

She had a sudden image of herself standing outside her bedroom closet in the dark. Something had caressed her neck then, too. "What song?" she repeated. "Old Springsteen anthems, loud. You?"

His arm brushed hers as he reached for the cup she'd just filled. "Yeah, Springsteen," he agreed. "Jungleland. Backstreets. Promised Land."

"Youngstown," she added. "Thunder Road." She had to resist the urge to rub her palm across the spot where their arms had met. It felt as if all the tiny hairs were standing at attention.

"Born to Run," he countered.

"No Surrender," she said.

"I'm on Fire," he whispered. "Human Touch."

She tried to see his face in the reflection, but it was impossible. *Are we still talking about songs?*

"Working On a Dream," he continued.

"Dancing in the Dark?" Ella didn't mean to say it. The title just slipped out.

Chet leaned against her, briefly, in the pretense of picking up the spoon she'd just laid down. The metal jittered along the edge of his cup as he stirred nothing into his black coffee.

The heat of his lean body reminded her of the strip of warm sunlight soaking into her quilt yesterday morning.

From the television, the sound of canned laughter shattered the moment into a million impossible pixels of doubt.

They both moved away at the same time.

"Sorry," he said.

"It's all right," she replied.

They took their coffee into the living room and avoided looking at each other for ten minutes. When the program ended, Ella practically leaped to her feet.

"Time for bed—" she began.

"Got to be going—" Chet said.

They looked at each other.

He handed her his empty cup. "See you at The Drugstore."

"Sounds good," she replied.

Nick yawned loudly. "Thanks for the cap," he said. "I can't wait to check out those gloves." He started toward the bathroom totally oblivious to the tension permeating the room.

Chet was already on the porch. "Thanks for the coffee."

"Anytime," Ella murmured. "Drive carefully."

He strolled to the Mustang and folded his lanky frame into the driver's seat.

Ella waved from the porch.

Chapter Eighteen

Nick read her a few paragraphs from *The Sorcerer's Stone* and ended up falling asleep with the book open, on his chest.

Ella smiled when she removed the book. He was such an original. A reader, a gamer, an athlete. He was going to make some girl very happy someday.

She propped his backpack against his bedroom door to make certain it would remain open, and then she went back to the kitchen to rinse out the coffee pot.

Chet's visit had been a little strained. But that wasn't what worried her.

She was afraid the noises were going to start up again. The way they had almost every night.

Turning up the volume on the radio, Ella hummed along with Adele. In moments, the kitchen was back in order.

She clicked off the radio and started her nightly door and window check.

The silence in the house was unnerving. *Have to get a television for my bedroom. It always kept me company on the nights Anson stayed away from home.*

All the doors and windows were secure except for the window over the kitchen sink.

Ella was appalled to discover she had never relocked it since the day she'd let in the cool fall air. *How could I not have noticed? I've checked doors and windows a zillion times since then.*

She glanced up at the key hanging at the top of the attic doorjamb. Careless, she scolded herself. Stupid, too. Still chastising herself, she continued her nightly check.

Outside the living room window, the yard was silvery. The trees stood black against the moonlight. Looks cold, she thought.

When the phone rang, Ella's heart skipped a beat.

And then adrenalin kicked in and she dashed to the kitchen to pick it up before it could wake Nick.

"Hello?" She was breathless from the sprint—or from the certainty that it would be a hang-up, or worse, a heavy breather. Or even *him*.

"Did I wake you?"

She clasped the receiver tightly. "Chet. Thank goodness it's you."

"Everything all right?"

"Oh, yes," she replied. "I just didn't know who might be calling this time of night."

"Hope it isn't too late. I could call back tomorrow."

"No, no. I – well, it's a long story. Just trust me when I say I'm glad it's you."

He chuckled. "That's a relief. I know I wasn't very good company tonight."

Ella tried to think of the best way to respond. She decided honesty was the best policy. "You did seem preoccupied."

Chet did the man version of a sigh. It came out as something between a snort and a laugh. "That's putting it nicely. I came over to tell you all about Charlie and her problems, so you wouldn't get the wrong idea about the two of us. But when I got there, I realized it wasn't a fit topic for Nick." He hesitated. "Besides, I wasn't sure you would really want to hear all that old water-under-the-bridge stuff."

"I would love to hear it," Ella murmured. She took the phone to the sofa and turned the TV on low. A re-run of *Friends* was playing. It was "The One Where Joey Speaks

French." Ella grabbed the remote and pushed the record button. This episode always made her laugh out loud—no matter how many times she watched it.

Chet was quiet.

"Are you sure you want to tell me this?"

He mumbled affirmatively. "Just climbing into bed," he said. "I guess you noticed Charlie was a little tight when she walked into The Drugstore."

Ella thought back to that moment. "I thought she was upset. Like she'd been crying or something."

"That, too," he said. "But it was the booze that was the worst of it. I can't believe she drove to the café in that condition. Lucky she didn't kill someone on the way."

"I didn't realize it was alcohol causing her eyes to be so red." But even as she said it, Ella realized she should have recognized the signs. Anson always got wasted when he was upset about something. "That's strange," she said.

"What do you mean?"

"I should have known what was wrong. My ex-husband was an emotional alcoholic. Always got drunk when something wasn't going his way. Or when I didn't do what I was supposed to. Or Nicky."

Chet sucked in a breath. It sounded like a hiss in reverse. "Was he? Did he. Hit you? Hit Nicky?"

Ella wished she hadn't mentioned it. She'd gotten caught up in the moment. "Only once," she admitted. "I may be dumb, but I'm not stupid."

Chet didn't reply.

"Sorry," Ella said. "I shouldn't—"

"Yes," he interrupted. "You should. You definitely should. Is there any chance he will show up here?"

"No. He doesn't know where we are. We left no forwarding address when we moved. No one knows where we are except my mother. And of course she wouldn't tell him. I changed my phone number, too."

"Wow," he said. "I felt there was something like that. Please, promise you will call me if you ever need me."

Ella could hear the sound of Joey speaking his garbled "French" in one ear, and in the other ear, she could hear Chet promising to be there if she needed him. It was comforting. "I will," she promised. But even as she said it, she was telling herself not to get dependent on another man. To change the subject, she said, "Weren't we supposed to be talking about you and Charlie?"

She heard the sound of Chet's bedsprings squeak and she pictured him leaning back against his pillows.

"First off, there is no Charlie and me. She's a happily married woman, even if she didn't give that impression tonight. We have a little history," he said. "To be blunt, we went together all through high school but when it came time for college, she didn't agree with my choice. She thought she was pregnant."

He seemed to be waiting for a reaction. Ella mumbled, "Oh, my." Of course, he didn't know Martha had already told her this.

"Yeah," his voice was flat, as if the trick still rankled. "I told her we should get married. I fully intended to take her and the baby with me to college."

"What happened?"

"She left me at the altar. There was no baby after all; in fact, she discovered she couldn't even have children. That's when she took off and started partying. We didn't see each other for years."

"Oh, Chet," I was astonished. "This sounds like a Lifetime movie."

He chuckled. "I went on to college and earned my degree." Now he stopped talking completely.

"Chet?" I had a feeling I knew what was coming. I just wasn't sure it was the right time for it. Weren't we barely friends?

"Sorry," he said. "I need to tell you this—among other things." He went silent again.

This time, Ella waited. On TV, a commercial for Male Enhancement pills made her cringe.

"I met my wife at college." Simple fact. Simply stated. Heartbreak still evident after all these years.

"Your wife?" She tried to sound surprised.

"It was love at first sight. I know how trite that sounds. But it happened just that way. I sat next to her in The Study of Genetics and that was all it took. We were married within the year."

Ella thought she should feel jealous, but she couldn't. The hurt in his voice was still so close to the surface she only wanted to smooth it over, take it away. "How long were you married?"

"Five years. I brought her home to Stutter Creek after graduation. She was a preschool teacher. We were ready to start our own family. She was looking forward to opening her own preschool right here. But she wanted to start our family first, because she knew how much I wanted kids."

Deep silence this time. Ella watched Joey, but the show no longer held any interest for her. She closed her eyes and tried to imagine how hard it must be for Chet to talk about all this. *And what does it have to do with Charlie getting plastered?*

But he wasn't to that point, yet.

"When Robin was two months pregnant, she became very ill. We went to the doctor together. In a matter of days, everything was shattered. She had ovarian cancer."

"Oh my God, Chet. I'm so sorry."

"It was bad," he muttered. "We had to choose between chemo and the baby." He fumbled with the phone.

Ella could hear him doing something. She pictured tears in his lashes, wiped moisture from her own.

"We chose chemo," he whispered. "But it didn't even matter. The cancer was too advanced." He took a deep breath. "The doctors assured me she wouldn't have been able to carry the baby to term even if we hadn't chosen chemo." Now his voice was completely frayed. "Then Charlie moved back and married the richest man in town. I was angry at first. I didn't think there was room enough for both of us in Stutter Creek. But mostly I was just angry because she was still here and Robin wasn't. Finally, I became numb. After a year or two, I was finally able to forgive Charlie. I didn't care anymore. Didn't care about anything for a long time."

"What brought you back?" Ella dove in. "You seemed so happy and content when I first met you."

"Grief therapy, a good façade," he paused again. "And you."

The room stilled around her. She could no longer hear Joey, or Chandler, or even the too-jolly voice of the commercial pitchman. It was as if time itself had come to a slow halt. "What do you mean?"

"I shouldn't have said that." He really did sound contrite. "I only called to tell you why Charlie was so upset. I didn't intend to rush things again. I just can't seem to help it with you."

Strained silence.

"Ella?"

She pulled in air. "I'm here. It's just...you don't know my past. With men, I mean. I haven't had much luck." She said the words quickly before she could back out. "I'm afraid to try again. Afraid for Nicky, mostly."

"And I haven't started off very well, pushing you. Going too fast."

She heard the squeak of bedsprings again.

"Charlie was quite drunk," he said. "I'll just tell you this part, then I'll be done." His voice dropped, as if he had to whisper it even to himself. "She and Roger have been trying to adopt, but she keeps sabotaging herself with the agencies. She really does have a drinking problem, and she has a couple of DUIs. Adoption agencies don't like that."

"Oh, no. I had no idea." She was reminded of that old saying about walking a mile in someone else's shoes. On the surface, Charlie appeared to have everything. But in truth, her life sounded almost bankrupt. "Does she always seek you out when she drinks?" *That might be a little too much baggage—even for me.*

Chet laughed. "Only when her husband is out of town."

"Oh—"

"I know, I know," he interrupted. "You don't even have to say anything. I've let it go on for far too long. I guess misery *does* love company. The bad thing is I'm afraid she really will hurt herself one day. Or kill someone else driving that damn Mercedes when she's had too many."

"Yeah, it sounds like she has a death wish."

"Yes—"

The line went dead.

Chapter Nineteen

Ella looked at the phone in her hand. *No! It can't be dead. It's my only link to the outside world.*

The house seemed to come to life around her. She could hear every rasp of branch on glass, every hum and whir of every appliance, every whisker twitch of every imaginary mouse inside each and every wall.

The phone rang in her hand and she almost threw it on the floor.

"Hello?" She could barely hear herself over the pounding of blood in her veins.

"Sorry!" Chet said when she answered. "My cell died. I had to dash into the other room and grab old faithful."

"Oh, thank God. I thought my line had gone dead—it's the only phone I have, you know. My cell doesn't work out here. Wouldn't, even if it weren't trashed."

"Are you frightened?"

"Yes," she admitted. "I keep seeing this tan car. Everywhere we go I catch a glimpse of it. Like an apparition that appears when you least expect it, then disappears when you look right at it."

"Damn."

Ella heard the sound of the phone being laid down, *clunk*, on some piece of furniture. "Chet? Are you there?"

His voice came from a long way off. It sounded tinny. Speaker phone, she thought.

"I'm here. Pulling my jeans back on. Be there in a few minutes."

Her first instinct was to say no. "No, no, no. That isn't necessary—"

"I've seen that car. I wondered about it—small town, you know? We usually even get to know the tourists, but not this one. Never see the driver out anywhere. Just see the car, driving."

"Yes. I – I thought it followed us home tonight." She bit her thumbnail. "I thought you were him, pulling into the driveway earlier."

Cursing. Followed by the sound of car keys jangling. "No wonder you seemed so on edge. I'm on my way," he said. "I'll charge my cell phone in the car."

Ella was still on the fence. She wanted him to come. But she didn't want to be needy. *Do I need him, or just want to see him? Does it make a difference?* "Okay," she said. "Okay. Be careful."

*

She watched for his car.
She wished for another bottle of wine.
She brushed her hair, and her teeth.
She watched for his car.
She turned on the radio—again.
She checked on Nick.
She watched for his car.
She wished she'd told him not to come.
She wished he'd hurry and get there.
She watched for his car.

After fifteen minutes, Ella decided he had changed his mind. She turned off the kitchen light and sat on the sofa. The TV light always soothed her somehow. She thought she heard a car, but she had made certain to position herself so that she could see out the big window.

She stood and peeked out anyway.

Nothing was coming down the road from town, but there did appear to be headlights shining from the other direction—from past her house. To see them, she would have to go out in the front yard.

No.

She sat back down on the sofa and scanned the muted channels for another *Friends* rerun. Or something similar to occupy her mind. *Maybe he realized what a bad idea this was. Maybe Charlie called again. Maybe he just backed out.*

She glanced toward the window.

The house was so quiet. She could barely hear the radio from the kitchen. She unmuted the TV just as she heard the squeak of a door opening somewhere in the silent house.

Icy tendrils of fear gripped her in a wintry embrace.

She stood slowly, remote control falling from her nerveless fingers. It landed on the sofa with a soft *plump* sound. "Nicky?" she called.

There was no answer.

Car lights stabbed the sheers and she dashed to the window.

The blue Mustang was in the driveway. The growl of its engine was loud near the window.

Ella glanced over her shoulder toward the kitchen.

There were no more sounds.

She cracked open the front door for Chet, and then she forced herself to walk back into the hallway off the kitchen.

The attic door was closed. It couldn't have squeaked.

She twisted the knob.

Locked, as always.

"Everything all right?" Chet spoke softly.

Ella turned and he opened his arms as if they'd been lovers for decades.

She crossed the few steps between them and his embrace was as strong and tender as she'd expected.

Her head found his broad chest. "I thought I heard a door open." That's not what she'd meant to say, but that's what came out. "I need to check the rest of the doors and windows. Pretty sure I heard *something*."

For a moment, he just held her.

"Okay," he said. He put her back a step, gripping her upper arms in his workingman's hands. "Let's go."

Ella lifted one forefinger and touched the hard edge of his stubbly chin. "Thank you for coming back."

He took hold of her hand and pressed the backs of her fingers to his lips. His navy-blue eyes never left hers. "Thank you for finding me." Still holding her hand, he led them softly down the hall to Nick's room.

Nothing appeared to be amiss.

Ella crept in and tucked the cover a little closer about his boyish form. She leaned down and lightly kissed his forehead.

At the door, Chet took her hand again.

They checked the bathroom and her bedroom. All was as it should be. A stack of books made a good doorstop. The bedroom door was wide open, just the way she'd left it.

"I must be jumpy," she said when their inspection was complete.

Chet checked the back door lock, and then held his hand out. "Key to the attic?"

Ella pointed to the nail at the upper corner of the doorframe.

"Clever," he said.

"I was afraid of losing it."

Without another word, he unlocked the door and tiptoed up the stairs. Ella was amazed that he could be so quiet.

She wanted to go up with him, but she wasn't comfortable leaving Nick sleeping unattended. Maybe I am overprotective, she thought. *But if someone is up there, I want to be down here to grab Nicky and run.*

"All clear," Chet said when he came back down a few moments later. "Not even a trace of raccoon, rat, or squirrel." He hung the key back on its tiny nail. "We did a good job on those vents."

"Must've been my nerves." Ella led the way back to the living room. "I feel like an idiot."

Chet caught her hand from behind. This time he spun her around to face him. "I didn't want to leave earlier. But I felt like I was crowding you." As he spoke, he was slowly pulling her back toward his chest.

"No, I—"

He brought her hand up to the side of his neck and placed it there so she could feel the pulse of his heart. His hands found their way to her hair. He pressed it away from her face with ultimate gentleness. His thumbs caressed the contours of her face.

Ella felt herself relax. The feel of his hands on her skin was like waking in the middle of a good dream. She didn't want it to end.

They stood that way for an eon, just holding on to each other, eyes locked in silent communication.

When he finally lowered his lips to hers, she closed her eyes and let the worry slip away. His mouth was soft and firm and the kiss was like cotton candy—dangerously sweet and gone too soon.

She opened her eyes and brought his mouth back to hers.

This time the kiss was a bit more urgent.

When they parted, he ran a broad thumb across her bottom lip. "You don't know," he murmured.

Ella was confused. "Know what?"

He steered her toward the sofa and pulled her down beside him. "You don't know how long it's been since I've felt anything."

Ella caressed his hair. The waves intrigued her fingers. "I'm still afraid," she said. "What if I told you I'd *never* felt this way before?"

Chet pulled her onto his lap and covered his mouth with hers.

"Mom?" Nicky called.

Ella drew back as if she'd been scalded.

Chet grinned and ran his thumb over her lips again.

She caught it with her teeth; nipped it playfully.

"You're beautiful," he whispered.

She stood, somewhat shakily. "I'm right here, Nicky. You okay?"

There was no answer.

Ella hurried down the hall toward his room, Chet close behind.

Nick had wiggled around and got one leg out from under the covers, but he wasn't awake.

"Just a dream," Ella said when she backed out of his room for the second time. "I probably woke him when I kissed him on the forehead earlier."

"You certainly woke me," Chet said when they were back in the living room. "Kiss me again."

Ella ducked her head. She could feel the heat rising from her neck into her face. "You like to tease me, don't you?"

"Oh yes," he said. "You wear that shade of pink so well." He chuckled. "The first time I laid eyes on you—that day, on your porch—I began to pray."

"Pray?" That was the last thing she'd expected to hear.

Chet clasped her to his chest and placed his chin on top of her head. "I prayed that I would be able to wrap you in my arms like this." He pulled her even tighter. "I prayed that you were unattached."

She felt his lips on her hair.

"I prayed that God had sent you here just for me." His strong arms encircled her like a safety net. They swayed together in the liquid moonlight seeping in through the sheers. The radio was so low there were only particles of music drifting about on the super-charged air.

"Chet..." Ella didn't know whether she should believe everything he was saying, or whether she should run backwards from the possibility that he was Stutter Creek's biggest player.

"It's okay," he said. "It isn't too soon. It's been way too long." He stopped swaying to the far off music and tilted her face up to his. "Tell me you feel the same way, Brown-eyed-girl."

Ella crushed the doubt threatening to strangle her. "I do," she said. "I feel the same—but I'm not sure if I should."

"Trust me," he said. "You can trust me, Ella Webb."

She raised herself on tiptoe and met his lips with her reply.

Neither of them noticed as the tan car sped away from the scene. Its headlights were off, but the driver didn't need them to see. Ella and Chet were perfectly silhouetted in the moonlit living room window.

Chapter Twenty

Chet stayed a while longer. He would've stayed the entire night, but he couldn't risk folks starting rumors about Stutter Creek's newest business owner. "We'll have plenty of time," he told Ella. "The house is locked up tight. You and Nick are safe here. But if you hear anything else—don't hesitate to call."

What he didn't say was that he was not only worried about the small town rumor mill, he was also worried what Charlie might do when she found out he was seeing Ella. He knew he should have made it clear to Charlie that her welfare was no longer his concern. He should have done it long ago. Should have done it the first time she'd threatened to harm herself. But he hadn't. And now, he was really afraid she might make good on some of her threats.

He hadn't told Ella about the threats. He felt like the village idiot, allowing Charlie to have this kind of emotional hold on him. If he told Ella that Charlie had said everyone would be better off if she just "drove off the mountain," he was convinced Ella might think he was still involved with her.

In truth, as soon as they'd left The Drugstore, he'd simply called her husband to make sure he was back in town so he could deliver her home safely.

It was then that Roger told him how the adoption agency had said they were closing their file, because they discovered her DUIs.

"I told her there are other agencies," Roger said. He had just arrived home when Chet drove her Mercedes into the spacious garage. "You know, with enough money we'll get a baby. We may have to hire an attorney and arrange a private adoption, but if Charlie wants to be a mother that badly, then by God she will." The smell of bourbon rolled off the older man in amber scented waves.

Chet shook his head and vowed to wash his hands of the both of them. "Well, I just wanted to make sure she got home all right." He took out his cell and called Stutter Creek's only taxi. Roger had taken Charlie right up to her bedroom.

"Mindy will take care of her," he'd said when he returned.

Chet raised an eyebrow. "Mindy?"

Roger poured himself another drink. "You know, Mindy. The housekeeper."

"Oh, sure," Chet replied. He'd had no idea they had a live-in housekeeper. "Well, I'll just wait outside for the taxi." He tried to hand the keys to the Mercedes over to Roger.

"You didn't have to call a cab." Roger waved the fob away. "Just take the Mercedes. I'll have someone pick it up tomorrow."

Chet shook his head and laid the keys on the hall table. "Very generous of you, but I've already called. They'll be driving up at any moment." He glanced out the floor to ceiling windows, which flanked the massive front door. "In fact, here they come now."

"At least let me pay for the ride," Roger insisted, wallet in hand.

Chet stepped outside and waved good-naturedly before entering the yellow car.

When he got home, he'd climbed into his beloved Mustang and attempted to drive the blues away. That's how he'd ended up at Ella's house. But the blues had clung to him like lint. It was only after his visit that he began to feel better. Seeing Ella and Nick always had that effect on him.

Their relationship was so special. No wonder Charlie was desperate to have that, he thought.

He'd picked up the phone and called her without giving himself a chance to back out. When she told him about the tan car, he knew he'd been right to call.

But he hadn't seen anything. Thankfully, everything had been locked up tight. Then there was that moment when they kissed. And kissed. And kissed.

He'd had to force himself to leave.

For the first time since Robin died, he felt hopeful again.

*

Ella answered on the first ring. "Hello?"

"Just wanted to let you know I got home safely. And say goodnight. Again."

Ella laughed. She was lying in bed. "Goodnight. I feel much better now. Thank you."

"Doctor love," he replied. "Call me anytime. Kisses guaranteed to cure what ails you."

Ella groaned. "All right doc. I think – I think I may need a prescription. My condition might be chronic."

"Ahhh!" Chet said. "You're killing me."

"I've got the cure for that," Ella countered. "Kisses work both ways you know."

"Goodnight, Brown-eyed-girl." His voice was soft. "Can't wait to see you tomorrow."

"You, too, Blue-eyed-boy." Ella clicked the off button on the cordless receiver and lay back in her pillows.

Tuesday morning came around much earlier than she wanted. Once again, she dragged herself out of bed and put the coffee on. She hoped the bright sunshine meant the weather was going to hold off a day or two. The weatherman was predicting snow before the week was out.

She drank her first cup of coffee sitting at the kitchen table reliving the events of last night. As the memories stole over her, she absently traced the outline of her lips with her forefinger. She was in now. In deep.

"You didn't wake me," Nick said.

She turned and he was standing in the doorway, scratching his head, yawning.

"Just giving you an extra five minutes," she said. "Here, sit down and tell me what you want to eat. She stood up and the scuff of the chair on the linoleum reminded her of the moment Chet had stood behind her at the sink.

"Mo-o-m," Nicky's voice was petulant. "Where are you?"

Ella came to herself. She was standing behind the red chair, holding on to the back as if for dear life. "Sorry," she said with a smile. "Just haven't had enough coffee yet." She poured a second cup, and that's when she saw the smudge of dirt on the counter top. "Nicky," she said. "Did you set something up here, something dirty?"

Nick was yawning and stretching. "Whaddya mean?"

He wasn't nearly awake enough for interrogation.

Ella wiped the offending red dirt away with her dishcloth. She distinctly remembered cleaning the kitchen last night. There's no way that red smudge would have escaped her.

She tossed the dishcloth into the sink. *Oh well. Could have been anything.* She turned to get Nick's cereal from the cupboard. When she pulled the white-painted door open, it gave off a very distinctive *squeak.*

That's it. That's the sound I heard last night.

Chills coated the back of her neck so suddenly she actually shivered.

With some trepidation, she reached into the dark recesses of the over-the-counter cupboard. Frosted Cheerios were there somewhere. She'd bought the large box at the store the day Norma had helped them move in.

Her fingers met something small and furry.

She jerked her hand away and closed the cupboard. Whatever was in there was cold. Cold and dead.

Nick was surreptitiously sipping her coffee.

"Let's go to The Drugstore," she said brightly. "I'm craving one of those wonderful ham and cheese omelets." She pretended not to see Nick plop her cup back down.

"Are you serious?" he asked.

"Sure, why not? Heck, we own the place."

Nick got up and started for his bedroom to get dressed.

"Go ahead and brush your teeth," she said, already reaching for the garbage can from beneath the sink.

From the drawer she took her yellow rubber gloves. She'd used them to clean the refrigerator when they moved in last week. *Has it really been only a week?*

She tugged the gloves on and listened for the sound of running water from the bathroom. She took a deep breath and yanked open the cupboard door.

It was a small raccoon.

Is it the one we saved? Did it try to come back? Is that what I heard last night; Chet said they use their paws like little hands.

Eyes smarting, tears starting, she held the kitchen trashcan up to the bottom of the open cupboard and scraped the little black and gray corpse into it with a gloved hand.

She tried not to gag. It didn't smell. It hadn't been in there that long. But there was blood on its little face, not much, just a little. And the head lolled from side to side as if it was no longer connected properly to the neck.

Ella whispered, "I'm so sorry little one. I wish I could take you out back for a proper burial, but Nicky doesn't need to see you this early on a school day. Especially not on the second day of a new school." *Naturally it would have to be right there in Nicky's cereal cupboard. On the other hand, if it hadn't been, I might not have found it until tonight. That would have been bad. As it is, I'll have to throw all the boxed cereals away and sanitize the cupboard. Then I'll ask Chet how it could have gotten in. Is there another broken vent somewhere downstairs?*

It was only after she'd taken the bag and disposed of it in the dumpster that she began to wonder how the little animal became injured. *I hope we didn't injure it in the trap that day, but it shot out of there so fast I never even got a good look at its little face.* She shuddered and hurried back inside to give the cupboard a quick scrub with Clorox. She also took a moment to check the other cabinets, just to be certain that was the only one.

As she worked, she suddenly recalled the red smudge on the counter. She'd thought it was red dirt smeared around. *Whatever it was, it's getting Cloroxed!*

By the time all that was done, Nicky was dressed and ready to go.

Ella took a two-minute shower, skipped the makeup, and clipped her thick hair up with a giant clip. She stepped into jeans, her favorite fleece top, and Asics walking shoes.

"Got everything you need in your backpack?"

Nick nodded. "What about my lunch?"

Crap. Totally forgot that. "Can you eat at school today?"

"What are they having?"

"I have no idea," she admitted. "But we are really pressed for time. Oh, duh." She stopped and rolled her eyes. "Bring your lunch box, kiddo. We own a diner."

Nick's eyes lit up. "I can make my lunch while you make my omelet."

"That's right. Have we got it made, or what?" Ella made her voice sound cheery.

They got in the Jeep and headed out. She made it a point not to look when they passed by the dumpster. Life in the country, she thought. Gotta toughen up, I guess.

The morning smoothed out after that. Nick ate a good breakfast, made himself a great lunch—he piled the turkey *high*—and went to school happy.

Ella turned up the CD player and broke into song on the way back from dropping him off. She was trying to erase the image of the little raccoon from her mind.

She was seriously thinking about checking to see if there were any rentals in town. This constant problem with wildlife and iffy phones and power was beginning to seem insurmountable.

This isn't how it's supposed to be, she thought. Living in town might solve some of those problems. But she'd signed a six-month lease. And she was really loath to try and talk to Charlie about it. Especially after what Chet had divulged last night.

Thinking about everything in between snatches of Bon Jovi and Jason Aldean, Ella never even noticed the tan car when it pulled out of the parking lot of The Antlers Motel. She was eager to get back to The Drugstore and get busy. The booths had been filling up when she left.

Chet stopped by around nine thirty. He seemed to know that's when the breakfast crowd began to thin. He brought the newspaper and sat at the counter to eat.

"Shouldn't you be out catching things?" She filled a thick white ceramic mug with coffee and set it before him.

His blue eyes sparkled. "I caught what I wanted last night." He sipped the coffee and let the steam obscure his stare.

"That's funny," she replied. "I caught something last night, too. And it was still in my cupboard this morning." She hadn't meant to make a joke of it. Sometimes things popped out of her mouth without her brain's knowledge.

He set the mug down with a *clunk*. "What do you mean? A mouse, a rat?"

Ella shook her head. Tendrils of hair escaped the clip and tickled her neck. "Small raccoon." Her eyes misted over. "Darn it. I wasn't going to cry. But I think it might've been the one from the attic. You know, the one we trapped."

Chet frowned. "It was in the cupboard? Did it leap on you when you opened the door—hey! Maybe that was the noise you heard last night."

Ella nodded and poured herself a cup of coffee. The place had been so busy she'd barely had time to think. "It was dead." Her voice sounded heavy even to her own ears.

"You're kidding—is it still there?" Now he sounded professional.

"I bagged it and put it in the dumpster."

He was taking money from his wallet, pulling on his jacket. "I've got to go get it," he said. "Have it tested. Something about it just doesn't sound right."

The blood drained from Ella's face. "Oh my God. I never even thought about it being sick. I'm such a city girl. I saw that it had injured itself so I just assumed that's what killed it."

Chet shook his head. "Better safe than sorry. Did you clean the area where you found it?"

"Of course," she mumbled. "I washed the whole cupboard with bleach water." She hesitated. "Was that right? Or do I need to do something else?"

Chet handed her a five-dollar bill. "You did the right thing. Did Nick see it?"

She shook her head. "I didn't want him to start the day with that image in his head."

He nodded. "Call you later, after I get it to the vet's office."

Ella's good mood was gone for good. "Okay. Sorry I didn't think of that. I should've called you."

"Not a problem," he replied. "You'll get used to calling me, eventually." He smiled and started for the door.

"You forgot your change," she called. "You only had coffee." She glanced in his cup. "And not much of that."

He just waved. "I'll be back."

An hour later, when they were prepping for lunch, he called and told her he'd found the bag and took the animal to the veterinarian. "She's sending it to Albuquerque for testing."

"I feel so bad for the little thing. Did you look at it?"

"I did. And I don't think it was sick. It did appear to be injured. I really hate that. I think it may have been injured by the trap and then it was trying to go back to its nest."

"Oh, that's so sad." Ella dabbed at her eyes with a paper napkin. "I hope no more come in. I just, well, I don't like to cause anything harm."

"Me, either, brownie. Me, either."

She giggled in spite of herself.

"Okay if I stop by for supper tonight?"

Ella was surprised he would even have to ask. "You mean here at The Drugstore? Of course."

"Great. I've got to check out a report of a black bear getting in the dumpster out at Copper Lake Campgrounds, but I'll be back before closing time."

"Bears?" she asked. "I can't wait to hear all about it."

Chet laughed. "I'll have to take the two of you out there for a picnic someday. Ever heard of Crybaby Bridge?"

"No. But it sounds like a place that would be right up Nick's alley. Mine, too, actually. Is there really a crying baby?"

"I won't say anymore. You have to experience it for yourself."

"Fine," she teased. "I'll just ask Martha."

Chapter Twenty-One

The day flew by and before she knew it, Ella was on her way to pick up Nicky from school.

"Great day," he said, climbing into the car. He had walked out with the same kid again only this time the boy had waved at her, too. "Seth wants me to come over this weekend and play video games. He's got the new NFL game."

Ella smiled. "We'll see," she said. "Don't forget, you have a job to do on Saturday, and we sort of made plans with Chet on Sunday."

"Oh yeah," he replied. "I did forget." He shrugged. "Oh well, there's always next weekend."

She patted his knee. "I am glad you've made friends so quickly. I'll have to meet his parents, though."

Nick grinned. "I told him you'd say that. He said they already know all about you because of The Drugstore. They're going to come in for supper one day this week."

"Well that sounds great," she said. "What are their names?"

They continued with the small talk all the way back to The Drugstore where Nick waltzed in and claimed his table. He laid out his books and put his earbuds in.

When she went over to take him a snack, Ella asked what he was listening to.

He took out one bud and held it up so she could hear.

"I don't hear anything," she said, perplexed.

Nick laughed. "I just use 'em to block out the sounds so I can get this stuff done."

Wow. Is that my kid? Where'd he get all that common sense? Not from me, that's for sure. She gave him a verboten public hug—very brief—and strolled back behind the counter with a new spring in her step. *I love this place!*

When the supper crowd began to arrive, Nicky donned his apron and began to bus the tables without even being asked. Belinda Montoya, the part time evening help, showed him how to place the glasses and flatware in the ancient dishwasher, and how to scrape the food into the two large wheeled garbage cans. "When we close, I'll show you how we dump these monsters in the dumpsters out back." She grinned. "I call them ugh and ugly. But you can call them what ever you want. Trust me, after a few days of lifting these bad boys, you may call them things you don't want your mom to overhear."

Nick grinned back at her. Being treated like the equal of a high school athlete was quite a confidence builder.

"I think he's enjoying his job," Martha whispered when Ella passed by. "Belinda seems to have taken him under her wing."

Ella's eyes filled with moist emotion. "Martha, you don't know what that means to me, to see my boy blossoming like this—wait, do boys blossom? Or is that reserved for girls?"

Martha laughed. "I'm not sure, but I can see it happening."

Ella hoped it would always be this way, but she knew that was too much to ask for. *I'll just take it one day at a time. I won't do the what-if and if-only routines. Nope. Enjoy it while it happens. That will be my new middle name.*

Chet walked in around six-thirty and Ella was certain she knew the minute he came through the door. Something made her look up from the table she was serving. He took up just the right amount of space in the atmosphere. Like that old water-displacement experiment they'd done in junior high school science. How many pebbles, pennies, etc. does it take to make the water flow over the edge of the glass?

"Sit anywhere," she called out. "I'll be right with you." Seeing him was like seeing a blade of sunlight through a raincloud. She turned back to her customers, hoping they didn't notice anything unusual.

From the corner of her eye, she saw Chet wave to Nick.

Nick stuck his chin up in acknowledgement. His hands were full of plates and glasses.

"Looks like you've joined the workforce," Chet said.

Nick mumbled something in reply.

Ella couldn't see his face from where she was standing, but she thought it a safe bet that he was smiling.

"So," she said after turning in the other customer's order. "How'd the bear hunt go?"

Chet sat back in the corner of the booth with one knee cocked up in the seat, and one arm slung along the back of the booth. He was the picture of nonchalance. His hair was wind blown and wild; tiny bits of leaf debris and pine needles called it home. Smudges of dirt had slipped into the crinkles around his eyes and the vertical laugh lines bracketing his mouth. It only served to give him an even more authentically weathered look.

Ella wanted to sit and study him like a model in Life Drawing 101.

"They were there, all right," he said. He took out his phone and showed her pictures of a mama bear and two cubs climbing in and out of the dumpsters near the campsite.

"Oh, they're so thin." Ella was dismayed to see the animals up close. "I don't know what I expected, storybook bears I suppose."

Chet's face agreed. "It isn't good. They're not usually this close to civilization. It's the drought that's causing them to come down from the mountain."

"And the dumpsters are easy pickings I suppose."

"Exactly right," he said.

"What will you do? Remove them somehow?"

Chet was saved from answering when Nick came up and dropped into the opposite seat. "Can I take a break, Mom?"

He looked beat.

"Of course you may," Ella said. "How about a root beer float? I think you've earned it."

Nick nodded enthusiastically.

She'd known that would liven him up.

"I'll have one of those, too," Chet said. "Along with a BLT." He flashed a pearly smile made even brighter by the grime on his face. "But first, I think I'd better wash up." He stood and started toward the restroom. "Save my place, Nicky-boy."

Nick grinned and turned around until he was sitting the same way Chet had been sitting, one knee cocked, one arm riding the back of the seat.

Ella hurried to get their floats and Chet's sandwich.

That night, Chet stopped by the house after he'd gone to his own home to shower and shave.

Ella was just tucking Nick into bed.

Chet listened from the living room as Nick read his mom a few more pages of *The Sorcerer's Stone*, but it was as if Nick was reading himself a bedtime story. He was so tired he kept drifting off.

When he closed his eyes and let the book fall to his chest, Ella marked his place and turned out the light.

She walked back into the living room, looking forward to a bit of adult conversation and perhaps a little more.

Chet had fallen asleep on the sofa.

Ella smiled and covered him with a blanket. She touched his curling hair. It was still damp. It reminded her of shiny little springs standing out here and there because he'd obviously been in too much of a rush to dry it.

She thought about waking him, but he was obviously as exhausted as Nick. *I'll get my own bath first, and then see if he's awake.* But he wasn't, and he didn't. Not until dawn.

When her alarm went off the next morning at six, there was a note on her pillow. *You're an angel. Thanks for the sleepover.* It was signed with a goofy smiley face and a tiny heart.

Ella got up and looked out the window to make sure his car was gone. Then she tucked the note into her dresser drawer beneath her undies. *What will the townspeople think of me now? Oh well, too late to worry about that. For all I know, he might've even left as soon as I went to sleep.*

She yawned and stretched. It had been the best sleep she'd had since they'd moved into the house on Lilac Lane. There hadn't been a single noise. Not one.

"Today's the day we find out how many are coming to the fundraiser," she told Nick over breakfast. "It will be our very first catering job. We have to make it as near perfect as possible."

Nick shrugged and shoveled in another bite of French toast. "I want this for breakfast every day," he said. "Do you make this at The Drugstore?"

"Yes," she said. "I don't know why I don't make it for you more often. It was always one of your faves."

He nodded and downed half a glass of milk. "I dreamed Mr. Boone was here last night."

She laughed. "He did stop by right after you'd gone to bed. But you were so tired I didn't tell you. I guess he was tired, too. He fell asleep on the couch."

"We work hard, Mom." He smiled. "I meant all of us. You, too."

"Thanks, sweetie. When you enjoy what you're doing, it doesn't even seem like work." She tweaked the cowlick standing up on the back of his head. "That's why you have to go to college and get your degree. So you can do whatever your heart desires."

"Like Mr. Boone?"

"Exactly," she agreed. "And now, me, too."

On the way to school, they discussed how one decides what they want to do. "Just think about what you like to do when you aren't working," she said. "That will point you toward your passion."

"Passion?" Nick's eyebrows went up.

"Yeah, you know, the thing that excites you the most." She glanced at his reflection in the windshield. His face said he was really thinking it over.

"Right now reading is my passion. And playing video games." He appeared a bit confused. "But playing football is also my passion."

"That's the good thing about youth, you get to try out all these things. Find out which ones stick with you, and which ones get forgotten along the way. There's no hurry. It's not like you're going to college tomorrow."

His body relaxed. "And now for some music." He began to fiddle with the scan button. His mom's habit of using music as a segue for changing the subject had apparently rubbed off on him, too.

"Sixty three!" Ella squealed when Beth Stockton caught her in the parking lot.

"Yep, not a bad turnout for such short notice, if I do say so myself." She patted herself on the back. "But I think we should plan for at least ten or twenty more. There are always quite a few parents who forget to return things, or who never get the notices in the first place. Then they just show up. It happens at the class Christmas party every year."

"Okay." Ella was thinking out loud. "I think we should plan for an even one hundred. We have to include ourselves, too. Right?"

"That's right," Beth agreed. "It's a good thing you're in charge of the food and not me."

Ella nodded, barely listening. "We'll do one hundred box lunches. One hundred desserts. Then there's the tea, soft drinks, water. Should we have coffee, too?"

Beth laughed. "I'll let you and Martha work all that out. She did a fundraiser for us last year, for the library."

"Fantastic," Ella replied. She was still lost in thought when she arrived back at The Drugstore.

All morning, she and Martha planned menus and wrote down ideas. By ten o'clock, they were almost ready to place their order.

"We just have to keep it simple," Martha instructed. "And present a variety. Turkey clubs, ham and cheese, pimiento cheese, veggie deluxe, egg salad, maybe chicken salad; it's always one of our best sellers."

"Whoa," Ella gasped. "This is keeping it simple?"

Martha chuckled. "You're right. I always get carried away, besides, it's really your call now."

Ella shook her head. "It may be my call, but it's your experience I'm depending on." She tugged at her apron strings as she talked. "I want a variety, but I don't want a lot of people choosing the same thing and leaving us with a bunch of not-so-popular items left over."

"Absolutely right," Martha agreed. "Let's see..." She tapped a pencil against the counter.

"I've got it," Ella exclaimed. "We'll do our two most popular sandwiches, and then we'll have premade salads, too. I mean, it's going to be mostly women, right?"

"There you go," Martha said. "You are exactly right. I don't know why I never thought of it myself."

"And we'll have to have some finger sandwiches for the kiddos. You know, with the crusts cut off. And maybe cookies, or brownies for dessert?"

"Perfect." Martha was writing as fast as she could. In moments, they had figured out the amounts for each food. Martha was like a human computer when it came to totaling their weekly food orders from the wholesalers. This was just another day for her. "It's like ordering a whole day's worth for one event," she said.

Ella was beyond excited. "Oh, we mustn't forget the extra boxes and napkins. And the cups for tea, too."

Martha smiled and held up the notebook where she was listing amounts. When she was finished, she handed the lists to Ella. "Time for you to learn how to order." She pointed toward the phone and the old fashioned Rolodex. "Meats are behind the letter M. Bread behind the letter B. All paper goods can be found in the P section, you get the idea."

"Wait," Ella sounded a little panicky. "Don't we do this by computer. You know, fill out a form, pay with a credit card?"

Martha laughed until tears blurred her vision. "I expect you *will* be doing it that way before long, but me and Joe did it this way for years. It always seemed to work for us.

Besides," she indicated the Rolodex again. "The vendors all know us by name. They are expecting you to call. I've already told them all about you."

Ella dropped her forehead into her palms, crumpling the list slightly. "Oh, Martha, I don't know what I would do without you. Thank you for not leaving me in the lurch."

Martha patted her sympathetically. "This is a good way for you to get your feet wet."

Ella rolled her eyes and laughed. "That's putting it mildly.

Chapter Twenty-Two

Wednesday night, Ella and Nick decided to make the short drive to Pine River to pick up her new phone. "I don't really know if it's necessary to even have a cell phone when I can't use it half the time. But since I've still got over a year left on my contract, I might as well take advantage of it."

"Don't forget, Mom, it's also your camera and your calendar." Nick was always the voice of reason.

"You're right," she said. "I did forget that. The store is open until nine, so I think we can get the phone and then grab a bite of dessert at Dairy Queen. If you aren't too full from supper, that is." She let her voice trail away as if she thought there might really be a chance that he would turn down ice cream.

"I could probably choke down a chocolate dipped cone, or a hot fudge sundae." He grinned. "If I tried real hard."

Ella shifted up to fourth gear. "Sounds like a plan, then." She turned up the radio and in moments they were singing along.

The night wind scraped past the Jeep's windows and took away all their cares. "I kinda like it here," Nick murmured in the break between songs. "How about you, Mom?"

Ella smiled. "Just hearing you say that you like it makes me sort of love it."

The rest of the trip was spent in companionable silence. The stop at the phone store was surprisingly brief and fruitful, and Ella gave herself a pat on the back for having bought the phone insurance.

After a stop at the local Dairy Queen, they headed back to Stutter Creek, tired, but content.

When they got home around eight-thirty, Norma was just leaving their house. She saw them pull in so she turned around and came back. She was driving a dark colored older model Chevrolet Caprice.

"Hey, you two," she called as she stepped out of the car. "Long time no see!"

"I can't believe how time flies around here," Ella replied. "Getting Nick in school and spending every day learning about the restaurant has kept us so busy." She unlocked the front door. "Come on in." "Nicky you go ahead and jump in the sh—"

She stopped midsentence.

Norma and Nick stopped, too.

"Did you hear that?" Ella asked. She had her head cocked to the side like a spaniel.

"Hear what?" Nicky replied.

Norma didn't say anything at all. She just peered around Ella in an attempt to see what was going on.

"Sounded like a door closing. Or maybe a window, you know how it sounds when you go to close one and it slips and drops down with a bang?"

"C'mon." Norma put her hand in the pocket of her jacket.

Ella looked at her questioningly.

Norma shrugged. "Just like American Express, I don't leave home without it."

Ella understood her to mean she was carrying a handgun in her pocket.

"Don't worry," Norma said. "I've got a concealed license."

"I wasn't really worried about that," Ella said. "I'm actually beginning to think I should do the same."

Norma nodded and began to move through the dark house.

Ella turned on the living room lamp, and then they went on to the kitchen, bathroom, and each bedroom. She flipped on the lights in each room.

Everything was secure.

"Do you guys ever go into the attic?" Norma asked, jiggling the locked doorknob.

"Not since Chet came and replaced the broken vents. We always keep this door locked." She was a bit breathless. "Must've been my imagination." She felt terrible that she might have frightened Nick again. After the wonderful evening they'd had going to Pine River, she felt ridiculous bringing it all tumbling down.

"Probably another critter," Norma said. "When they hear someone moving around, they go scurrying. Don't feel bad. I wonder if Chet checked under the house, and inside the walls?"

Ella shrugged. "I don't know for certain. But I will talk to him about it the next time I see him. Funny thing is, he was here last night and we never heard a thing."

Norma smiled. "Hmmm, spending some time together, huh?" She gave Ella a knowing look that dissolved into a womanly giggle. "He's a really good guy. I'm glad you two have hit it off."

Ella ushered Nick into the shower, promising to leave the door cracked open so he wouldn't feel alone. *I hate being such a coward, always thinking I hear something.* She thought of Nick's face when he asked if she'd leave the bathroom door cracked open "just a little." *I see how it's impacting my son.* She vowed to stop it, there and then. *From now on, I will simply ignore those hackle-raising feelings and remember that there's a logical explanation for every creak, groan, and bang in this old house.*

"I think he's a great guy, too," she admitted to Norma, pushing the odd noise from her mind. "But really, we're just friends. He's going to teach Nicky how to play baseball this summer."

Norma accepted the glass of tea Ella offered. "You don't have to tell me anything about it." She sipped her tea. "It's no one's business what two consenting adults get up to on their own time."

Ella giggled and swatted her with a cup towel. "Oh, you," she said. "I'm serious. No matter what anyone thinks, we're just good friends. And you know what?" Her voice grew wistful. "It's really nice to have friends for a change."

Norma looked through her. "You didn't have friends in Albuquerque?"

"Wasn't allowed to." Her eyes widened when she realized what she'd said. "I mean, with work and everything, there just wasn't time."

"Uh huh," Norma said. "I understand. Completely." She held her tea glass up. "Nothing new under the sun, chickie. Nothing new under the sun. Just remember, you aren't that girl anymore. Why, look at all the friends you've already made here."

Ella smiled. "And you're one of the best," she said.

"Yes, I am. You can count on me, which reminds me of the reason I came over this evening. Poor Mrs. Benefield fell and broke her hip. She's in the hospital and will be for some time, so if you don't see her out puttering about, that's the reason."

"Oh, that's so sad. I hope she'll be all right." Ella pictured the old woman lying alone in that big house and it made her inwardly cringe. "Was she able to call for help when it happened? Or did someone find her?"

"Luckily, she wore one of those Life Alert necklaces and she actually had the presence of mind to push the button. Her daughter told me the poor thing simply stumbled getting out of the bed. Got her foot tangled up in the spread or something."

"My goodness. Glad to hear those Life Alert things really work. I guess it happened in the daytime when we were away from home, or we would have seen the ambulance."

"Yes, Becky said it happened yesterday around nine a.m."

"I appreciate you telling me," Ella replied. "Is there anything I can do to help out?"

Norma smiled sadly. "No, I don't think so. After surgery, she'll be moved to the rehab hospital for a couple of months. So if you see any strange people coming and going, it may be her daughter, Becky, or her husband—I didn't catch his name. Becky said they might be in and out a few times getting clothing and personal items. Watering the plants and what-have-you." Her mouth turned down. "She said they are also wondering if it's time to go ahead and place her in a nursing home after she recovers. I got the impression they were going to start packing up some of the nonessential items in the house. Just in case."

"Oh, my goodness. That's too bad. I suppose with the dementia, it's sort of inevitable." Ella barely knew the woman, but the news was depressing nonetheless.

It wasn't until Norma had gone home that she realized the tan car could have been one of Mrs. Benefield's family members. That would explain why she kept seeing the vehicle on Lilac Lane.

I'll have to ask her about it the next time I see her, she thought. But by the time she got Nick into bed and her own bath taken, she had forgotten about all about it.

The next day Ella awoke bright and early. She was ready to tackle the day. In fact, today was going to be the first time she opened up on her own.

Nick seemed to feel her enthusiasm. They ate cereal and headed toward The Drugstore; anxious to see when the supplies they'd ordered would be coming in.

"Surprise," Martha said when they arrived. "I came down early because I had a feeling the paper goods would be arriving."

Ella peeked around her stout form and saw a lanky young man stacking brown cardboard boxes in the prep area. "Sure you don't want me to take these up to storage?" he asked, one hand on the handle of the red dolly. "It's no trouble."

Martha shook her head. "Not this time, Jake. We'll be putting the supplies to use very soon. Got a catering job at the school this Saturday." She looked him up and down. "Surprised someone hasn't contacted you about volunteering."

Ella laughed at the older woman's audacity.

"Oh," Martha said, as if Ella's laugh had reminded her they weren't alone. "Here, what's wrong with me? Let me introduce you to the new owner of The Drugstore." She held her hand out toward Ella. "This will be the new boss—she will be running the place and doing all the ordering from now on. Ella Webb, meet Jake Patterson." She saw Nick sitting at his usual table. "And that handsome young man is her son, Nick. He's employed here, too."

Nick looked up and smiled when he heard what she'd said. "Hi." He held up one hand in greeting.

"Nice to meet you both. I've known Martha for sometime now, so if it seems I'm doing things out of habit when I bring your order in, I probably am. Just tell me if you need it done differently, otherwise, I'll keep on doing it the way I know how."

Ella nodded. "At this point, I'm sure you know more about this place than I do. So feel free to carry on." She glanced up the stairs toward the storage area. "Except for today of course." They all laughed. "This special order is very exciting since it's the first catering job for me."

He nodded. "Now, what was this about me volunteering?" He looked at Martha for an explanation.

She told him all about the Rent-a-Gent fundraiser. "And while I know you're actually based in Pine River, I also know Beth would love to auction you off if you aren't doing anything on Saturday."

Jake threw back his head and laughed. "You should have been in sales," he said. "Okay, you've convinced me. Give me her number and I'll give her a call. Better yet, here's my card. Just tell her to call me if she wants another victim. Tell her I'm very experienced at lifting and carrying."

They all laughed at the obvious job qualifications.

They were still laughing throughout the day as they folded and put together the food boxes, which were shipped flat, and then started filling them with the bagged chips, paper napkins and plastic ware.

"Having the boxes made and half-filled in advance will make our last minute work so much easier," Martha explained. "Tomorrow, we'll start baking the cookies and brownies, and then Saturday morning, we'll come in early, put the sandwiches together, wrap them in plastic wrap, place them in the boxes, make the tea, and then load everything up to transport to the school."

"Whew," Ella said. "I can't believe we're going to do all this." She looked around at the boxes stacked high on the prep counter.

"Yep," Martha said. "The biggest problem is always finding the space to put everything before we transport."

"I see what you mean," Ella agreed. "Maybe I should invest in one of those long fold up tables just for events like this. Then when we're finished, just fold it and store it."

"That would be perfect," Martha agreed. "I even have one at home. We used to use it when all the kids and grandkids came for the holidays. It was the kids' table." Her eyes took on a misty shine. "The kids always loved having their own table. I would put a pine cone turkey or a popcorn ball Santa for the centerpiece." She blinked and looked away. "I don't know why I never thought to use it here. We always need the work space when we have catering events or even large takeout orders during ski season."

Ella patted her forearm. "The main thing is, we could really use it now. But it's no problem for me to stop and pick one up after I drop Nicky at school."

Martha laughed. "Actually, it might be difficult to find one. I think I bought that one at Wal-Mart in Pine River. They *might* have one at the hardware store here, but most likely they'd have to special order it."

"I love this town," Ella said. "But I am going to have to get used to the limited shopping opportunities." She chuckled. "Maybe it will save me money in the long run."

"Yeah," Martha laughed. "Or cost you even more having to run back and forth to other towns."

Ella grimaced. "You're probably right. In fact, we had to make a quick trip to Pine River last night to replace my damaged cell phone."

"Touché," Martha said.

Chapter Twenty-Three

There didn't seem to be enough hours in the day for everything they had to do to run the restaurant, keep up with Nick's homework, and get ready for the upcoming fundraiser.

Nick wasn't having any trouble keeping up in school, but Beth Stockton fully believed that her students should learn to study on their own time regardless of how easy the classwork seemed. "I want every kid in my class to go to college," she said. "And once they're off on their own, I want them to know how to succeed without someone standing over them with a whip." Every child had a required reading list based on his or her level of understanding, and each book required a complete report. They had to turn in one report each month, but they could turn in more than that if they wanted.

Nick loved the challenge. He was determined to be the first one in class to finish his list. But he also loved earning his own money at the restaurant, and of course he had the daily homework to keep up with as well.

For her part, Ella simply checked his folder each day to make sure he was doing what he should. He still needed occasional help with story problems in math, but even those seemed to be more of a welcome challenge than a headache.

The only thing missing during this time was Chet.

He stopped by and offered to help on Thursday evening, but after a few minutes, he received a call on his cell. "I'm sorry," he said. "I've got to run, but I'll be back tomorrow." He shot Ella a glance that told her absolutely nothing, and then took off without another word.

If Martha thought it odd, she didn't say.

212 | Ann Swann

Ella pushed it to the back of her mind where the odd noises and strange happenings resided, and vowed once more not to worry about things outside her control.

That night, they went home tired, but happy. Things were coming together. All the food had come in right on time, the boxes were prepped and ready, now all they had to do was finish making the desserts and tossing the salads. And of course that would be done at the last possible minute so the veggies would be fresh.

"I think it's going to work," she told Nick on the way home.

"Me, too," he mumbled. "Danny said he was going to bring some board games to play in the school library while the auction is going on. Should I take my checkers?"

"You bet," she said. "And a deck of cards, too. You can practice your card tricks and play Spades or Hearts." She looked at him sternly. "But no poker, got it?"

He grinned. "Yes, ma'am."

"And absolutely no betting of any kind."

He nodded. "I know, I know, we had this talk already, remember?"

Ella ignored the sarcasm.

Nana had taught him the game of poker one weekend when he stayed with her. She'd thought it was a hoot, winning all his pennies (she had a whole jar full of change on her dresser), but Ella was afraid not every parent would want their kids learning how to gamble. Especially not at a school function.

When they drove into their own driveway, she was once more reminded that it would be nice to have a timer for the lights. After this event, she told herself, I'll make a special trip to the hardware store. If they don't have one, maybe they will order it. If not, Pine River has a Radio Shack.

"It's really dark," Nick said as they stepped out of the Jeep.

"Clouds over the moon," she said. "I was just thinking how we should invest in one of those timers that turn on your lights at dusk."

"Yeah," he agreed. "That'd be cool. Maybe Mr. Boone knows how to put it in. We could make it turn on the front porch light, too."

Ella laughed and held her new cell phone up so the light illuminated the keyhole on the front door. "Yep, that would be nice."

The house was toasty warm inside, and for once, she didn't hesitate on the threshold.

They relaxed, Nick got ready for bed, and she listened as he read to her from the novel, *Hatchet*, by Gary Paulsen. It was the first one on his list. "I thought Mrs. Stockton would let me do my reports on my Harry Potter books, but she said she knew I'd already read them and she wanted me to read some books I might not have chosen for myself."

"I think that's good," Ella said. "It's always best to push yourself in new directions."

"If you say so." Nick opened the book. "I kinda like it already. This kid has to learn to survive by himself in the wilderness."

"Oh, my," Ella murmured. "I hope it isn't too exciting to read at bedtime."

Nick snuggled down into his blankets. "Nah, not for me, Mom."

She laughed and settled in beside him. "Okay, read on McDuff."

Nick began.

She let him read two whole chapters before she called a halt and made him put the book away.

"Wow," he said. "This is awesome, isn't it?"

She nodded. "And kind of gross, too."

"Yeah," Nick giggled. "That's what I like."

She kissed his forehead and reached over to turn on his nightlight. "I'm not surprised that's your favorite part," she laughed. Then she headed down the hall toward the bathroom for her own shower. Nick didn't ask her to stay this time, he simply turned over and mumbled goodnight.

No noises, Ella thought, crossing her fingers. *Please, Lord, let it be a no noises night.* She smiled at her own silly alliteration, but she checked every door and window just the same.

As she bathed and got ready for bed, Ella ticked off the list of things she had to do at the restaurant the next day. She and Martha were making refrigerator drop cookies. They already had four big batches of dough covered in plastic in the restaurant's fridge. They had enough for almost two hundred cookies. We'll be baking all day, she thought. *Do we even need brownies?*

As she strolled back to the living room in her robe and slippers, she tried to keep from wondering why Chet had left so suddenly after the mysterious phone call. She felt certain it had something to do with Charlie. On the other hand, there was that problem with the bears. Could it have been work related? If so, why wouldn't he have told her?

Ella wanted to put it all out of her mind. She had plenty of other things on her plate just now. No need to go looking for someone else's worries.

As if on cue, the phone rang. She was carrying it in her hand, just in case. "Hello?"

"Hey, Brown-eyed-girl." Chet sounded tired.

"Well hi, Blue-eyed-boy, how's it going?" She sat down on the sofa and put her feet up. This was what she'd been waiting for, no matter how much she hated to admit it.

"Here I am, calling to apologize again. About running out on you earlier, I mean."

Ella thought he really did sound sorry. "Is everything okay?"

There was a moment of silence and then his voice, flat and terrible. "I had to do something I really hate."

"Oh, no," she said. "Do you want to talk about it?"

"I don't even want to think about it, but I have to tell you so you'll understand why I left so quickly."

Ella braced herself for something horrible. *He's going to tell me he's still in love with Charlie after all. He's going to say he hates admitting it, but once Charlie saw him getting close to Nick and me, she convinced him they should still be together.*

In her heart, Ella had known this would happen. She had tried telling herself it was too soon. He sounded contrite, but hadn't he already demonstrated how much he cared for his old flame by taking care of her the night she called him drunk?

Those were big red flags, just like with Anson. Only, this time, Ella told herself, things would be different. She was no longer a desperate single mother, she wouldn't put up with any excuses for shoving her and Nick into the background.

"You did leave in an awful hurry," she replied. She tried to inject a note of chill into her tone. *It's time I start standing up for myself.*

There was no reply. No reply at all.

Ella looked at the receiver in her hand.

"Chet?" No response. "Chet, are you still there?" Silence. *Had he fallen asleep?* She listened closely for sounds of breathing, or perhaps snoring. But there was no sound at all. She pushed the on/off button expecting to hear a dial tone when she broke the connection, but there was nothing. She was listening to dead air.

Dread filled her mind. *Not this again.*

She sat, gripping the phone, waiting for the noises to begin, wondering if the lights were going to go out.

Nothing happened.

Trying not to make any noise at all, as if it would make any difference, Ella stood very slowly. *I don't have to check any doors or windows, she thought. I know they're all secure. But I need my new flashlight just in case. It's in the bedroom with the hammer.*

She started down the hall, tiptoeing in to Nick's room to gaze, briefly, at her sleeping boy. *Maybe this is just another fluke. Like before, when Chet's cell phone died and he called back on his landline.* She held onto that thought as she continued down the hall to her bedroom.

The hammer and flashlight were under her bed. She'd put them both in a flat open box left over from when they moved in.

Now, when she pulled the box out, the sound it made sliding across the hardwood floor reminded her of the scraping sounds that sometimes emanated from the attic. Please, she thought, not tonight.

Weapon and flashlight in hand, she started back to the living room recalling how she had slept in the recliner on their first night here. I can do that again if I have to, she thought. She went back and grabbed her bed pillow and the fleece throw from the foot of her bed and snapped off the overhead lights.

After putting the TV on low, Ella arranged her pillow and blanket in the recliner, made certain she had her phone, her hammer and the flashlight, then she settled in to see if she could doze.

A glass of wine, she thought. It helped last time. And on the heels of that thought was one more. *After the Rent-a-Gent Fundraiser, I will seriously talk to Charlie about finding a house in town. One way or another.*

As she threw off the blanket and prepared to sit up, Ella heard the snick of a key turning in a lock.

"By God," she muttered, "that's *enough.*" She jumped to her feet and rushed toward the kitchen. She was certain the sound had come from the back door—it couldn't have been the front door, she was sitting right there in the living room when she heard it.

Hammer and flashlight in hand—in case the lights suddenly went off—Ella dashed across the hallway and stopped.

There was a soft puddle of light on the floor outside her bedroom door.

I turned that light off. I know I did.

She stood indecisively. *Is someone in my room? Did someone come in and hurry right past me while I was arranging my little fright nest in the recliner?* If anyone had gone down the hall, they would've passed Nick's room, too.

She gripped the hammer and started down the hallway again. *I was just in there. But now I have to check on Nicky, again. And see why my light is on. I know I turned it off—I'm positive.*

All at once, an idea invaded her brain like a terrible disease. *Someone is trying to terrify me. Someone who has a key to my house. Someone who knows when I'm here alone. Nothing ever happens when another person is here. Especially not when Chet is here.*

Chet and Charlie.

Charlie and Chet.

Is there something more here than meets the eye? Is this small town that seems too good to be true harboring a couple that gets their kicks out of terrifying the new tenants? Maybe that's the reason the house was so cheap, just to lure in a single woman, or even a single woman with a child? Maybe that's why it was so convenient for Chet to be the one to take care of the attic noises. Then he turned right around and called Charlie afterwards. And the next day, a dead raccoon appeared in the cupboard.

Ella's fear went round and round in her head, churning her emotions into near panic.

Scrape

Thunk

She stopped outside Nick's room and gazed up at the ceiling. *Someone is up there now. Someone opened the door with the key and went right up into the attic after turning on my light just to frighten me and lead me away. Perhaps just to let me know they were right here with me.*

It isn't Anson. He's in jail. Can't believe I have to keep reminding myself of that.

That leaves only Charlie or Chet, or the pair of them, together.

She felt sick at her stomach.

The hammer seemed suddenly flimsy and ridiculous. Anyone who would go to this much trouble to scare her might really be dangerous. Or at least, really crazy. She could think of no other reason. Unless Charlie was doing it without Chet's knowledge, in order to get her and Nick to leave.

She stepped into the bedroom.

Nick was sleeping just as she'd left him earlier. This time, however, she leaned over him to make certain he was actually breathing.

The closet was next.

Without giving herself a moment to reconsider, Ella pulled the door open and shined the flashlight inside. A couple of hangers talked to each other, but that was all. There was nothing else. It wasn't even a walk-in closet so there really was no place for anyone to hide.

She stalked down the hall to her own bedroom, her anger growing with every step. Now that she thought she'd figured out what was going on, fright was giving way to bright red fury.

She stepped into her room ready for action. Hammer held high, she checked every inch of the room. But she'd heard the scrape and thunk from overhead. Either there are two people, one down here and one up there, or there was one person working alone who has discovered a way to get in and out of the attic with ease. It always seemed to culminate with the sounds from above.

I have to go up there, she thought. *I have no choice.*

Ella walked back to the attic door and pulled the key off the nail.

Taking a deep breath, she fit the key into the lock and turned.

Snick

That was definitely the sound she'd heard earlier.

Ella removed the key and then hesitated. Nick was asleep in his room. She would be all the way upstairs in the attic. What if there *was* someone hiding downstairs somewhere? At this point, with everything that had happened so far, Ella was afraid anything was possible.

Her attention was suddenly diverted by the rumble of an engine toward the front of the house.

It's the Mustang, she thought, picturing the compact blue sports car from last night. But is it coming or going?

She dashed up the stairs and flipped on the attic light just as the sound of the engine stopped. It was right outside her house.

Glancing quickly around, Ella was not surprised there was nothing to see. They had cleaned up all the dust and old boxes so even if someone had been up there, they would've left no prints and there would've been nothing to move around. So what makes the scraping-thunking sound, she wondered.

She wanted to stay and examine the entire attic; it wasn't nearly as scary as she'd imagined it would be. Not with the overhead light on. But there was a car in the drive and she was almost positive it was Chet. *Come to think of it, Chet is the person who always checks out the attic. How convenient is that?*

Ella fixed a neutral expression on her face. She wanted to present a cool façade. There were too many unanswered questions. Too many coincidences concerning him and Charlie and the key to her house. *I'm not going to fall into his arms this time. It's way too easy. Too questionable. Should I even let him in? Or just send him away? For that matter, should I simply cut my losses and run back home to Mama? No, that's too close to Anson. Stuck here. Gotta make the best of it.* For the first time since they moved in, Ella felt a twinge of real regret.

All the way back down the stairs, she kept expecting to hear the doorbell or a fist pounding on the door.

Instead, she heard the roar of an engine come back to life.

She got to the porch just in time to see the Mustang fishtailing out of the driveway headed back toward town.

Chapter Twenty-Four

Ella took half a step onto the porch. She was dumbfounded to see Chet speeding away from the house.

Another half step took her all the way outside. That's when she was able to see the red taillights of a different vehicle as it crested the hill almost a mile away.

She didn't know what to think. She watched as Chet's taillights grew smaller and smaller until they, too, appeared at the same spot where the first set had been only an instant before.

I give up, she thought. Whoever was in the house must have gone out the back door—that was the *snick*, not the attic door. They obviously have a key. Chet must have seen the car, or perhaps a rendezvous was already planned.

I'm beginning to think this town that seemed so perfect is absolutely crazy. Or maybe it's just this house. But now that she was becoming convinced it was Charlie, she wasn't quite as frightened anymore. Jealous women she could handle. Violent ex-husbands were another matter. *But he doesn't know where we are. Have to keep that in mind.*

She turned and stepped back inside, locking the door behind her. Through the living room, she could see the attic door. She'd left it standing open like a portal to another dimension.

"Dammit," she muttered, standing in the vague glow at the foot of the stairs. "There really should be a light switch down here. Maybe I should just leave it burning up there all night. The way my luck is running, someone would come along and turn it off anyway." She laughed at her own morose joke. Then she started up the stairs again, still holding her hammer and flashlight.

Her anger had dissipated with the disappearing taillights.

She glanced around the attic without going all the way inside, then she turned on the flashlight and flipped off the overhead light switch.

Going back down in the darkness, with the flashlight pushing its narrow beam ahead of her down the steps, Ella felt her nervous fright returning.

Her feet barely touched the last three steps as she hopped down and closed the door quickly behind her. She jammed the key in the lock and twisted it hard, giving the knob a quick jiggle to make sure it had engaged.

For the first time in days, she shoved the red chair under the knob. *But how can I secure the front and back doors if someone—Charlie—has a key?*

Turning the problem over in her mind, Ella hurried down the hall and checked on Nick for the umpteenth time.

Finding him exactly as she'd left him only a few short moments earlier, Ella slumped against the doorjamb, completely deflated.

Glass of wine, couple hours sleep, get through the next few days, and then we are leaving this house if I have to take out another loan to do it.

She pulled her second bottle of Moscato from the fridge and poured a small glass. *This was supposed to be for a housewarming, she thought. I envisioned Norma and maybe Martha helping me drink it. Maybe I'll get another bottle for the housewarming at our new place.*

She placed the new blue bottle back in the fridge and debated calling Marissa at the police department. *Even if it's too late for them to do anything, I may need police reports if I'm going to try and break my lease.* She settled into the recliner just as headlights torched the living room drapes.

In another second, the sound of the Mustang reached her ears.

Ella debated turning off all the lights and pretending to be asleep. But she was afraid Chet would knock, or ring the bell, and wake up Nick.

She lugged herself from the chair and made it to the front door just as he exited the car. Watching him cross the yard, all her convictions turned to doubts. He can't be a bad guy, she thought. He just can't. She opened the door and waited.

After taking the porch steps two at a time, he drew her into his arms without question. His face was lit by the porch light, but his height made it impossible for her to see into his eyes.

Ella pulled away and stepped back into the doorway. She didn't invite him inside.

"Ella?"

She heard the confusion in his voice.

"I – I don't know what's going on? We were talking on the phone, and then—"

"I was on my way here. I was calling you from my cell, but of course I lost you at the edge of town." He pushed one hand into his thick hair. "I knew I was going to lose you, but I thought we had another minute. You were telling me something and the line just went dead." He peered at her as if she'd lost a marble. "It happens all the time. I know you know that." He dropped his gaze. "That's why I wasn't too worried about it. I knew I'd be here in a couple more minutes."

Ella looked away. "Why did you pull into the drive, and then leave?"

He looked down the road. "As I pulled up, I saw a light colored car headed toward town."

"Was it the same tan car? Was it my ex-husband? Could he be out?" Ella's blood pressure shot up so quickly she thought her eyeballs might explode.

Chet must've seen the distress on her face. He stepped forward and placed both hands on her shoulders. "No, no, it wasn't him. When I caught up to it, it turned out to be a white car. I flagged it down anyway. It was Mrs. Benefield's daughter, Becky." He shook his head. "The poor old woman fell and broke her hip. Becky was at the house gathering up some more nightgowns for her. Apparently, she had surgery and now she is wanting her familiar things—"

Ella waved her hand in front of him, a look of consternation on her face. "I know, I know. Norma told me all about it." She felt tears prick the backs of her eyelids, but she was determined not to cry. It had been another emotional evening and she'd been certain it was either Chet or Charlie or Anson. Now here stood Chet looking heroic and despondent all at the same time.

She continued to stand in the doorway. It might take every ounce of strength she ever had, but she was determined to send him away. "Chet, I'm tired. I'm going to bed. It's been a very stressful night and we have the fundraiser event coming up."

He was extremely close to her again.

When she looked up, the porch light creased his face into deep origami folds of worry.

"It was the bears." His voice was almost inaudible.

"What?" Ella leaned forward. "What do you mean?"

Chet swiped the cuff of his sleeve across his eyes. "People kept feeding them at the dumpsters. I knew it was going to happen. Even though I posted signs not to feed them. Even though I used recorded dogs and air horns to try and scare them away—nothing worked."

Ella felt her earlier nausea return. She watched as tears reappeared at the corners of his dark blue eyes. "What happened?" She didn't want to care. But she couldn't help herself. She had to know.

"Someone got too close to the cubs. The mama bear charged at them. Chased them back to their car. Idiots got it all on video. They were videoing each other—daring each other to get closer and closer—teasing them with fruit and potato chips." His voice broke behind a sob.

Ella pulled him into the house and steered him to the sofa. "Here," she said, offering the glass of wine she had poured earlier.

Chet sipped and then gulped.

Ella took it into the kitchen and refilled it.

When she retuned, he was standing beside the window, looking out. "I'm sorry." His voice was raw. When he turned to her, his face matched his voice. His eyes were naked, lashes clumped into wet spikes. He wouldn't look directly at her.

"You had to euthanize her, didn't you?"

He nodded.

"Oh my God," Ella said. "That's horrible. She was only protecting her young. Couldn't they be relocated or something?"

Chet shook his head. "Park policy says when a wild animal harms or threatens a human..."

"I'm so sorry." She didn't know what else to say.

He lowered his voice. "What's worse, the cubs are on their own now. They took off, but they'll probably be back and start the whole cycle over again."

Ella wrapped her arms around his waist. She couldn't understand how people could be so stupidly, ignorantly cruel. "I'm so sorry," she repeated. "I just *hate* people sometimes." She hadn't meant for her voice to sound so vehement, but Chet seemed to understand. He pulled her even closer.

"When the Sheriff called me, down at The Drugstore, I knew it was going to be bad. He told me the two boys—not teens, but not too far on the other side—barely made it to their car before they sped away." He set his chin on top of her head. "I knew what I was going to be forced to do. It isn't the first time—nor will it be the last."

She shook her head at the horrific images he'd invoked.

"I didn't want Nick to know," he said. "And I didn't trust myself to tell you in front of him." He hesitated. "My defenses don't seem to exist when I'm around you."

Ella wiped her own eyes and took him by the hand. There was no way he could be behind the strange things that had been happening. No one with his level of compassion could do something so mean.

"We need to talk." She led him back to the sofa. "I think someone is trying to scare me into leaving." She watched his eyes. "I think it may be Charlie."

He sat quietly while she detailed everything that had happened tonight. She expected him to automatically defend Charlie, to say it couldn't possibly be her. When he didn't, Ella began to trust him again.

"I hate to think it could be her," he said. "But she has been drinking a lot since the adoption company dropped them." He rubbed his upper lip as he spoke. "Roger says he will get her a baby no matter what it costs." He closed his eyes and leaned back. "But I wonder what kind of life that child would have."

"But why would that make her resent me? Because I have Nicky? Oh my God, you don't think she wants Nicky, do you?" The horror of that thought sent Ella into new depths of confusion, despair, and finally, the beginnings of a cold rage.

Chet opened his eyes and looked right at her. There was no deception in them. "I think she may be jealous." He took her hand. "She knows how I feel about you. And Nick."

"What?" Ella began. "What do you mean?"

He took both of her hands in his. "I've been trying to show you how I feel," he said. "But there's always something getting in the way."

Ella waited. This wasn't going the way she'd planned. Not at all.

"I think of you all the time, Brown-eyed-girl," he continued. "And Nicky," his face softened. "Nicky's such a great kid."

The silence was impenetrable after he stopped talking.

At last, Ella squeezed his hands. "I want to believe you," she admitted. "But I'm so confused with everything that's going on."

He caressed the backs of her hands with his broad thumbs.

"Do you really think it could be Charlie?" she asked.

He appeared to choose his words carefully. "I don't want to accuse her unjustly. I know she has some emotional problems that need to be addressed by a professional." His thumbs stopped caressing. "I think she needs serious treatment for her drinking. I really do." He looked into Ella's eyes. "But I've never known her to be mean. Never."

Ella exhaled. She didn't realize she'd been holding her breath, waiting to hear the verdict. "Maybe it isn't her at all." *Oh my God, am I defending her now? Maybe I'm the one who needs treatment.*

"I know what we can do," Chet said. He sat up straighter. "I want you to call a locksmith and get the locks changed. And don't give a key to anyone. I want you to have the only keys."

Ella began to nod. "That's a great idea." She thought of all she still had to do for the catering event. "It may be after the fundraiser, but I will do it. Then, if the nonsense stops, I'll know for sure it was Charlie. She's the only other person who has a key."

"I really hope it isn't her." Chet squeezed her hands gently. "But we have to put a stop to this—whatever it takes."

"Thank you," Ella said. She squeezed back. "And Chet..."

He waited.

"I'm really, really sorry about your bears. It just makes me sick."

He pulled her into his arms and held her tightly.

Chapter Twenty-five

Friday dawned cloudy and cool again.

Ella and Chet had fallen asleep on the sofa. She had conked out first, her head on his shoulder. When she awoke later, her head was on the bed pillow she'd brought in to make her "fright nest."

He'd stretched his mile long legs out on the coffee table and the blanket was somehow covering them both. "Morning," he said when she raised her head.

"Hi." Ella immediately put a hand to her hair.

He grinned and smoothed her rough locks gently. "Looks beautiful, Brownie."

"Is it really morning?" She glanced toward the window, but the day was so overcast it was hard to tell.

Chet turned his wrist over and examined his watch in the dim light. "Five o'clock," he said.

Ella stood. "My alarm will be going off any moment." She was self conscious in the early light.

Chet reached for her hand. "I'll take off before Nick gets up."

She leaned down and pressed a kiss onto his forehead the same way she did Nick every night. "We've got to stop meeting like this," she teased.

"Hah!" He threw his head back, but did not let go of her hand.

Before she knew what had happened, she was on his lap again.

"I agree," he crooned. "*This* is how we need to meet." He kissed her soundly, morning breath and all.

Ella sat contentedly for a few seconds. She couldn't resist smoothing his squiggly hair with her fingertips. "Did you know I almost had myself convinced you and Charlie were in on it together, trying to scare me away."

He caught her hand and brought it to his face. Eyes closed, he pressed his lips to her skin. "I'm going to be here every night until we find out what's going on. No one will be scaring you again."

Ella was saved from replying by the sound of the alarm clock beeping in her bedroom. She hurried down the hall to turn it off.

When she came back, Chet was folding the blanket and preparing to leave. Without a word, he swept her into his arms. "See you at The Drugstore, Brown-eyed-girl." He kissed her again, almost chastely.

"I'll be there." Ella opened the front door and stood aside.

He stopped in front of her. "Thank you for understanding about my job," he said. "You always make me feel better."

Ella stood on tiptoe and took hold of his collar. Without allowing herself to think twice, she pulled his face to hers and gave him a kiss that would last him all day. "There," she murmured. "Take that with you."

"Argh," he rumbled playfully, picking her up and twirling her like a child. "I'll be back for a refill this evening."

She laughed and pummeled his shoulders until he plopped her back on her feet.

Ella watched him as he backed the Mustang sedately out of the drive. *I won't think. Not going to second guess anything. Too much to do today. Too much to do.*

She went down the hall to wake Nick and get their day started.

An hour later, they were on the way to the restaurant where Nick was looking forward to French toast and hot chocolate. The morning was growing foggier by the moment. Trees and bushes loomed out at them at every turn, and once they hit town, the wink of brake lights reminded Ella of Chet chasing the red taillights down the road the night before.

She took a deep breath and said a silent prayer that they would be able to get through the next two days so that she could get the locks changed and put an end to the mystery of who was trying to frighten them away.

Martha greeted them with a smile, but she didn't linger for small talk. "I'm baking cookies," she said. "I brought the work table." She indicated a long gate-legged table set up in the storeroom. "We'll cool them there and then wrap them in plastic to go in the boxes."

Ella felt a tingle of excitement course through her veins. "I can't believe we're really doing this."

"I can't believe I don't get to help until after school," Nick replied.

Martha went back to her work and left the customers to Jan and Ella. Nick finished his breakfast and Ella took him to school. By the time she got back to the restaurant, all thoughts of the crazy goings on at home were completely out of her mind.

While they waited on customers and packed boxes, the day slipped past. Before she knew it, noon was upon them and Chet was sitting at the bar watching her work.

"Hey, Blue-eyed-boy," she whispered as she passed by. "You hungry?"

"Starving," he said. "But I can't decide if I want a ham sandwich or a dozen cookies." He dropped his voice. "Or just you."

Ella would have blushed if she had time. Instead, she set a glass of ice water before him. "Cool off while I make your ham sandwich." Her dimples deepened. "And if you're a good boy, I'll treat you to a cookie or two."

Chet ducked his head, but his shoulders shook with laughter. "I'll be good," he mumbled. "That's a promise."

They had little time for any more banter after that. The lunch crowd swelled and eddied around them and Ella barely knew when he signaled for his check.

She hurried over.

"That was mighty tasty," he said. "I like watching you work."

"Glad you enjoyed it." Ella totaled his purchase and took his cash.

"See you for supper," he said as he headed out the door.

Ella was left standing behind the counter already looking forward to suppertime.

She wiped her brow. Somehow, everything was getting done.

When she picked Nick up from school, he went right to his favorite booth and started on his homework. "When I'm finished here," he called. "I'll start helping you guys."

Ella glanced his way, but he'd already gone back to his math book. *He's seriously liking this.* And sure enough, within half an hour, he was behind the counter tying on his apron.

"What should I do first, bus tables for Belinda or help Martha with the boxes for tomorrow?"

Ella looked around the dining room. "If you'll clean booths three and four, I think we'll be caught up in here. Then you can see about helping Martha."

The next time she looked up, Chet was sitting on his same stool at the bar.

Ella plopped onto the stool next to him. "Mind if I join you for supper?"

He smiled. "Only if we move to my favorite table." He stood and walked to Nick's place in the front window.

"I'm having soup tonight," she said. "Cheese broccoli. How about you?"

"Sounds great. The weather is getting colder and colder." He looked out the window. "Won't be long till the snow flies. Then you'll be serving soup day and night."

Ella dished up the soup and added thick chunks of toasted French bread.

"Where's Nick?" Chet asked between bites.

"Oh, he's in the store room—what is now called the work room—helping Martha finish the boxes for tomorrow.

Nick appeared out of the back as if she'd called him.

He headed straight for them. "Mind if I have a bowl?"

Ella stood. "Of course not. I'll get it—"

Nick shook his head and rounded the end of the bar. "I got it, Mom." He was careful not to burn himself on the hot pot.

"Bread's in the warmer," Ella called out. "Good and crusty."

She smiled as he added a glass of milk to his tray. "I can't believe this is the same kid I brought with me from Albuquerque," she whispered. "But don't tell him I said that."

Chet watched Nick carefully arrange the items on his tray so they wouldn't spill as he carried it to the table. "He seems to really enjoy this."

Ella nodded. "He just needed to be needed. Or maybe valued is a better word."

"Don't we all," Chet agreed. He looked at his watch. "I'm going to take off in a bit. Go home and shower. I'll see you in about an hour." He glanced up as Nick approached. "Hey, buddy. How's school treating you?"

Nick set the tray down and gave him a thumbs up. "You were right, I really like it." He sat beside Ella.

She picked up his math book and took out the paper that was folded into it. "Looks good, kiddo," she said after checking it over. She put it in his backpack. "Any other homework I need to see?"

Nick shook his head. "No, not on Friday. But I think we got all the boxes done and the salad stuff cut up." He took a huge slurp of soup. "All we have left to do is put the sandwiches together and put them in the boxes. Then we'll be ready to go."

"What time do you and Martha think we need to be here in the morning, in order to get all this done, I mean?"

Nick shrugged. "She said she was going to be here at six as usual." He looked at her over his bowl. "It's a regular work day, too, Mom. Remember?"

"Oh, that's right? How could I forget?" She chuckled. "Don't worry. Both Belinda and Jan are coming in to work while we get everything finished. Then we'll deliver it to your school."

Chet stood and laid a twenty on the table. "Nicky, you keep things lined out here, would you?"

Nick nodded. His cheeks were a little pink, but he was such a good sport he didn't mind the teasing.

Chet clapped him on the back. "After you ring up my soup, put the change in your pocket. You are a hard worker."

"Thanks," Nick said. "I try."

"See you later," Ella said. "Glad you stopped by." Neither of them noticed the gold Mercedes backing out of the slanted space in front of the restaurant.

Nor did they see the tan car parked in the shadowy space between the buildings across the street.

At quitting time, Ella locked the front door behind the last customer.

"Whew!" She wiped a hand across her brow dramatically. "I have to admit, I'll be glad when this thing is behind us." Martha laughed. "It's a lot of work. But you'll see the reward tomorrow." She held up her wrist. "Shall we synchronize our watches?"

Ella grinned. "First, I'll have to start wearing one."

"I'm heading out," Belinda called from the back room. "See you guys in the morning."

"Me, too," Jan echoed. "See you bright and early."

Nick yawned. "Dishes are all caught up. Breakfast stuff stocked and ready to go."

Ella strode to where he stood. "Nicky, you are amazing." She looped her arm around his shoulders. "C'mon, let's get home and get some rest."

"Mom," he began. "Didn't you say we were going to have brownies tomorrow, too?"

She laughed. "That was me being overzealous."

Nick looked confused. "Overwhatus?"

Martha laughed. "She means she almost bit off more than we could chew."

Nick still looked somewhat confused. "Does that mean we're just having cookies?"

Both women nodded.

"I'm learning," Ella sighed. "Learning as I go."

Martha patted her shoulder. "You're doing great. Both of you." She stepped past Nick to turn out the dining room lights. "Let's head out, kids." She dug her keys from her sensible black purse. "I think we've done all the damage we can do for one night."

Together they went out the back door and waited as Martha locked up. "Ella," she exclaimed. "I'm so sorry.

You should be the one locking up. I just did it out of habit. Guess I'm even more exhausted than I thought."

Ella laughed. "You don't have to apologize. I've told you before that until you decide otherwise, you are still as much a part of the restaurant as we are."

Martha smiled and climbed into her car.

Chapter Twenty-Six

Chet arrived at their house within moments after they got home. The evening was crisp and cloudy. When Chet rang the doorbell, Ella allowed Nick to answer. She'd seen the arrival of the blue Mustang through the picture window.

"Got time for a quick game of catch before bed?" He held out a couple of old gloves.

"Heck yeah!" Nick grabbed his jacket and rushed outside. The sun was gone but the living room light fell through the picture window and illuminated a perfect rectangle of summer on the crackly fall grass.

Ella stood in the doorway and did her best not to feel any trepidation. She knew Chet was a good guy, but this was her Nicky, she didn't want him to become invested in something that wouldn't last. On the other hand, Chet had promised to coach Nick in baseball, no matter what happened between him and her. We do have to live here, she thought. And he is one of the coaches.

In the yard, Chet was showing Nicky how to catch the ball with both hands when he felt it hit the glove. "Cover it with your free hand," he was saying. "Never let it pop back out of the glove."

Nick nodded, his little face serious in the soft glow of light.

Chet tossed the ball into Nick's glove.

Nick covered it with his free hand just the way Chet showed him. Then he threw it back.

Ella saw the surprise on Chet's face when Nick threw it directly into his glove.

Chet backed up a bit and threw it to Nick, harder. The boy caught it and pitched it back on the run. In moments, a true game of catch ensued complete with grounders and fly balls and heaters.

"You amaze me, Nicky," Chet called. "I believe you're a natural."

Even in the dim light, Ella could see the sweet smile that bloomed on her son's face at the unexpected compliment.

Chet draped his arm around Nick's shoulder and together they entered the house.

"Hot chocolate, Mom?" Nick asked, rubbing his hands together.

"You bet," she answered. "It's beginning to get cold, isn't it?"

Nick nodded. "Mr. Boone said I'm a natural. I can't wait for baseball season to start."

"I heard that," she said. "And I agree. You did look like a natural out there. I bet you'll be a natural hitter, too."

They sat in comfortable silence, Nick drowning each tiny marshmallow with the tip of his index finger.

When the chocolate was gone, Ella sent him to bathe and get ready for bed.

There were no noises, and the lights never even flickered.

Ella looked at Chet. "Isn't it strange how nothing ever happens when you're here?"

He thought it over as he helped her wash and dry the mugs. "That sounds bad doesn't it?"

She quirked an eyebrow at him.

"Well, I mean, it sort of sounds like nothing happens because I'm here where you can watch me so naturally I can't make anything happen."

"Oh, I didn't mean that," Ella began. "I just meant that—" She stopped in midsentence. "But now that you mention it, that does make sense."

He dried the last mug and set it in the cupboard. Then he twirled her around so that she was facing him. "You know I think the world of you and Nicky." He had her trapped against the sink, but he wasn't touching her.

"I know." She dried her wet hands on a cup towel. "I was just going to say that whoever is doing it must be a real coward. They don't even attempt anything when a man is around."

He leaned in and gave her a quick kiss. They could both hear Nick banging around in the bathroom, humming a tuneless tune.

She touched his full bottom lip experimentally.

Chet pulled her against him and kissed her again. This time he held her firmly.

"I'll make up your bed on the couch," Ella said. "We need to be at The Drugstore early. We still have to toss the individual salads and build all the sandwiches."

"And I suppose the restaurant will be running as usual?"

Ella nodded. "I hope it all works out." She couldn't keep the nervous fear out of her voice.

"It will," he replied. "Between you and Martha, everything will be perfect."

Ella stepped away from him as she heard Nicky open the bathroom door. "Will you be there? I mean, has Beth tapped you to volunteer?"

He ducked his head as a deep blush spackled the back of his neck. Curving his hand over the offending area, Chet admitted that he was going to be one of the Rent-a-Gents.

Ella was about to make some snarky remark when Nick walked in with his ball cap on his wet head and his *Hatchet* book in his hand. "Ready to read, Mom?"

She smiled. "You bet. Hey, you want to read in here so Chet can hear, too?"

He nodded shyly. "I bet you'll like this book," he said. "A kid is stuck in the Canadian wilderness."

Chet examined the cover of the book. "Hey, I've read this. It *is* a good one."

Ella grabbed a blanket from the hall closet and tossed it around Nick on the sofa. She removed the cap from his head and settled in beside him. "Now, where were we?"

Nick opened to the bookmarked page and started reading.

Chet leaned back in the recliner and closed his eyes.

In moments he was breathing deeply. When he let out a gentle snore, both Nick and Ella giggled.

She motioned for Nick to bring his book. They tiptoed to his bedroom where Ella tucked him in and kissed his forehead.

"Mom," he said as she turned to go.

Ella stopped.

"We've been forgetting to say our prayers."

She turned back to his bed and kneeled beside it. "You're right. Our routine has been interrupted so often that I've completely forgotten." Of course she didn't mention how often she'd let it slide because she was hurrying back to the living room to see Chet as soon as Nick was asleep.

"Now I lay me down to sleep," he began.

Ella listened as he asked God to keep them safe and sound. She smiled when he stopped and included "Mr. Boone and Martha" in his prayer. "And don't forget about Nana," he said.

"Amen," she echoed. "That was very sweet, Nicky."

He looked up at her from the depths of his bedclothes. "They're good people. Just like me and you."

She leaned down and kissed his forehead like always. "I love you, buddy."

"And me, you," he said. It was his stock reply, sort of a mother son thing.

She walked back to the living room where she discovered Chet hadn't moved a muscle. For a moment, she simply stood and looked at him. Nicky trusted him completely. Her gut told her she could, too. But it was her once-bitten-twice-shy emotional mentality that kept her from being wholly convinced. She was beginning to think that mentality had become part of her makeup, maybe part of her psychological DNA. Especially since she'd actually made *two* mistakes where men were concerned. *Of course I can't really consider Tag a mistake. Without him, I wouldn't have Nicky.*

She covered Chet with the blanket and dropped a kiss on his forehead like she'd done with Nick. His lips curved up at the corners, but he didn't wake. Ella clicked off the overhead, but left the appliance light burning over the stove. Then she went to run her own bath.

Tonight feels like a precipice. Tomorrow the fundraiser will be over and I will be forced to decide what to do about the house.

After a relaxing bath, she donned her least-sexy knit PJs and made one more foray through the house to check the doors and windows. She was surprised to find that even though Chet had changed positions, he was still snoring.

She grinned and tiptoed back to her bedroom. *I hate to admit it, but I do feel much safer with him here. Yeah, I'm really an independent woman. She sighed and vowed not to become to dependent on Chet, or any man for that matter.* Then she grabbed her Kindle and tucked herself into bed, certain she wouldn't fall asleep for hours.

It was dawn when she awoke with her Kindle in sleep mode on her chest.

She could hear movement in the kitchen but the beep, beep, beep of her alarm drew her attention and she rolled over and pressed the button to turn it off.

When she rolled back over, Chet was standing in her bedroom doorway wearing her old cornflower blue apron over his plaid shirt and jeans.

Ella covered her mouth to keep from guffawing.

He crossed to the bed and threatened to spank her with his spatula.

She scooted to the middle so he could sit on the edge. "Sleep well?" she asked.

"Like a rock." He cupped her chin in one hand and ran one thumb under her eye.

She closed her eyes and lay back, allowing him to explore her face.

"I was going to sneak into your bed in the middle of the night." He was so close his breath warmed her cheek. "But you were sleeping so soundly, I didn't have the heart to wake you."

Ella opened her eyes and he was right there, his blue eyes inches from hers. "It would've been nice," she said.

He pressed his lips to hers and she responded with an ardor that surprised them both. Chet pulled back and looked into her face, a question drawing his brows together.

Ella pulled him down beside her and he slipped his hands beneath the blankets, exploring and caressing as his mouth sought hers once more. She pulled him even closer, reveling in the feel of his hard chest pressed to hers.

In no time their breathing had quickened to the point that she began to wonder about a stopping point.

Chet must have sensed her sudden recalcitrance. He pulled away reluctantly, his gentle hands sketching the form beneath her knit pajamas one last time. "I like these," he said, his breath preceding his lips on her throat.

"Mmm," Ella replied. "I like your apron. It brings out your eyes." She took his head between her hands and pulled his lips back to hers. "For some reason, it also makes me hungry."

He groaned and pressed himself the length of her. "You're asking for trouble, Brownie."

"Oh, yeah?" She licked his upper lip. "How's that?"

Returning the moist affection, he murmured, "I think my toast is burning."

He jumped up and ran to the kitchen.

Ella laughed when she smelled burnt toast accompanied by mild cursing.

By the time she dressed and made it to the kitchen, Nick was sitting at the table eating a bowl of cold cereal; his Eagles cap perched firmly on his head.

Ella avoided Chet's eye, and Nick never even questioned what he was doing there so early, wearing his mother's apron. She and Chet joined Nick in having cereal—just in case they didn't have time to make anything at The Drugstore—and then the three of them strolled out of the house as if it was no one's business.

"Thank goodness it's Saturday," Nick said. He had packed his checkers, some books, and a deck of cards in his backpack. "I hope Danny brings his Knock-Knock book."

"Are you taking your Nintendo?" Ella asked.

Nick thought about it for a moment. "Nah, everyone always wants to play with it. And I hate saying no all the time. I'd rather just leave it at home."

"Smart kid," Chet said.

They didn't kiss when he left, but the way his gaze lingered on her lips, she almost felt as though they had.

He gave Nick a salute and crawled into the Mustang, backing out and waiting for them to get in front of him so that he could follow them all the way to town.

So strange that nothing happens when he is at the house, Ella thought. The idea wouldn't leave her alone even though she kept telling herself she wasn't going to think about it. Today was going to be all about business and making a good impression on the patrons at the fundraiser.

She smoothed her hair and freshened her lipstick in the rearview mirror. Nerves were beginning to rear their pointy little heads. She said a silent prayer that everything would go according to plan.

For once, they were the first ones at the restaurant. But it was only a minute before everyone else arrived.

After awhile, breakfast customers began to trickle in and Martha and Jan handled them while Ella, Belinda, and Nick made the individual salads and put together the sandwiches.

They wrapped each sandwich in cling wrap and stacked them in the big refrigerator. By this time, it was eleven o'clock.

Nick had the good idea to open all the boxes and set them side by side on the long table. "Now I can just go down the row and plop the sandwiches in while Belinda comes behind me and closes the box." He waited for someone to contradict him. "You know, like Henry Ford's assembly line."

Ella clapped him on the back. "Good thinking, son." She finished stacking the last of the Styrofoam salad bowls in the fridge. "We've got white tablecloths and the plastic ware already packed in my Jeep. Martha's going to put down the seats in her Suburban, and I think all the food will fit in there." She looked around. "Beth said the kids made fall table decorations in Art class, so I think we're all set."

Chapter Twenty-Seven

"Who'll give me five? Five dollars for this fine specimen?" The auctioneer was also the principal of the elementary school, Marsha Dixon.

"I will, Ms. Dixon," Norma called, waving her number paddle in the air.

"There are five dollars going once, but really folks. This is Officer Rod for goodness sakes. Not only does he wield a mean paint brush, he also likes to rake leaves and clean out flower beds—"

"Ten dollars," his wife called. "And I will hold you to all those things."

Officer Rodriguez rolled his eyes. "Please, someone offer fifteen, my wife will work me to death if she has to shell out ten bucks."

"Fifteen," Norma yelled. "My weeds are plumb out of control."

Ms. Dixon grinned. "That's more like it, ladies. Who'll give me twenty?"

Someone in the back row raised her number paddle and Officer Rodriguez pumped his fist in the air. "Yes!" he crowed.

Suddenly there ensued a heated bidding war between Norma, the lady on the back row, and the officer's wife, which drove Officer Rod's price up to almost one hundred dollars.

"Sold—er, rented, to the lady in the back row. Sheila Jenkins, claim your gent!" Everyone applauded and Officer Rodriguez hopped off the stage to give the winner his contact card.

Ella watched the proceedings with disbelief. *Did anyone really live this way?* She checked her watch. Beth had assured her it would be a lot of fun, this Rent-a-Gent fundraiser. And it was; watching the volunteers sashay around in waiter's uniforms reminded her of Chet in her apron this morning.

But it was when the guys walked the stage in front of the audience that the fun began. Jake the deliveryman was a huge hit. He strolled across in his uniform, pushing Ms. Dixon on his freight dolly.

She told the crowd that he was ready, willing, and able to handle anything.

When he doffed his cap and leered, he was also rented for one hundred dollars.

Ella was pleased that nearly all the boxed lunches were eaten, and most of the salads as well. Folks devoured the cookies and there was plenty of iced tea for all. The kids in the library were also given boxed lunches, although the librarian drew the line at iced tea. She provided bottles of water instead.

As the fundraiser progressed, Ella hooted and clapped right along with the best of them. Especially when Ms. Dixon joked about the men's abilities according to their individual professions. But somehow, Ella still felt disconnected.

When she noticed John and Beth Stockton holding hands and treating each other so tenderly, she just couldn't tamp down that old green-eyed monster called envy. *How does one find that certain someone? That soul mate? Could Chet be mine, or was that asking too much? When he was nearby, she thought it was highly possible, but the moment he was out of sight, the doubts came creeping in.*

Her mind wandered back to high school, to Nicky's father. They'd been a couple for months when she finally gave in and slept with him on—of all things—homecoming night. She hadn't been the queen, but she had been a member of the court. It seemed so tawdry and ridiculous now, but back then, it had seemed like a fairy tale come true. Tag had been her world.

What a mistake.

When two months passed and Tag learned of her "condition," it had been nothing but *adios*. He offered to pay for an abortion, but that was it. She was so ashamed that she didn't tell her folks until Tag was already off at college in another state.

She didn't want *him* if he didn't want *them*. But her mom didn't see it that way at all. "He has a financial responsibility," she said time and time again. "It costs a fortune to raise a child—you can't let your pride deprive your child of a decent life."

But Ella didn't agree. And for once, she didn't give in. She simply went to work in one restaurant after another, putting every penny she could in a bank account for "after." Her college dreams fell by the wayside.

She and her mother had a huge falling out. They didn't reconcile until little Nicky was born. And when her father died unexpectedly, Ella moved back home. But it was hard, being treated like a child again—especially when she was a mother herself.

On top of that, her mom knew everything about raising a baby—or so she thought—and she never hesitated to let Ella know it. In her eyes, Ella could do nothing right.

Is that why I was so desperate to find love, and to find Nicky a father? Is that what kept me from seeing that cold hard streak running through the middle of Anson's psyche? He'd seemed so perfect—love at first sight perfect—until they'd been married awhile and his resentment over raising someone else's child began to come out.

Had there been red flags before they were married?

Ella asked herself that very question time and time again. What she now saw as controlling, back then had simply seemed like love. The fact that he didn't want her to work, well, that seemed too good to be true to a young mother, at least until he began to complain about their finances.

Every time there was a bill from the doctor or dentist, or even new cleats for Nick's first football season, Anson would make some snide remark about child support. And the firm hand he had with her son, the one she'd thought would be good for Nicky—who had become quite spoiled at Nana's house—was actually more like a mean streak masquerading as firmness.

After a few months, Ella had begun to think of Anson as The Bully. And still, she made excuses for his behavior.

She wasn't proud of it, but after much soul searching, she knew it was true. She'd only lived on her own for a brief while after Nicky was born, right after high school. Then over the years, Anson had convinced her she couldn't get along without him.

Ella bit the inside of her lip to put an end to the unwelcome memories. *Nothing to be gained by looking back.* She had Nick and now she had her own diner. *Life was good, and it would get better and better.*

She glanced up toward the school stage where Big John was climbing the steps. They'd even allowed Turk to come in with him. Ella had a feeling it was Beth's caveat—no Turk, no John.

"And now, ladies, let's hear some bids for Big John Stockton and his faithful sidekick, Turk the Wonder Dog!"

Everyone applauded and someone wolf-whistled, Ella thought it might have been Beth, then the principal said, "Big John, so called because of his ahem, *height* (more wolf-whistles), can be hired to paint, clean gutters, rake leaves and do other odd jobs requiring a man of his stature." She laughed. "Changing light bulbs is his specialty."

"What about Turk the Wonder Dog?" someone called out. "What's his specialty?"

"Eating," John replied jovially. "If you rent us, you have to supply the dog biscuits."

Everyone applauded again, and Ella was amazed at the affection granted the huge dog. Even the canine appeared to be smiling.

"Remind me to tell you about Turk the Wonder Dog," Marissa whispered, leaning over conspiratorially.

Ella nodded, a look of confusion on her face.

"He really is a hero," the dispatcher said. "For *real.*"

Ella would have asked for details, but several hands went up and another bidding war was underway. Beth kept driving the price up, saying she couldn't bear for anyone else to benefit from her hubby's expertise, and the emcee kept shooing her hand back down. "You're price gouging," Ms. Dixon cried. "At least, I think that's what it's called."

Beth laughed and put her hand down. It was all in good fun, and for a good cause.

Martha simply waited until everyone else was done, and then she put in the winning bid. When John hopped off the stage to present her his business card, she said, "I've got the ladder ready, and the eaves are waiting." She winked at Beth, and then turned her attention to Turk. "And as for you, ya big ox, I've got a nice rump roast in the freezer."

"Wait a minute," John joked. "I like roast, too."

Martha swatted his arm and tucked the business card in her purse. "I'll be calling you—soon."

Ella smiled, an image of Mayberry springing to mind again. She watched as Beth and John laughed together over some comment one of them had made.

Maybe I'll have someone like that. Maybe someday.

252 | Ann Swann

She hooked one foot behind the other, leaned back in her chair, and relaxed.

And then the next Rent-a-Gent walked onto the stage and her mind went blank.

Chet Boone swaggered across the stage in his khaki uniform. He carried a comical critter net over one shoulder, and on his face was a self-deprecating smile.

"Here he is, folks," Ms. Dixon announced, "Stutter Creek's most eligible bachelor, Wildlife Biologist and our resident critter catcher, Chet 'Take 'em Alive' Boone!"

Chet bowed and swept his Indiana Jones hat from his head all in one smooth motion. "At your service," he said.

Catcalls and whistles abounded and Chet's face turned redder than a fall apple. He stood upright, moving somewhat jerkily, and executed a quick turn, heading back to mid-stage at record speed.

"All right, ladies, who will start the bidding—"

"I bid twenty-five bucks," someone in the back called out.

"Fifty!" another countered.

"Seventy-five!" a third interrupted.

Ella kept her lips pressed together tightly. The price had already risen well out of her budget, and besides, the "take 'em alive" comment had really thrown her for a loop. All she could think of were the tears in his eyes when he told her about the bears. But Ms. Dixon probably didn't know about that.

She glanced up to see if his face was still flaming, and was surprised to find him staring straight at her. He wore an expression not unlike the one she'd noticed in her bed this morning. Good humor mixed with something else—an underlying question perhaps.

Ella tried to decide if he was really looking at her, or if he was looking at someone behind her. She didn't want to be the dork that turns around and actually glances behind, but she was almost to that point when he mouthed something that looked like, "What? No moola?"

She raised her hands to show that they were empty. There was no doubt he was talking to her. His navy blue gaze seemed to bore right into her flesh. Ella shook her head and made a sad face, and that's when she realized the bidding had stopped.

She glanced around and every eye in the place seemed to be looking at her. Now it was her turn to blush. She felt as if every kiss she'd shared with Chet was tattooed right on her face. Great, she thought, everyone already knows. That's just the sort of impression I hoped to make as the newest business owner in town. But there was nothing she could do except grin and bear it.

Dispatcher Marissa came to her aid. "I heard our new café owner had an unwelcome visitor in her house—and on her first night here, too. That's not a fun way to start out—maybe we could all chip in and rent the critter catcher for her. Just for a day or two." Everyone laughed, but it sounded like a good-natured laugh. Even Ella chuckled.

"I believe the current bid is seventy-five dollars," the principal chortled, delighted at the prospect of raising even more money.

"Eighty," Marissa cried, raising her hand.

"Eighty-five," the woman near the door yelled back.

"Ninety!" Marissa countered.

"One hundred dollars!" the unseen woman practically shrieked.

Ella did turn then. She felt certain Charlie was the woman doing the bidding from the back row near the door. But a tall woman sat between her and the other "bidder," so she couldn't really see.

"Go for it, Marissa," Beth Stockton whispered. "We'll all chip in." She glanced around the area at several of her friends and fellow teachers. "We can't let Charlie win just because she's loaded."

So Marissa went for it.

When the bidding was over, Chet Boone had been rented for $200.

He stepped down from the stage and tried to hand Marissa his card. His face was once again in flames.

"Oh, no," she said, pushing his hand away. "You belong to our new café owner, lock stock and barrel—or at least until she gets our two hundred dollars worth."

Everyone roared with laughter, except for Charlie who stalked out without a backward glance.

Chet turned to Ella and presented his card.

"But, but—" she meant to say she could never repay that amount of money, even for a good cause, but he shushed her gently.

"Now, don't worry," he said. "Catching critters is not my only talent." He hung his head when he realized he'd just uttered another racy double entendre, but he forged gamely ahead. "I mean, I've got lots of other talents—"

The women sitting around them began to giggle.

Ella couldn't help herself. She took the proffered card and attempted to stifle her own laugh with the back of her hand. "Well, thank you," she replied, nodding at Chet and at Marissa. "I'm sure I'll find lots of ways to use you."

That did it, the place erupted and Ella simply sat back and covered her eyes. Chet grinned and fled back up the steps to Ms. Dixon who was holding the microphone down at her side to try and stifle her own mirth.

Few people noticed Chet's quick scan of the room as he topped the wooden steps. For a moment, his eyes stopped on the empty chair where Charlie had been sitting. An unreadable look clouded his eyes and temporarily stilled his features. Then Ms. Dixon grabbed him by the arm and turned him around to face the rest of the crowd once more.

The ladies in the audience cheered and whistled, and then Chet Boone was ushered off into the wings.

The next Gent was a fireman named Sam Burdett. Ms. Dixon said he was very skilled with his hose. The women went wild.

Chet Boone's chart topping bid held up for all of five minutes, then the record was shattered.

Chapter Twenty-Eight

The fundraiser ended around four o'clock and Ella, Martha, and Nick stuck around for another hour and visited with all the patrons.

Nick had thoroughly enjoyed himself, but they were all exhausted and ready to go home. Nevertheless, the three of them headed back to The Drugstore to make sure Belinda and Jan were ready to close up.

Chet had whispered that he would meet them back at the house after they closed the restaurant.

Around dusk, they were finally headed home. It was almost impossible to believe the Rent-a-Gent fundraiser had culminated the first week of school and work.

When they turned into the driveway, Ella realized she was beat. *What a week it's been!*

Nick took the house key and ran on ahead of her. He wanted to get inside and get the TV tuned to the latest installment of X-Men. One of the boys in the Library had told them it was on the movie channel.

Shaking her head, but with a smile on her face, Ella locked the Jeep doors and followed her son up the wide steps. "Oh," she muttered, recalling the book of recipes Martha had sent home with her two days earlier. In all the excitement, she kept forgetting to take it into the house.

She clicked the remote to unlock the Jeep and was hurrying back down the steps when a cold certainty that she was being watched stole over her shoulders like a dense shadow. She glanced up just in time to see the silhouette of a man step behind a tree at the end of the drive.

Ella gasped, grabbed the spiral-bound cookbook, and began to back cautiously toward the porch. It took every ounce of courage to turn her back on that figure, dash up those five steps, and dive through the front door.

Once inside, she whirled around and drove the deadbolt home. Then she leaned to the side and peered out through the curtains.

The silhouette was standing rock-still behind the too-narrow tree.

It's him. He's found us. Somehow, he got out.

She tried to tell herself she was being paranoid; Anson couldn't be out. And even if he was, he had no way of finding them. But in her gut, she knew that he had. *I don't know how, but I know that gut feeling.*

After watching the silhouette for a few more seconds—during which time it didn't seem to move—Ella went from room to room checking each window and door lock, again. She also checked the view from each window. She was looking for an old blue and white Dodge pickup. She tried her best to be stealthy; she didn't want to alert Nick just yet. Didn't want to frighten him. Let him watch his movie. Let him live in innocence a few more minutes before he had to learn to be afraid again.

But there was no old blue and white pick up anywhere.

There was nothing at all.

She wound up back in the living room foyer, breath heavy as steel in her lungs.

Standing to one side again, she twitched the edge of the curtain and peered out once more.

The silhouette still hadn't moved.

How can he remain so perfectly still?

She moved back into the kitchen for another view from a different angle. *Is it him?* Her rational mind tried to convince her that the shape she was seeing was nothing more than a tree shadow—one standing just behind the other.

But he was there, she told herself. *He was. I saw him move.*

She grabbed the cordless phone and dialed her mom's number.

When Viola answered, Ella was blunt. "Mom, have you heard anything about Anson? Could he be out of jail?"

Viola gasped. That was the last thing she'd expected to hear. "Oh, honey. He got out on probation or something. He came to the house, pushed his way right past me and came into the house. But of course I didn't tell him anything. I was going to call you, but I knew he couldn't find you there."

Ella closed her eyes and pushed the bangs off her forehead. "I feel like someone is watching us." She laughed bitterly and walked back to the living room to look out the window. Nick had the throw pillows in the floor in front of the TV. He loved Wolverine.

She peeked out the curtain again.

The shadow was gone.

Maybe the lowering sun changed the angle?

Biting the tip of her thumbnail, she debated telling her mom exactly what she'd seen. But there was no need to worry her before they had good reason. What could she do from Albuquerque?

"Ella? You still there?" Viola's voice sounded very concerned.

"Still here, Mom." She kept her voice low. "Just wondering how he could possibly have gotten out on probation. And if there is any way he could know where we are."

Viola said, "Hold on a sec." She laid the phone down with a clunk.

Ella held her own receiver away from her ear. She could hear her mom moving away from the phone. In seconds, she was back.

"Oh, no." Viola's voice had changed drastically in the space of a few seconds.

Ella's heart seemed to stop. "What? What is it, Mom?"

Her mother exhaled shakily. "I - I put your new number on my fridge. Now—it's gone. Along with the magnet Nicky made me in Sunday school."

"But that doesn't mean—"

Viola cut her off. "Yes, it does. That's exactly what it means. I went out the front door to my neighbor's house to get away from him. He went out the back. To do that, he had to go straight through the kitchen." She stopped for a breath. "I could understand misplacing the slip of paper, perhaps. But honey, I wouldn't misplace that and the magnet that was holding it." She sounded as if she were on the verge of tears. "He took it, Ella. He knows where you are. Stupid me. I should have thrown the paper away after putting the numbers in my cell phone. All he had to do was call the diner and ask whoever answered where they are located."

"Oh my God." Ella couldn't say anything else. She was too shocked that her safe haven had been breached so easily.

"You have to tell the police," her mom insisted. "They have to be on the lookout."

As if they have nothing else to do, Ella thought. "I'll ask Martha if anyone has called wanting the address, if not, maybe I can just change the phone number. That would solve the problem, wouldn't it?"

Viola didn't speak right away. She didn't know a lot about computers, but she knew enough, and she was fairly certain that the phone number would be listed on The

Drugstore's website. After a moment, she voiced her concerns to Ella.

"You're right," Ella said. "I even looked it up once, didn't I?" She chewed her thumbnail. "I'll check into it tomorrow," she said. "That's one thing I like about Stutter Creek—not everyone is online. In fact, we don't even have a computer here at the house. Haven't been able to replace the one he trashed."

Viola sighed. "I am so sorry, baby. I can't believe I wasn't more careful."

"Mom—" Ella interrupted. "You didn't do anything wrong. It's him. He's the one who forced his way into your home and then stole—"

"I know. You're right. Nevertheless, it's done and I feel as if I'm to blame. If anything happens to you or Nicky because of my stupidity, I'll never forgive myself."

Ella was almost paralyzed by disbelief. "Mom," she interrupted again, "nothing will happen. I'm calling the police right now."

"Good!" The relief in her mother's voice was apparent. "I'll go ahead and hang up then. You call me, you hear? Let me know you're safe."

"I will, Mom, I'll call you every night. Deal?"

"Deal," Viola agreed. "And if I don't hear from you, I'll be calling you. In fact, I think I'd better just come on out there."

Ella thought it over. "Can you take off work that easily?"

Viola sighed. "I wasn't going to tell you this, but I fell and sprained my ankle a few days ago."

"Oh, Mom! What happened? Why didn't you say anything?"

Viola sighed. "I didn't want to tell you, because you have so much going on right now, I didn't want to worry you. Besides, it's only a bad sprain. I just can't drive yet. I'm supposed to keep it elevated as much as possible."

"Oh my goodness, I need to be there to help you. Who is looking after you? Cooking, cleaning—"

"Now, calm down El. My neighbor across the street is looking after me. She's doing a very good job, too."

"How did it happen?"

Viola chuckled. "Like an idiot, I missed the last rung on the stepladder at work. Tumbled right down." Viola worked part time at a plant nursery. "The boss was so nice. I think he thought I was going to sue or something. But it was definitely my own fault. Hurt my pride more than anything."

"Oh, Mom. I'm so glad you're okay. Don't you worry about us. In fact, I'm hanging up now—"

"So you can call the police, right?"

"Right." She laughed darkly. "I'll talk to you tomorrow. Don't *worry*. Everything's going to be okay. And you stay off that foot." She couldn't believe she was the one comforting her mother instead of the other way around.

Because in reality, she was absolutely terrified.

She immediately hung up and dialed the Stutter Creek Police Department.

Chapter Twenty-Nine

Marissa wasn't working, but Officer Rodriguez had gone to work right after the fundraiser was over.

Ella was glad he was the one who responded to her call.

While she waited on him to arrive, she told Nick everything that was going on.

And then she repeated it all to the officer just a few minutes later. She told him everything that had happened. Especially about Anson going to her mom's house and then everything else that had happened at their house. She made certain to tell him about the Aramis cologne and the lights being turned on and off. While she spoke, Nicky's eyes grew wider and wider.

"Sounds like someone's toying with you all right," Officer Rod said.

"That's what I thought," Ella agreed. "But I could never understand how he could turn the lights on and off at will."

"Simple," the officer responded. "In addition to an indoor breaker box, some houses have a main switch out back. It turns off everything in one fell swoop."

Ella felt like an idiot. She'd never heard of such a thing. "But how could he have gotten in to leave the cologne, and hide things, like my hammer, and my coaster?" she asked. "I'm very careful. I check these doors and windows every night. I never unlock them—" she looked at the kitchen window. Officer Rodriguez hadn't made it that far yet, but he didn't have to. Ella vividly recalled that brisk fall day when she had opened the window to let in the breeze. The day Chet Boone had arrived. *Did I lock it back? Surely I did. Why wouldn't I?* It finally occurred to her that perhaps the old window had fallen back down on its own and she simply hadn't noticed that it wasn't locked. Or maybe Nick had seen it open and took it upon himself to close it. She thought about all the times she'd checked that window since then. *I know it was locked every time I checked it. It's locked right now. But that one day, I don't think I locked it. I don't remember even shutting it.*

"I think I know how he might've gained entrance," she said. She led the officer to the kitchen window. "I unlocked it one day to let in the fall breeze. Then something happened and I forgot to go back and lock it. I don't even remember closing it that day." She unlocked it now and raised it a few inches, and then turned it loose. After a few seconds, it fell back down with a *thunk*. That sound, Ella thought. *I've heard that before. But not on that day. I was sitting out on the porch drinking coffee when Chet drove up. I do remember that.*

"Look here," Officer Rod said. "Are these scuff marks on the sill?"

Ella reached out to touch the faint black marks on the otherwise pristine windowsill.

"Is it possible?" the officer asked. "Could he have hoisted himself into the window?" He leaned over and looked out. "It's easily five feet off the ground."

Ella nodded. "Oh, yeah. Anson is very athletic. He played sports and worked out with the guys all the time. He is one of the few people who had a gym membership and used it." She laughed sarcastically. "He even had one of those chin up bars in the doorway." Her eyes were moist. She didn't want to fall apart in front of Officer Rod. She turned her head away. "He was always showing off, telling me I needed to work out like he did." She hesitated for a moment, and then plunged on. "He was so arrogant. Once, we were watching NCIS or one of those other crime shows on TV and he started laughing at the medical examiner who was identifying a burned body."

The officer stopped what he was doing and listened closely.

After checking to make certain Nick really was absorbed in his movie again, Ella rushed on, feeling as if it was very important to get this out. "He was saying if you really burn a body no one can ever identify it—if you know how to do it right."

"What else did he say?" Officer Rod asked softly.

"That—that the main problem would be the teeth and bones. Get rid of the teeth and make sure the fire is hot enough to burn the bones, he said." She put a hand on the wall to steady herself. She suddenly felt very faint.

"Was he ever married before?"

That's a strange question to ask, she thought. Especially since I just told him—a bulb went off in her head. "Yes, once." She looked at the officer with horror in her eyes. Eyes that seemed able to see all the way into the past. "He said she took off on him after only a year of marriage. Said she disappeared without a trace."

Officer Rodriguez took a couple of pictures with his phone. If he was alarmed by her words, he didn't show it. "Going out to see if there are any tracks outside."

Ella nodded and wiped her nose. "Do you think he would've locked the window after he left? Does that make sense?"

The officer gave her a look that could have meant anything. Then he went out the back door.

He was back in only a few minutes. "It's impossible to find any tracks," he said. "But the ivy at the base of the trellis is trampled completely flat."

Ella inhaled sharply. "The trellis under the attic window?"

He nodded. "Could be he made a copy of the attic key. You said you left it laying on that same windowsill for several days." He indicated the one where they'd found the scuffmarks. "Then he just went up and unlocked the attic window. He probably tried the key on every door in the house first." He peered at the windowsill again. "Then he could have come and gone at will. Coming up the trellis, through the attic, and down the stairs. If he had a key, that is."

Ella had to sit down. The vision of Anson in their house while they were gone made her physically ill. "And he would relock the attic door behind himself so I wouldn't know. That would be so like him. He always played pranks on us. He would jump out of closets, lock us out of the house so we had to stand there begging to be let in. He would even scare us by pretending to lose control of the car going over bridges. Anything to make us squirm." Her eyes narrowed. She stood. "He isn't going to get away with it anymore." She unlocked the attic door and started up the stairs.

Officer Rodriguez followed close behind. And then he touched her back. "Stop right there. Let me go first. From what you've just told me, it sounds like we're dealing with a real psycho."

She flattened herself against the wall to let him pass.

At the top of the stairs, Officer Rod flipped on the light. He checked the entire attic before allowing her to proceed. "I don't want to be up here with Nick alone downstairs," she said. "I just want to see if the window is unlocked."

"It's not locked." Officer Rod reached over and flipped it up with two fingers.

Scrape

He turned it loose and it fell back down.

Thunk!

"He must've loved that sound," Ella said. "We heard it many times over the last few days. But we could never figure out what it was." She quickly crossed the attic and looked at the window. When it was down, it appeared to be locked.

"Look here," Officer Rod showed her the window lock. "Even when it is unlocked, it appears to be locked." He twisted the mechanism. It had been filed off just enough so that even when it was in the locked position, it no longer touched the frame.

"Anson did that," she said. "I just know he did."

The officer looked around the attic. "You go on downstairs. I'm going to find a board or something to put in here to secure the window."

Ella caught on immediately. "How about a broom handle?"

"That'll work," he agreed. "We'll have to cut it off so that it fits between the upper sill and the frame."

"I don't have a saw," Ella said. "But I've got a large steak knife."

Officer Rodriguez laughed. "We'll make it work," he said. "Have you got a measuring tape?"

Ella got the measuring tape, the steak knife, and Nick, and hurried back up the stairs.

Nick watched curiously as the officer measured the height of the window from the middle to the top, and then marked the same length on the broom handle. He started sawing away at the wooden handle with the steak knife. When he'd made a fairly deep cut, he cracked it over his knee. It broke cleanly.

"There you go." He handed the remainder of the broom back to Ella. "I've ruined your broom and your steak knife." He handed the knife to her also. "But it will have to do for tonight."

Ella eyed the jury-rigged window with suspicion. "Thank you, Rod, I don't want to seem ungrateful. I mean I really appreciate everything you've done." She cut her eyes at Nick. "But the more I think about everything that *he's* done, the more I think we should just gather up our stuff and go spend the night in town—"

Her little speech was interrupted by the crackle of the police radio. "Unit Six?"

"Excuse me," he said. He tilted his head to one side and spoke into the mic attached to his epaulet. "Go ahead."

"Unit Six, we have a major 10-50 northbound lane Highway 385 just south of the loop. DPS requesting traffic assistance."

"10-4 Headquarters. Unit Six responding."

"Go," Ella said. "I don't know what a major ten-fifty is, but it sounds serious." She shooed at him with her hands. "Go ahead. I promise, we'll be fine. We're just going to grab our overnight bags and go to town."

"A 10-50 is a vehicle accident," he said. "The word major means there are injuries. If she'd said minor, it would've meant no injuries." He tested the broom handle he'd stuck above the window. "If you get your things quickly, I'll walk you out to the Jeep."

Ella told Nick to run and pack his stuff. "Grab your swimsuit," she said. "Maybe the hotel will have a pool."

Officer Rodriguez followed them downstairs.

They were nearly at the bottom when his radio crackled again. "Unit Six?"

"Go ahead," he responded.

"Estimated Time of Arrival?"

He looked at his watch. "ETA ten minutes," he said.

"10-4. Be advised, Life Flight is en route. Traffic control needed immediately."

"10-4. ETA *five* minutes." He turned to Ella. "I have to go now."

She locked the attic door and shoved the red chair under the knob. Then she ushered Officer Rod toward the front door. "We're coming. Go ahead." She grabbed her purse. "Nicky! Let's go."

Officer Rodriguez was on the porch as Nick came running, lugging his duffle bag behind him.

The officer opened their doors and checked the interior of the Jeep.

Ella locked the front door behind Nick and they dashed to the vehicle and climbed in. "Thank you for everything," she told Officer Rodriguez. "Drive safely."

He gave them a little salute, climbed into his car and flipped on the lights and siren.

As they backed out of the drive, they could see him talking on the radio.

In seconds, they were all headed to town with him leading the way.

Chapter Thirty

"Whew." Ella slowed the Jeep. "Sorry I rushed you so, Nicky. I have to run back in the house. I totally forgot my cell phone."

"But Mom—"

"I know it doesn't work out here," she said. "But it will work in town, and it has all my numbers in it. I'll need them to call people when we get to the hotel. Have to let them know where we're staying." She was mainly thinking of Chet, who was supposed to be over later. But she'd also promised to call her mom, and she certainly didn't want to pay long distance charges from a hotel phone. Not when she could call from her cell for free.

She hopped out of the Jeep. "C'mon," she said. "It won't take but a sec."

Nick started to argue, but something in his mother's tone told him not to bother. He jumped out and followed her back into the house.

"I laid it on the kitchen table." She hurried to the kitchen, grabbed her cell and was surprised to see the red message light blinking on the landline.

That's not good news, she thought. She took a deep breath and pushed the button to listen.

"Ella?" It was Chet's voice. "I'm on my way to Pine River." He left a slight gap. "Charlie was at the fundraiser, drunk. Apparently she was pretty upset when she left. The state police say she crashed into the back of an eighteen wheeler." Now his voice was softer. "Thankfully, the truck driver is okay, but she's in a helicopter on the way to the Pine River Hospital. Roger is coming in from Seattle." He paused one last time. "I will head back as soon as Roger arrives. I'm sorry. This is the last time, I swear."

Ella stood looking at the phone for what seemed like an hour. Poor woman, she thought. That's the major 10-50. Poor Chet. She's really messed up and he's really tied to her. *On the other hand, I guess this proves she wasn't the one standing behind the tree.*

She smoothed her forehead with her fingertips. *Can't worry about that now. First things first.*

She thought about trying to call Chet back, but she didn't want to be in the house any longer than necessary. *I'll call from the motel just like I planned.*

Nick was looking at her with a question in his eyes.

"I'll tell you about it on the way," she said. "Let's go."

After locking the front door again, they walked quickly back to the Jeep.

Ella felt as if the night had grown even darker. It wasn't a comforting feeling. He could be anywhere, she thought.

They got in and locked the doors and for the first time, she wished they had chosen a hard top instead of a soft top. In her mind, she could easily see Anson ripping into the canvas with a steak knife like they'd just used to cut the broom handle.

She backed out of the drive.

"Is our landlady going to die?" Nick asked.

Ella shifted gears. "I hope not, honey. But she was driving drunk and ran into the back of a semi-truck." She glanced at his face to see how he was taking it.

"Is she related to Mr. Boone?"

That was unexpected.

"No, but they've been friends for many years."

"What did he mean, this will be the last time? On the message—"

"Nick." Ella's head swiveled around. "Did you see that car we just passed?"

Nick turned in his seat and looked behind them. "You mean that tan one going the other way?"

Ella nodded. "Yes. That one." She pressed the gas a little harder. "It may have been Anson."

"Go faster, Mommy," Nick always reverted to mommy when he was upset. "Let's get to the hotel."

Ella glanced down to check her speed, and her heart dropped into the pit of her stomach. Their gas gauge was on empty.

She looked in her rearview mirror. *Did the car's brake lights come on?* Maybe it was turning into the Benefield's driveway.

That has to be it. It wasn't Anson. It was probably Becky, Mrs. Benefield's daughter. It's just talking about him with officer Rodriguez that made me think that. Well, that and the fact that we suddenly seem to be out of gas.

"Hey, Nicky," she made her voice light.

"Yeah?"

"We're out of gas. We don't have enough to make it into town." She was already looking for a place to turn around. "I know we just filled up the tank, but somehow, we don't have any now. We have to go back to the house."

"But what about Anson? I heard you and Officer Rod talking. I know he's the one who's been making all the noises to scare us."

Ella gritted her teeth. "Yes, but we can't take a chance on running out of gas between here and town."

She pulled to the side of the road and executed a quick turn around. *Is it possible someone siphoned the gas while I was parked at the elementary school? I filled up just yesterday. Maybe someone siphoned it out last night, right in my own carport?*

Her mind whirled with possibilities as they neared their own house again.

What if we had run out of gas beside the road? Maybe that's what he wants. Maybe he intends for us to disappear like his first wife.

"Okay, here we are." She turned into their driveway a bit sharper than she intended. Ella didn't want to alarm Nick unnecessarily, but what if it really was Anson and he bullied his way inside like he had at her mom's house?

"Honey," she said, as she opened her door. "I think Anson siphoned the gas out of our tank."

Nick looked behind them as he got back out of the Jeep.

Ella waited for him to come around the vehicle, and then she pushed him in front of her as they ascended the porch steps. "When we get inside, I'm going to call the police department again." She jabbed the key into the lock and shoved Nick inside as soon as she had it open.

"Why are you so sure it's him?" Nick asked.

"I think you already heard me telling Officer Rod that something made the lights go on and off. And all those noises in the attic? Officer Rod and I just discovered that someone had broken the lock on the attic window. Whoever did it could come in using the trellis whenever they wanted." She shuddered involuntarily. "Then there's that tan car. I've seen it on our lane more than once. I thought he was driving it. I just didn't want to believe it."

Nick rechecked the deadbolt on the door she'd just locked. "He probably is the one who's been sneaking around in here—I wonder what he wants, just to scare us?"

Ella gave him a shrug on her way to shove the chair back under the attic door. "Could be," she said. "Or maybe he wants revenge for me having him arrested and put in jail."

Nick nodded. "Guess he got our number off Nana's fridge and tracked us down." His voice was low, as if he were speaking to himself.

Ella nodded. "And I'll also tell you this," she glanced at the kitchen window. "I had stupidly left that window unlocked and Officer Rod found a footprint on the sill."

Nick's eyes got larger and larger as she spoke.

"We think he got in, saw the key to the attic, and had himself a copy made." She thought back to all the things that had happened. "That could be how he gets through the attic door after coming in through the attic window." She recalled the touch on the back of her neck. *Wonder why he didn't just kill me then? Maybe that would've taken the fun out of it. Or maybe that was before Chet spent the night. Could that have pushed him over the edge?*

Nick rushed to the kitchen window and checked to make certain it was locked now. "Maybe he wanted us to think the house was haunted. Or maybe he wants us to give up and go back home to Albuquerque for some reason." He looked at his mother shrewdly. "Maybe he's trying to scare you into giving up so you'll go back to him."

Ella winced. "I don't think so, sweetie. Besides, nothing on earth could ever make me go back to him. *Nothing.* Do you understand? You never have to worry about that. I'm just sorry he had to hurt you before I finally got up the courage to leave."

Nick looked at the floor. "It wasn't just me he hurt."

Ella pulled him to her side just as headlights stabbed the room with light. They both ran to the living room window. The lights had been filtered through the sheer curtains, but it was obviously the same vehicle they'd passed a few moments earlier.

"Is it him?" Nick's voice shook—but only a little.

Ella watched the car pull into the end of their drive and sit with the lights facing the house. "Stand to one side, Nicky," she said, pulling the heavier curtains closed. "I think it is him, but he isn't coming up the drive."

The car was simply parked with its lights shining on the front of the house.

"Get me the phone," she told Nick.

He ran to the kitchen, grabbed the cordless phone and dashed back to where Ella was hiding behind the drapes.

"Here, Mom." He tried to make sure he didn't get directly in front of the picture window as he pushed the phone at her.

Ella put it to her ear. "It's dead. Was it on the charger?" Nick nodded.

She dashed to the kitchen and checked the phone base to see if it was still plugged into the wall. Then she pushed the on/off button a couple of times, but there was no dial tone. Her skin went cold. "We have no phone," she said. "But it was working just a few minutes ago."

"He's leaving, Mom," Nick yelled.

She hurried back to the living room just in time to see the car reverse and head back toward town. "Where is he going?" she muttered. *Bastard!* She wanted to scream and shout and call him all sorts of bad names, but she didn't want to fall apart in front of Nick.

"Should we get back in the Jeep?" Nick asked.

Ella stood, chewing the tip of her thumbnail as she thought the situation over. "I don't think so," she said. "Our gauge is right on empty. What if we didn't make it? We'd be stuck on the side of the road. At least here, we're safe."

Nick nodded, but his eyes were troubled. "Are we really safe? He's already been in the house. What if he comes back? What will we do?"

Ella pulled him to her side. "First, let's check all the windows again, make certain they're locked up tight." She smiled to show him she wasn't afraid. She hoped her quivering insides didn't give her away somehow. "And we stay together, okay? Remember, Officer Rodriguez has already been out here, so as soon as I figure out a way to call the PD, we can have them come back."

Together they checked all the windows in the kitchen, living room, and bathroom, then they moved on to the bedrooms.

When she flipped on the light in her room, she was shocked to see her lingerie drawer upended on her bed. All of her undies, bras, and hosiery were scattered across the counterpane in drifts of delicate color.

Embarrassed for her ten-year-old son to see her most personal things, Ella immediately began to gather all the items together. The large drawer was upside down on the bed. Nick helped her right it, and together they managed to plug it back into the dresser where it belonged. She glanced around for the note from Chet. She had tucked it into this very drawer. But it was nowhere to be found. And as she gathered the lingerie, something sticky met her palm.

She drew back, about to cry out, when she realized what it was. *Oh, that sick bastard!* She couldn't believe he'd been in her house and pleasured himself in her private things in the five minutes they'd been gone.

Wait, she thought, that's impossible. Officer Rod fixed the attic window before he had to leave, there's no way he could've gotten back in. Unless he simply broke the window and removed the broomstick.

She thought about going back into the attic to check, but first she quickly separated the soiled items—two pairs of silky peach colored panties—and wadded them into a ball in the corner of the dresser drawer. She didn't want to have to explain to Nick what had occurred. *I'll give those to the cops when I can.*

Maybe it's over now. He was probably waiting for my bedroom light to go on. He was probably just hanging around to see what I'd do when I found his mess—

The house went dark.

Chapter Thirty-One

"Mom!" Nick's voice was hoarse with fear.

"Right here, honey." Ella felt her way around the bed until she found him. The darkness felt alive, as if it were Anson's ally, his cohort.

She gathered Nick in her arms and placed a finger over his mouth. "Not a word," she whispered. "He did this before, when you were sleeping. We'll just wait him out. He'll go away." She crossed her fingers when she said it. Ella didn't really think he was going to go away this time. He'd made certain they were isolated, no gasoline, no phone, no lights. She was afraid he was following some sort of plan this time. Not just playing around.

Nick's chest heaved and she squeezed him tighter.

"It'll be okay," she said. "Mommy's here."

He's only ten years old, God. Help us, please. If that is Anson, and he's coming after us, please, please—

They both heard the thud of heavy boots on the attic floor above them.

"Mommy!" Nick's voice was a strained whisper, but how long before he broke down and began to scream hysterically?

How long before she did? *Or before I run out the door screaming?*

"Nicky?" she whispered directly in his ear. "Can you do something for me?" She was walking him around the bed to the other side as they spoke.

Nick nodded. "I'll try."

They both heard the unhurried clomping as someone crossed the floor above them. It was as if he were making as much noise as possible. *Nothing stealthy this time.* No thud, no scrape. Just Clomp! Clomp! Clomp!

Ella reached down and pulled the new hammer out from under the bed. "I want you to get under the bed. There's a flashlight there, but don't turn it on yet."

Nick began to shake his head. "I wanna stay with you. Are you getting under, too?"

"No, I'm going to lure him away." She tried to hold the hammer down so he couldn't see it. She fully intended to knock a hole in Anson's head if she could. He had no right to come in her home and terrorize her and Nick. He'd taken away all their options for help. She was no longer that wimpy little girl he'd married. This time, she was ready to fight. There was really nothing left to do. He'd taken away all their outs.

"He'll kill you, Mommy." Tears coated his words.

Ella gave in and showed him the hammer. "He won't see me until it's too late. Now, get under there and don't come out until I say it's okay." She knew her voice was stern, but if she didn't make it stern, he might not take her seriously. She didn't want to leave him there alone, but what else could she do?

Nick got down on his hands and knees and then onto his belly. With little effort, he crawfished all the way under the big bed.

"Nicky?"

"Yeah?" His voice was muffled.

"If something goes wrong and you have to run, you go straight to Norma's house through the woods. Can you find it?" *Oh my God, what am I telling him? Maybe we should both try and go there, right now.*

In response to her question, Nick whimpered, "I think so."

The footfalls started down the stairs.

That door is locked, she thought. And we put the chair under the knob—he can't come through there.

Heart pounding, she dashed from the room and ran to the kitchen. *If he manages to come through that door, I'm going to do my best to kill him.*

An idea occurred to her. "Anson," she yelled, carefully pulling a second chair over beside the attic door and climbing up on it. "I know it's you." She tried to steady her voice. "If you don't leave, I'm going to blow your head off!"

The horrid footfalls clomped down the remaining stairs at top speed. They were accompanied by a laugh that froze her insides as surely as if she'd drunk a gallon of ice water.

"Yeah?" He laughed again. "Prove it!"

He shattered the old wooden door from the inside with one well-placed kick from his size twelve boot.

The chair was still beneath the knob, but the entire top panel of the door had splintered. In the moonlight coming through the kitchen window, Ella could see his massive silhouette.

With another kick, the entire door disintegrated. Shards of wood flew in all directions. The red kitchen chair went scooting across the floor until it hit a piece of debris and flipped over on its side. Its chrome legs reflected the moonlight as Anson came through the splintery hole with something in his hand. Ella suspected it was either a gun or a knife, she couldn't tell for certain.

With all her might, she swung the new hammer at the back of his head.

He didn't expect her to be taller than he was, and positioned behind him as he broke through.

The hammer connected with his skull with a satisfying crunch. She'd swung it so hard, the thing flew from her grasp even as Anson crumpled to the floor.

282 | A n n   S w a n n

As he fell, he twisted around and reached for her. Instead, his fingers found the edge of her chair and he yanked it over with his flailing two hundred plus pounds.

She tumbled to the floor with him.

Blood poured from his scalp, but still he was conscious. "*Bitch*," he yelled. "I'll kill you and that worthless brat, too!"

Ella scrambled away as soon as she hit the floor. He's going to get up, she thought. *I can't let him get up. He can't get to Nicky, no matter what.*

Those thoughts went round and round in her head as her eyes darted about the room in search of the hammer. She spied it in a heap of broken wood just to the right of the attic doorway.

As she dove for it, she thought she heard movement in the bedroom.

Anson was doing his best to sit up. His head and face were covered with blood and he was moaning about the present he'd left for Nick in the cabinet.

Ella realized he was telling her he'd put the body of the little raccoon in the cereal cupboard. That made her even more furious.

Stay down, she thought. *Just stay down.*

She stood and lurched toward the hammer just as his hand closed around her ankle. Ella kicked and stomped at his hand with her other foot, but he let out a sickening laugh and swept both feet right out from under her.

She went back down with a *whoof*. Still, she struggled to regain her balance and make a grab for the hammer at the same time.

"Mom?" Nick's voice was shrill.

"Run, Nicky, run. Don't look back, go where I told you!" She did her best to get upright again, but it was hopeless. She couldn't get her ankle free. His grip was so tight it was supernatural, as if Frankenstein's monster had grabbed her instead of Anson.

Kicking and scratching, still lying on her side, Ella twisted her head and tried to see her son, but the moonlight didn't reach that far. Was that the sound of his sneakered feet, running? She couldn't be certain, but just in case, she did everything she could think of to keep the monster's attention focused on her so that Nicky could escape.

Anson tightened his grip and yanked her toward him.

Her skin burned as she slid across the hardwood, her shirt hiking up under her armpits. "Bastard!" She kicked at his face with her free foot.

She connected with something solid, but she thought it was his shoulder. The hammer was still out of reach. With great effort, she got her hands beneath herself and tried to shove her torso upright. The floor around the attic door was becoming slick with his blood and she went down again, cracking her chin hard enough to bring stars to her eyes.

This time, she couldn't even yell; she just lay like a caught fish, gasping for breath. *Nicky*, she thought. *Get Norma. Hurry.*

Chapter Thirty-Two

Nick took one look at the scene in the hallway outside the kitchen before running to his room and throwing up the window sash. His Mom was down, but so was Anson. *If I had a weapon, I could help her.* He flung his leg over the sill and dropped easily to the ground.

He thought of all the things Chet had stored in their carport storage shed. Bound to be something in there, Nick thought. *If not, I'll go to Norma's, but that's two miles round trip. If I go there now, Mom might not be alive when I get back.*

Like a flash, he was around the house and fumbling with the lock on the storehouse door. Just like the attic door, the key was hanging on a nail. This one was hidden behind a loose section of the doorframe. His mom thought she'd kept that knowledge from him, but she wasn't very good at hiding things.

After grabbing the key, Nick unlocked it and flung the door wide in search of some kind of weapon. The tangle of antique traps fell out at his feet. One was the old bear trap Chet had showed him. "Cruel thing," Chet had said, shaking his head sadly. "The animal often tried to chew off its own paw to get away."

Nick looked down at the rusted steel trap. He envisioned Anson with his foot caught inside.

Nick had heard Officer Rod say the ivy was all trampled beneath the attic window. Could he lure Anson there again somehow? We used traps to catch the raccoon, he thought. *Why not trap this animal, too? He's way more dangerous than any raccoon.* Nick involuntarily recalled the off-the-cuff way Anson had backhanded him and shoved his mother into the door hard enough to crack her cheekbone. *He's not going to get away with it again!* He'd never even told his mom about the time Anson threatened to "crush him like a bug" if he didn't behave. Later, Anson had told Nick not to mention it, he'd only been joking. "That's just how grown men talk," he'd said.

Nick reached down and took hold of the old bear trap. It was amazingly heavy—solid steel. *Thing must weigh thirty or forty pounds.* He let the trap clank back down to the concrete floor of the storehouse. I know where to put it, he thought. *But how will I get it there when I can barely pick it up?*

His eye caught another rusty glint of moonlight on old metal. *His little red wagon.* When they moved, he'd almost left it behind, but at the last minute, he'd run back to Nana's garage and hauled it out. She had given it to him on his fifth birthday. He'd used it to haul many rocks and loads of dirt around her house.

That's it. He pulled it out into the open and wrestled the bear trap into it. The trap's heavy chain clanked against the metal of the wagon and Nick shot a quick look at the front door to see if anyone had heard. *Why is it so quiet in there? He'd better not hurt her.*

His mom had told him to run down to Norma's house and call the police, and he intended to do just that, but he also knew Officer Rodriguez was busy and he needed help now.

He found a short length of wood and a can of WD-40 and added those items to the wagon. Chet had used the WD-40 to lubricate the rusted hinge on the 'coon trap. Nick thought it might help with the old bear trap, too.

Taking up the handle of the wagon, he took off around the back of the house at a quick walk. He made certain to keep his head below the level of the windows.

Just another minute, Mom. Hold on one more minute, that's all.

Under the trellis, he saw the area where the ivy was almost bare. The moonlight pooled there as if to say *that's the place*. His breath puffed out in front of his face in the cold night air.

He heaved the trap out of the wagon onto the ground as the moon—it's work done—scudded behind a thin cloud. "Our father who art in Heaven," Nick murmured, hardly aware that he was whispering aloud, "hallowed be thy name." He always pronounced hallowed the old-fashioned way, hallow-ed. "Thy kingdom come," he took the wood from the wagon, "thy will be done." He sprayed the trap with the lubricant. "On earth as it is in Heaven." He placed one end of the board against one of the levers that would prise open the trap. When it gave a bit, he sprayed it with some more WD-40. Then he stood on the opposite lever—both had to be depressed at the same time to open the trap and set it—and placed the squared off end of the board on the other lever. He gripped the wood with both hands and leaned on it with all his weight while also standing on the opposite lever.

Slowly, the trap began to open.

Nick pushed down even harder.

If my foot slips off, I'm a goner. He curled his toes inside his high tops and concentrated. "Give us this day, our daily bread." His breath was harsh in his throat as the stringy muscles in his ten-year-old arms strained against his flannel sleeves. "And forgive us our trespasses..." he refused to finish that sentence. He wasn't in the mood to forgive Anson for his trespasses, maybe later, when his foot was in this trap and he was howling in pain and agony. After all, Nick thought, the guy really was trespassing—literally.

Clack!

Just like that, it was done. The trap clacked open, the latch caught just like it was supposed to, and for a moment,

Nick was teetering on the edge, in danger of falling onto the trigger plate because he was still pushing down with all his might.

"Thank you, God," he muttered, hopping off to one side and kicking a pile of dried leaves over it to cut the shine of the WD-40.

I can smell the lubricant, he thought. *But there's nothing I can do about that.* He took the can and the board and covered them with a drift of leaves inside his wagon. *Never know when I might need that again.* Then he quickly pushed the wagon into the shadow of the eaves at the corner of the house and wiped his flannel-clad arm across his brow. Sweat was trapped at his hairline, cooling his face in the moist mountain evening.

He was catching his breath, gathering his courage for the next step, when his mom's scream split the air around his ears. *It sounds like he's pulling out her fingernails!* He'd seen that in an old war movie on Channel 41 and the POW had screamed just like that before divulging all his secrets.

"Mom!" His feet found the lowest slats on the stout trellis. "I'm here! I'm coming up the trellis." He was yelling as loudly as he could, but he was terrified. He wasn't certain which direction Anson would come for him, from the top, through the attic window, or from the bottom, behind him on the trellis. He hoped it was from the bottom. That would be *ideal.*

*

Inside the house, Ella's plight was growing desperate. She'd kicked and scratched and hit, but she could not get loose.

Anson seemed to be graying in and out.

Every time she thought his hold was weakening, she would try to pull away, but he would rouse himself and yank her back again.

The last time he weakened, she'd made a lunge for the hammer and was almost able to get her fingers around it. But he'd fooled her. Instead of simply yanking her back, he'd managed to get to his knees. Bloody hair clotted his vision and he began to crawl up her body using her clothing for handholds.

When he yanked her back again, he fell flat, smashing the whole of his upper body weight onto her lower legs.

Something in her knee popped.

That's when she screamed.

"Mom!" Nick had answered back, beginning his ascent of the trellis.

"Nicky, get out of here!" she screeched. "Go where I told you. Call the police. *Hurry.*"

Anson seemed to rally then, either at the sound of Nicky's voice or at the mention of him getting the police. He reached for her face with his bloody hands. He couldn't seem to form words, but he was close enough that Ella could see murder in his eyes.

"I'm on the trellis, Mom!"

"No, Nicky, damn it. Do what I told you!" Ella was having trouble getting her words out, too. Anson's weight was smashing the breath from her chest.

He made another grab at her face, but he was slow, she saw it coming. The contact from his palm to her cheek stung, but it was nothing like the cracked bone he'd given her that last long night at their home in Albuquerque.

"You prick," she hissed. "You may hit me, but my boy's already outside. You'll never hurt him again. He's bringing the cops. Officer Rodriguez is probably on his way right now."

"That the one you're screwing now?" Anson ground the words out as if they were made of crushed glass. "I thought it was that Grizzly Adams asshole."

Ella used the slickness of the floor to try and slither from beneath him. His chopped and slurred speech gave her hope. *Maybe I got him a good blow. Maybe it gave him brain damage.* All the while he was talking, her fingers were scrabbling around behind her head, hoping to land on the hammer by some lucky chance.

"I'm coming in, Mom!" Nick yelled again. "The cops are on the way. I'm coming up the trellis. I'm afraid to come in the front door." He muttered a few more words of The Lord's Prayer and then he broke into a Hail Mary his Catholic friend, Sean, had taught him.

"Don't you come back in here, Nicky!" Ella couldn't figure out why he didn't mind her. She knew there was no way he could have gotten all the way to Norma's and back. If he had, Norma would be with him. Was he afraid to go through the dark woods on his own? She wouldn't blame him, but why did he keep yelling about the damn trellis?

"I'm right here, Mom. I'm coming through the window now. It was broken. He broke the window, Mom!"

The pressure on her legs suddenly gave way as Anson hauled himself to his feet. He was using what was left of the attic doorjamb as a crutch. "Kill him," he muttered. "Before the police come."

Ella thought he was going to try for the attic stairs, intercept Nicky there, but they must have appeared too steep to him now. All at once he turned and staggered toward the front door.

"Look *out*, Nicky. He's coming around the house!"

She heard Anson fumbling with the deadbolt just as her fingers found the hammer.

Got you now, you piece of—

She struggled to her feet and hoisted the hammer high overhead.

Anson was still grappling with the bolt. Apparently the combination of his bloody fingers and his head wound were making it very difficult to work the lock. He kept swiping his hand across his eyes to clear the blood away.

It must be true, what I've heard about scalp wounds, Ella thought. The amount of blood on him and on the floor was unbelievable.

Encouraged, she took a giant step forward, gripping the hammer above her head with both hands.

The pain in her knee was sudden and intense. She cried out as it gave way. The adrenalin in her body had allowed her to forget about the pop that occurred when he'd fell on her. Ella saw the floor coming up to meet her before she even realized her knee had given way.

"Run, Nicky!" she screamed as Anson finally got the door open.

He staggered onto the porch and lurched down the steps holding onto the rail.

Ella scooted over to the doorjamb in a sort of sideways crab walk and did exactly what Anson had done, used it as a crutch to get to her one good knee, and then to her one good foot. She never let go of the hammer.

"Nicky, are you in the attic?" she called softly.

"Shhh," Nick said. "Don't worry, Mom. I got this."

She heard him rattle the trellis against the house. "I'm stuck, Mom, I can't get up. I'm scared! Come help me!"

"Nicky!" she screamed. "Stay where you are, Mommy's coming!" She hesitated, unsure whether to try hopping up the attic stairs, or down the porch steps. *If he's on the trellis, I don't want to get trapped up in the attic.*

She began to hop toward the front door on her one good leg.

When she got to the porch, it was easy to see the dark trail of blood.

Anson was obviously headed to the trellis on the side of the house. "Don't you hurt my baby," she shouted as she hopped down the steps on one foot.

"Come on you big coward," Nick called suddenly. "You think you're so tough. But you can't get me up here."

Ella couldn't believe her ears. The boy was actually taunting Anson?

"Go back in the house, Mom. Lock the door. He can't get up the trellis. You must have whacked him good. Look at all that blood."

How can he know all that? Is he actually looking at Anson? She wanted to go back in the house, like Nicky said. But he was a ten-year-old boy. *Shouldn't he be doing what she said instead of the other way around?* She stood with her hand on the porch rail for another minute, and then she turned and went back in the house and ran the deadbolt home. *I don't think he can get up the trellis. Not in his condition. But Nicky must have gone out a window. I'd better find it and lock it.*

Nick continued taunting his ex-stepfather, calling him coward and wife-beater and child abuser until she was on the verge of yelling at him to shut up—she could only imagine the fury taking over Anson's bloody features. *You don't know what you're doing, Nicky. You're pouring kerosene on the fire.*

But Anson was not responding.

What's he doing?

"Come on, old man. You can't even make it up the first step. I knew you were worthless and weak. Only weaklings hit women and kids. That's what the school counselor said."

Then Ella heard it. A sound like a bull pawing the earth, getting ready to charge.

"Chicken!" Nick began to squawk like a hen in the barnyard.

She had made it back to her bedroom where Nick had gone out the window when she heard the wooden trellis bang against the side of the house. It sounded as if someone had grabbed it and slammed it against the siding.

"Hahaha!" Nick laughed maniacally. "You're so worthless! Can't even get one foot on th—"

There was a tremendous *WHAM!* Followed by a shriek of pain the like of which Ella had never heard—not even in her worst nightmare.

"Nicky!" She screamed his name as she hobbled back down the hall toward the attic door.

"I'm okay, Mom. It's not me."

Then she realized she could hear Anson moaning beneath the screeching. Moaning and *snarling*.

"What *is* it?" she demanded. "What's going on?"

Nick was laughing. A real laugh this time, but sort of hysterical, too. "It's him," he said, his hysterical voice somehow joyful. "I caught him. I caught him in a bear trap at the bottom of the trellis."

"Oh, my God," Ella murmured. "Are you in the attic?"

"Yes, it's okay, Mom. I can see him plain as day. The moon is shining right on top of him. He can't go anywhere. I think his leg is broken, I see something white sticking out."

Ella felt her stomach flip flop. "Stay where you are!" she instructed. She could barely hear Nick's words over the broken snarls coming from outside.

Undaunted, she began to crawl up the stairs to the attic.

Chapter Thirty-Three

It took forever to navigate the attic stairs with her bad knee. Ella was pretty sure the pop she'd heard was some tendon giving way when his two hundred plus pounds had landed on it.

When she finally made it up, with Nicky helping her the last few steps, Ella's back and chest were drenched with sweat and her head was pounding from exertion.

But what she saw out the attic window made it all worthwhile.

Anson lay at the bottom of the trellis, writhing in pain. Nick was right. The white something sticking out was a shard of bone. The steel trap had crushed the shinbone and shoved a piece of it right out through the meat.

At first, Ella thought she would throw up just looking at it.

She hobbled from the window and sat on a wooden crate. Her head was woozy. Her breath short. "We have to get out of here. Get the cops."

We need a plan, she thought. Anson's tough. He'll get up in a minute, he'll manage to get loose, and then he'll make us disappear like his first wife. She knew it was ridiculous, thinking he could come after them on that shattered leg, but she felt so dizzy. What if he did?

Nick was hooting and hollering, taunting him again from the window.

Watching him, Ella was very disturbed. She had no idea the hatred for his stepfather ran so deep. *Wonder if there are things that happened that I never knew about?*

"Nick," she said.

He didn't hear her.

"Nicky!" Her voice was sharp.

He turned from the window. What he saw must have frightened him.

"Mom." He ran to her side. "Your face is all white. Are you gonna pass out?"

Ella shook her head. "We have to get to Norma's house. Think you can help me drive the Jeep? I can't work the clutch with this knee, but you can."

"I will," he said. "I can do it."

She tousled his hair and pulled him to her briefly. "I know you can. You saved my life tonight. Do you realize that?"

Nick smiled. She thought he might be blushing, but his face was all broken shadows in the soft moonlight. "You're the one that whacked him. I don't think I could've got past him if you hadn't."

Ella laughed out loud. "I didn't whack him hard enough, though." She put her arm around his neck and stood. "C'mon. Let's go." They started toward the door. "But first," she put her hand on the jamb, "go look out and make sure he's still down there."

Nick grinned. His teeth were white, but crooked.

I see braces in his future, Ella thought illogically.

"He can't go far," Nick said. "That trap weighs a ton."

"Humor me." Ella waited.

Nick ran to the window and peered out. "He's still there, Mom. But you're right, he's doing everything he can to get the trap open." When he returned to her side, he wasn't quite as cocky. It had never occurred to him that the trap would not hold. After all, it was a *bear* trap. "I didn't chain it to anything," Nick murmured as a light bulb went on in his head. "He can drag it along with him, can't he?"

Ella didn't agree or disagree, but that's exactly what she was worried about. "Maybe he'll pass out from the pain," she said. "It's bound to be excruciating."

They made it down the stairs and to the front door. The worst part was the short few steps from the house to the Jeep not knowing if he was still lying at the foot of the trellis, or if he'd managed to get up on one leg and hop along like Ella was doing. *What if he's hiding near the Jeep? What if he grabs us, or swings the trap and hits one of us?* In her mind, the man had become superhuman. *Can I even get in the Jeep with only one leg? It's so high off the ground.*

Come to find out, she could.

At the last moment, as she stood there, waiting on Nick to climb in, Ella was certain she heard the rattle of the chain behind her. She shoved Nick forward and hoisted herself into the driver's seat in one herky-jerky motion.

"Get down on the floor," she commanded.

Nick hit the floorboard.

"Shove the clutch all the way in with your hand—no, both hands—don't let up until I tell you."

Nick did his best to get his arms behind her right leg, which she needed to depress the brake and accelerator, with enough power to push in the clutch. But the way he was twisted across the console and bent behind her leg, trying his best not to smash her injured left knee, made it impossible. He simply couldn't get enough leverage to push the pedal to the floor.

"I can't do it from here!" he cried. "Move over, Mom, let me sit there and you be the shifter and help me steer. I can push it in with my foot."

From out of the darkness on the other side of the house, Anson bellowed. "I'll kill you for this you worthless little punk!"

They could picture him struggling with the jaws of the trap.

That gave Ella the impetus she needed.

With great effort, she dragged herself across the console and fell into the passenger seat, crying out from the pain.

Nick leapt into the driver's seat and shoved the clutch down with his left foot. "Now what?" he demanded. He'd watched his mom start and operate the Jeep many times, but actually trying to do it was a new thing, indeed.

"Press the brake down, too," she said. She made certain the gearshift was in neutral. "Now, turn the key."

Nick did as he was told, but the engine just dragged.

Ella looked at his feet. *What am I doing wrong? I've never tried to tell anyone how to drive before.* "Oh," she said. "Let off the brake and press the accelerator gently, just a little."

Nick did.

The engine roared to life and the automatic headlights came on, illuminating the carport and part of the yard.

"Not so hard!" Ella yelled. "Let up on the gas." She shifted into reverse. *Now the tricky part.* "Okay, barely, barely, *barely* let up on the clutch," she cautioned. "We can't afford to stall."

But stall they did.

Nick let the clutch out too far without giving it any gas.

"Damn it," she said. "I forgot to tell you to press on the gas as you let out the clutch." She brushed hair off her forehead. "Push the clutch back in. All the way."

"Mom!" Nick's eyes were glued to a spot near the corner of the house. "It's him. He's coming!"

Ella looked.

Anson was dragging himself along on one side by digging his elbow into the earth. Somehow, he'd gotten the trap off his leg, but he wasn't able to stand.

Why isn't he bleeding to death? The teeth on that trap would've surely severed an artery. Then she saw the belt he'd fastened around his thigh.

"Hurry, Nick. Shove that clutch in, we've got to go."

Nick was sitting like a statue, watching the bloody man drag himself toward them across the yard.

Ella shook his shoulder. "Shove that clutch in, now!"

He looked at her as if from a dream. Then he pushed the clutch down. She twisted the key—hard—and ground the gearshift back into reverse. "Now, let up on the clutch and press gently on the gas—feel it as you go, Nicky. You can do it."

Nick fastened his eyes on his former stepfather and did just as Ella said.

The Jeep lurched backward and stalled again.

Ella opened the passenger door. She felt a tear roll down her cheek. It was too much to expect. The Jeep's transmission was just too touchy. "C'mon," she said. "Let's get out and run to Mrs. Benefield's house. I think we can make it over there. We'll break a window just like he did. Use her phone."

Nick snorted and seemed to come to himself. "What if they turned it off?" He stomped on the clutch. "Put it back in gear, Mom. I almost had it. I almost did. Help me. I can do it this time. I know I can."

Ella debated a moment.

She looked at the big man lying in the yard with his forehead on his arm. He had stopped to rest or pass out, she wasn't sure which.

The tire iron! It's behind the seat. I could hit him like I did before. Make sure he never bothers us again.

Only, she wasn't at all sure she could do it; wasn't sure if she had the stuff to just hobble over and beat him to death when he was already down. It was different when he'd been coming through the attic door threatening to kill them. Then, she'd only been attempting to knock him out, to protect Nicky. Now, looking at him half-dead with a belt for a tourniquet, it didn't seem like self-defense anymore.

But what are the other options? Sit here all night hoping someone will drive by before he gains the strength to get up again? Could I even get out of the Jeep without falling? And what if he's gathering his strength right now?

Nick made up her mind for her. He wiggled the gearshift around until he found neutral, then he twisted the key and the Jeep came to life once more.

Hearing the engine, Anson hoisted himself up on his forearm and looked her in the eye. When he realized Nick was the one in the driver's seat, he threw his head back and began to laugh.

Ella felt the balance of power shift. Where Nicky had been taunting Anson out the window only minutes earlier, now *he* was taunting Nicky—even though he was lying mangled and bloody on the cold, hard ground.

But the laugh spurred Nicky on. He forced the shifter into reverse, gave the Jeep another bit of gas, and held on as it lurched backward out of the carport.

Ella yelled, "Clutch, Nicky, clutch!" Then she twisted the wheel around to straighten them out in the middle of the drive.

Nick rammed his foot down on the clutch as she shoved the shifter into first. He tromped on the gas pedal and let off the clutch as if he'd been driving for years.

The Jeep shot down the drive and Ella had a fleeting glimpse of Anson attempting to get up on one knee.

Then they were past him and Ella was moaning and holding her own swelling knee. She had bumped it and twisted it several times as she helped Nick straighten out the steering wheel and change the gears.

In moments, they were approaching Norma's driveway.

"Slow down," Ella cried. "We'll roll off in the ditch if you turn too fast."

Nick hit the brake, but not the clutch and the Jeep bucked and lurched as they bumped down and then up the shallow dip that marked the place where the drive connected with the red dirt road of Lilac Lane.

Half on, half off the edge of Norma's immaculate lawn, the Jeep's engine spluttered and died.

Ella reached over and began to honk the horn.

Nicky started shaking as the adrenalin left his body. "I'll go." He flung his door open and fell out on the ground.

He picked himself up and dashed to the door just as it opened.

Norma stuck her head out, pulling her fluffy white robe tighter around her middle. She put her hands up just in time to grab Nick by the shoulders as he fell up the last step. "What on earth?" she began. Then she looked past him to where Ella still sat, honking the Jeep's horn erratically.

Honk-honk-honk, honk honk—honk—honk.

So close to safety, Ella couldn't seem to stop pounding the horn. She stuck her own head out the window. "Call nine-one-one, Norma. Tell them my ex-husband is trying to kill us!"

Norma's eyes widened in shock when Ella leaned out into the glow of the yard light. Blood was splattered all over her face and shirt.

Norma pushed Nicky into the house and ran to the Jeep. "Where is he?"

Ella opened her door and slid out onto her good right leg. "We left him in a heap in the front yard. He's injured, but I'm afraid he's not injured enough."

Norma seized Ella's arm and slung it around her own shoulders. "Lean on me," she said. "We'll get in the house and call."

Nicky ran back to help support his mom on the other side and together, the three of them made it back to the porch.

It took every ounce of her remaining strength to hop up Norma's two small porch steps. Once inside the house, she collapsed gratefully onto the overstuffed sofa. "I don't want to get blood on your—"

"Hush," Norma scolded as she picked up the cordless phone.

With the push of a button she had the emergency operator on the line. But even as she was telling her the problem, she was also opening the coat closet and removing a dark colored gun case from the top shelf.

Like the experienced shooter she was, Norma pulled the .38 revolver from the zippered case and inspected the ammunition. It held six rounds and she was confident that would be enough to stop any intruder. But just to be on the safe side, she reached into the closet and brought out a second case. This one held a pistol with a sixteen-shot magazine.

She handed the pistol to Ella, safety still engaged, and carried the revolver in her hand. "You know how to use that?" she asked.

Ella shook her head. "Not really."

"Then you just stay behind me," Norma said. "And hand it to me if I run out of ammo in this." She held up the revolver.

Nick was looking at Norma with a look of awe on his face. "You don't mess around."

Norma shook her head. "My husband has been a long-haul trucker all our married life. I learned early on that I would have only one person to depend on in times like these. Me."

Ella tried to stand on her one good leg.

Norma looked at her. "What happened to your leg?"

Ella gave up and gingerly let herself back down onto the couch. She was still clutching the pistol, pointed at the floor.

"I knocked him down, but then he fell on my knee with all his weight. I think something tore in there."

Norma nodded. "Should I call an ambulance, too?"

"Not until we know if it's safe," Ella replied. "Once the cops are here, then we'll worry about me."

Nick sat by his mom. "Should I go and check all the doors and windows?"

Norma shook her head. "You stay right here with your mom, we don't want to be split up. If I have to shoot someone, I want to know for certain it isn't you." She smiled to take the sting out of her words. "Besides, I have an alarm system. If anything is opened, it tells me."

"We'll have that, too" Ella said. "When this is all said and done."

Norma watched out the front window. She had locked the front door as soon as they were all inside. "I want to hear all about it, later," she said. "I'll bet money he's the one who's been behind all the strange goings-on at your house, right?"

Ella nodded. "Exactly right, I'll tell you everything, later." She looked over at Nick. He was leaning back into the plush floral cushions, eyes closed. *Thank you, God. Thank you for neighbors like Norma.*

Chapter Thirty-Four

Officer Rodriguez was still working the wreck so Officer Sara Stendal was the one who responded. She was met at Norma's house by Chief Brown and a sheriff's deputy. The county deputies and city cops often backed each other up when the incident occurred just outside the city limits.

Norma opened the door. "They're in here, but the break-in occurred at Ella's house further down the lane."

Officer Stendal came in and prepared to interview Ella and Nick. "Officer Rodriguez gave us your ex-husband's description, said you'd once had a restraining order on him."

Ella nodded. "He threatened to *get* us for putting him in jail. We thought he was driving a blue pickup truck. He's not. He may be driving a tan or cream-colored four-door car. I've seen it around town several times. I think he's been stalking us for quite a while."

The officer nodded and wrote the information in her notebook. "Did you get a look at the tags at all?"

Ella shook her head. "But you can find *him* lying in my front yard. I hit him in the head with a hammer when he broke into my house through the attic." She looked at Nick. "Then he accidentally stepped into an old bear trap underneath the attic window."

Officer Stendal's eyebrows went up and she exchanged an unspoken look with the Chief. "Is that why you're covered in blood? Or is that from an injury?"

Ella looked down at her shirt. "I think it's his blood. From the head injury." She wiped a hand across her cheek. "It knocked him down, but he wouldn't quit."

The Chief interrupted. "I've heard enough." He turned to the deputy. "Let's go get him."

He turned back to Ella. "Is he armed, do you know?"

Ella nodded. "He had something in his hand, it was shiny, but I never really saw what it was."

The Chief patted his hip. "Sara, you stay here, make sure he doesn't show up."

Officer Stendal nodded curtly. "Now, let's start from the beginning. Why did he go to jail in the first place?"

Ella sat up a little straighter and began to tell her story. When she got to the part about Anson saying his first wife had disappeared, the officer's demeanor changed considerably. But they didn't have time to discuss it. Chief Brown broke in on the radio.

"Sara?" His voice was calm, informal.

"Go ahead, Chief," Officer Stendal replied.

"Suspect is no longer at this address. No evidence of a vehicle either. We do see that he was here, however. Just wanted you to be aware." Then he clicked off and called headquarters and told Marissa to put out a BOLO for a tan colored 4-door sedan.

Ella's felt the blood leave her face. "He's gone?"

Officer Stendal nodded. "Apparently the car is gone, too."

Ella looked from Norma to the officer and back again. Then she found some inner strength and pulled herself together. "I never saw the car tonight. I don't know where he had it parked. But I don't imagine he can get very far." She sought Nick's eyes. "He was really banged up, had a tourniquet around one leg. Pretty sure that leg was broken."

"Mangled, you mean," Nick said.

Norma narrowed her eyes.

Ella decided she was trying to warn them not to say too much. Why, she didn't know. But maybe the other woman was right.

Taking Nick by the hand, she said, "We won't go home until he's caught—"

"That's right," Norma agreed. "You'll stay here with me."

Ella shook her head. "Oh, no. We can't impose like that. We'll get a room in town—the Antlers Motel, perhaps."

"Probably where he's been staying," Norma said matter-of-factly.

"I hadn't thought about that," Ella said. "Is there another one nearby?"

Norma shook her head. "Not during the off season. Now, when the snow flies and the bunnies hit the slopes, then you'll see all the seasonal bed & breakfast homes open up."

Officer Stendal spoke up. "I think it would be a good idea if we drove you and your son to the Emergency Room. I wouldn't be doing my job if we didn't get you checked out. Just for good measure." She smiled to soften the words.

"I'm fine," Ella argued. "Except for this knee." She tried to stand, stumbled. "You're right. I don't know what's wrong with it. I can't seem to put any weight on it." She looked at her son, but spoke to the officer. "Do you think we could go to the house and get some clean clothes?"

The officer nodded and went to the car for a camera. "We will need pictures of the crime scene and of you two." She indicated Nick and Ella.

"If it's okay, I'll come, too," Norma said. "Ella can barely hobble."

Officer Stendal nodded again. "That's a good idea. I could have the ambulance meet us there."

"I think I'll be okay for a while longer," Ella said as they trooped out to the car.

*

When they got back to Ella and Nick's house, the lights were still off.

Officer Stendal took a large flashlight from her stash of equipment and slipped it through a ring on her utility belt. She told the three passengers to stay put while she rechecked the house. The Chief and the deputy had already been through it once.

She informed the dispatcher of their whereabouts, and told her to hold all traffic until further notice while she checked out the house.

The Chief and deputy were driving the neighborhood in search of Anson or his car.

To Ella, their home felt different now, even from the outside. It felt violated. Strange. Not their own anymore. It crouched in the darkness like a stray.

Ella was glad when Officer Stendal found the main breaker switch and all the lights came back on. And when she came out and gave them the okay sign, Ella exited the patrol car gingerly. But with Norma and Nick at her side, the porch steps were not quite as treacherous as before. There were dark stains drying in smeary patterns across the wooden planks.

Officer Stendal was waiting in the living room. "You need to go through the incident with me step by step." She pointed at the splintered door and the thick swathes of blood everywhere. "When did you first realize he was here? Did he threaten you, give you warning, or what?"

It took a lot of courage for Ella to make her way back through the front door. She took a deep breath and started from the beginning. "After Officer Rodriguez came out earlier this evening, we locked everything up tight and started toward town." She leaned against the wall, thinking back. "I filled the Jeep's tank with gas just yesterday, but on the way home, we passed that tan car right out front, headed the other way." She looked down the road, envisioning the episode in her mind. "I'd seen that car around town several times, but I could never see the driver. That's when I discovered my gas gauge was on empty. He must've siphoned the gas out while we were in town."

Officer Stendal wrote in a notebook. "Go on." Unlike some more impatient officers, she didn't pressure the victim (or witness) to get to the point—in her opinion, important details were often overlooked that way—instead, she allowed the person to tell the tale naturally, as it had occurred.

"Well, just as we got inside the house, the car came back and parked at the end of the drive. That's when I knew it was definitely Anson." She carefully lowered herself to the sofa. "When Officer Rod was here, we figured out how he'd been getting in. He'd been moving things around, hiding things, just to let me know someone had been in the house." She shuddered, a quick flex of skin like a cat with a flea. "He even got close enough to touch the back of my neck one night. That's why I called earlier. But tonight, I realized I didn't have enough gas to go back to town so Nick and I made sure all the doors and windows were locked, then tried to call nine-one-one. But of course he'd already been here. He'd cut the phone line or something."

"Yes, I saw that out back," Officer Stendal said, nodding for her to continue.

"Apparently, he had come in through the kitchen window and made himself a key to the attic door. Then he simply broke the lock on the attic window—and I didn't even check up there because the inside door was still locked." She glanced toward the jumble of splintered wood that was once the attic door.

The officer used her camera to snap pictures of the destroyed door and the surrounding splotches of blood that had pooled on the hardwood floor. "How did he get up to the attic window," she asked. "The trellis?"

Ella nodded. "That's also how he got caught in Nicky's trap. But that was after he came through that door and tried to kill me." She looked at the hammer lying near the baseboard. It was sticky with drying gore. "That's where I hit him, and that's where he knocked me down and hurt my knee." She rubbed it without thinking.

Officer Stendal snapped more pictures, and then she leaned down to take a closer look at something on the floor. "Well, well, well, what have we here?" It was a hunting knife with a four-inch blade. It was barely visible beneath the clutter of broken wood.

She snapped a few more pictures and then ducked out to the patrol car. In a moment, she returned with a pair of disposable plastic gloves and a couple of brown paper bags.

After placing the knife in one bag and the hammer in another, she filled out labels and attached them to each bag.

"Where else was he?"

Ella pointed up to the attic and also into the bedroom. "You'll find DNA evidence in my top dresser drawer." She closed her eyes, hoping Officer Stendal wouldn't make her say it in front of Nick. "All my lingerie was dumped on the bed when we got home." She locked eyes with the officer. "I put it back in the drawer for safekeeping. The pieces you want are balled up in the corner. Peach colored."

Officer Stendal appeared to be on the verge of admonishing Ella for moving the evidence, but the look on Ella's face must have changed her mind.

Ella and Nick waited while she collected the things from the bedroom, taking pictures the entire time. Nick led the officer upstairs to the attic, all the while telling her how he'd trapped Anson to save his mother's life.

"That was very clever." Officer Stendal peered at the ground from the attic window. "Where'd you get the bear trap?" Her voice was conversational but interrogative at the same time.

"Chet," he said. "The wildlife biologist." His voice faltered as if he was afraid of getting Chet in trouble somehow. He hurried to explain. "He left a bunch of stuff out in our storehouse when he was working on the attic. After we first moved in. Our landlady hired him to get rid of some raccoons and fix the holes they made."

Officer Stendal nodded sagely. "I understand." She wrote everything in her notebook. The moonlight illuminated the small window, but even with the overhead light on, the attic was still thick with shadows. Inky shapes crouched in every corner. "I know Chet," she said. "And Charlie, your landlady." An inexplicable look of sorrow crossed her face, but she recovered quickly. "Seems to me finding that bear trap in the storehouse was a real God-send."

Nick breathed a sigh of relief. "Yeah. That's what I thought, too. Except, where is he now?" He looked out the window into the darkness.

Chapter Thirty-Five

Norma and Ella were sitting side by side on the sofa when Nick and Officer Stendal returned.

"You're lucky to be alive," Norma was saying.

Ella patted her hand. "I'm lucky to have such a resourceful son. I'm just sorry we brought all this violence to your neighborhood." She closed her eyes. "This is what we were trying to avoid."

Nick stood in the middle of the room uncertainly.

"C'mon." Norma pulled Ella to her feet. "Let's get you checked out. That leg needs attention."

The trip to the hospital was uneventful. It took almost an hour to get registered in the Emergency Room and get her vitals and medical history in the computer.

Finally, an orderly brought in a wheelchair to take Ella to Ultrasound. As they wheeled down the hall, Chief Brown stepped out in front of her.

"How are you doing, Ms. Webb?"

When Ella indicated that she was okay, he continued.

"We've found him and his car. A tan Chevy. Pretty sure it's your ex-husband. His leg is crushed. Got a pretty good head wound, too. Jives with everything Officer Stendal wrote in the statement you gave her."

Ella caught her breath. "Is he...is he alive?"

Chief Brown nodded. "Alive, but unconscious." He gestured toward the Emergency Room. "Ambulance just brought him in. Apparently he managed to get into his car, but actually driving didn't work out so well. Ran off in a ditch just the other side of your house."

The doors were flung open as a doctor rushed toward the Emergency department on the run. They all caught a glimpse of a bloody mountain of a man lying on a gurney, shredded clothing trailing from his lower leg.

Even though he was unconscious, Ella was paralyzed by fear as the gurney was wheeled into a curtained trauma room out of view.

"Are you up to identifying him?" The chief asked.

Ella shook her head. "No. I. Yes. I mean that was definitely him, that was Anson." She realized she was babbling, but she couldn't help it. The entire evening seemed to be crashing in on her. Until now, she hadn't really had a chance to process what had happened. "Nick," she said. "Where is my Nicky? I need him with me. I need to make sure he's all right." Her voice seemed to dissolve into frayed syllables.

Chief Brown placed a broad, warm hand on her shoulder. "He's with Norma and Officer Stendal in the ER. I'll get him."

"Yes. Get him, please. He can't be where Anson is. Never—"

"Wait right here," the chief told the orderly. "Don't go until I come back, understand?"

The man nodded and leaned against the wall. When the chief was out of earshot, the orderly said, "Wow. What happened? Was it another wreck?"

Ella raised her head, and looked past him toward the slowly closing doors through which the chief had disappeared. "It was a wreck, all right." She didn't feel she could elaborate just then. Maybe later. After she had Nick by her side.

In moments, the doors opened again and Nick rushed in followed closely by Chet and Chief Brown.

She opened her arms and Nick flew into them. "Did you see him, Mom? Did you see Anson?"

Ella nodded. "He can't hurt us now, baby."

Chet knelt in front of her wheelchair and put his arms around both of them.

The unexpected public display of affection brought surprising tears to her eyes and her hand automatically went to her hair. Stiff, sticky clumps met her fingers. *Is that blood?* She was certain it must be. Her mind slipped back over the last few hours. They'd picked up clean clothes at the house with Officer Stendal, but she had no idea where they were now. She swept a hand over her cheeks. Sticky spots met her fingers there, too.

When Nick stepped back, a wet, red smear adorned his face. It reminded her of the stinging handprint Anson had left there so long ago.

Chet straightened and moved back, hooking his thumbs in his front belt loops. He nodded at Chief Brown but didn't say anything.

"So sorry," he mouthed, when he caught her eye.

Ella tried to smile, almost made it. "We're okay now." She took Nick's hand.

"Can I go with my mom?" Nick asked.

The orderly nodded. "One person is allowed to accompany us."

She glanced at Chet and the chief. "We'll be back soon."

Chet stepped forward and placed a hand on her shoulder. Both she and Nick looked up into his deep blue eyes. "I'll be in the waiting room." He leaned down and pressed a kiss on the edge of her filthy hairline. "I'm so sorry I wasn't there."

She didn't know which was more miserable, his face or his voice. "How is Charlie?" she asked.

He shook his head.

Ella's vision blurred again. "Oh, Chet. I'm really sorry."

The orderly began to push her down the hall. Chief Brown and Chet watched for a moment, and then the Chief turned and ushered him back into the waiting room. "That's a tough pair," Ella heard him say.

Chet murmured something about how he should have been there.

"Not to worry," the chief replied. "You should see the other guy."

Ella smiled when she heard that. "We made it, Nicky." She squeezed his hand. "We took care of him, just you and me."

"But what if he wakes up?" Nick glanced back toward the ER doors.

Ella stared straight ahead. "Then we'll deal with that, too. If there's one thing I know now, it's this." She placed her other hand on top of his. "Together, we can do anything."

Nick smiled. "You're right, Mom. But I think Mr. Boone will be there if we ever need help again."

Ella's face grew thoughtful as she pictured Chet's deep blue eyes. "Maybe, he will," she said. "But even if he isn't, we've always got each other."

Coming soon

Copper Lake

Chapter One

The bones were wet. The clay in the soil trapped the moisture as efficiently as a layer of mulch in a flowerbed. When Edgar held the femur up to the moonlight, he was thrilled to observe how fully the dirt and mold had settled into the cuts and cracks. It created an inky labyrinthine abstract on the once-white surface. *Ecclesiastes says there's a time for everything . . . I think the time has come.*

He caressed the soil around the bones, and then he pulled on latex gloves and lifted the rest of them from their shallow bed. Time has come, he whispered. *Time has come.* He often repeated things to himself when his hands were engaged in pleasurable activities—and this was the most enjoyment he had in a long time.

He'd begun to think he was done with this sort of thing, but life has a way of surprising one. *Yes, it does. It has a way of surprising one sometimes.*

It took hours to finish his work. But it was all right. He didn't think of his other girl even once. Well, not more than once. Maybe twice at the most. The main thing was, the important thing was, Edgar no longer felt trapped. He was finally free. The irony wasn't lost on him. As soon as he'd begun to free the bones, he began to feel freer, too. His mood lightened. *No more depression. No more darkness. Guess I buried myself along with my girls.*

He felt so light by the time he finished; it was as if his feet never touched the ground. As he started back down the trail he hummed and murmured, murmured and hummed.

Halfway down, he realized he didn't want to leave.

An idea entered his brain like an arrow. *I don't have to leave. I have a sleeping bag in the car. I have water, a chocolate bar, half a sandwich.*

He grew so excited, the flesh of his scalp tingled. I'm doing it, he murmured. *I'm going to spend the night with my girl. My best girl.*

Sunrise coated the bones in gold.

The fleshless form now reclined on a soft bed of clover. Miniscule pink flowers cradled the skull, nature's perfect pillow.

Edgar awoke and gazed upon his work. And it is good, he thought. Then he whispered, "Now, pretty girl. Now you'll be found. I'm sorry I've kept you in the dark for so long."

He unzipped his sleeping bag and pulled out his phone. It had been too dark for photos last night, but this morning the light was perfect. He took pictures from every angle, recalling how he'd spent the entire night right beside her. I'd like to post them, he thought. *Show the world my best girl. Instagram, Twitter, FB. Something.* But he knew he wouldn't. That would be suicide, pure and simple. Paper trail, digital footprint, all that. *I'm too smart to do something that ignorant. Only a novice would do that.* And he was definitely no novice. This was his life. His passion. His everything.

Stowing the gloves in his workbag, he zipped the nylon duffle and rolled up his sleeping bag. After eating the chocolate bar and drinking a bottle of water, he made a pass around the scene. He was thorough. Nothing left to chance. He wanted recognition, not incarceration.

After he determined everything was perfect, Edgar hiked back to his car where he unzipped the duffle, blotted his brow with a paper towel, and then placed the bag in the trunk of his car. He dusted the dirt and leaves from his shoes and climbed into the driver's seat.

He blotted his face again but avoided looking into the mirror. He didn't like looking at his face. It was narrow, with all the features crowded close to the ridgeline of his thin, crooked nose. His eyes were the palest blue, an old man's eyes, as if they'd aged faster than the rest of him.

He thought back to the patterns of lines and numbers he'd carved into the bones. So smart, he told himself. *So smart. They'll never figure it out, but they'll wonder. Oh, how they'll wonder.*

Each one had taken hours and hours and hours. But that had been years ago. Now, they were aged to perfection. And it was time for the big reveal.

The big reveal, he muttered. *Time for the big reveal.*

*

Kendra Dean picked up her coffee cup and drained the cold dregs before drowning it in the soapy dishwater. There was nothing left to clean. That was the last dirty dish. She wiped all the counters with disinfectant wipes and checked the fridge to see if anything needed to be thrown out.

Yesterday she'd swept and vacuumed the entire house. Weeded the flowerbed. Washed everything in the hamper.

Unlike the last few years of her life, everything here was spotless and orderly.

The kitchen radio played classic hits from decades past. Journey's anthem to fidelity, *Faithfully*, wafted across her consciousness as she stood watching the soap bubbles swirl away down the dark throat of the stainless steel drain.

She tried not to see the parallel between the disappearing bubbles and the unraveling threads of her own world.

Anger bubbled up as the soap swirled away. She'd never been one for self-pity, had no time for those that wallowed in it.

She wiped her teary face with her wet hand and her peripheral vision caught movement outside the kitchen window. A car was pulling into the circle drive.

Drying her hands and her cheeks, Kendra stood and watched as the lanky detective climbed from the driver's seat and looked around. She could almost hear his thoughts as he sucked in a lungful of pine-sweet air.

Her heart thudded in her chest. *What's he doing here?* She straightened her spine and shoved her salt-n-pepper hair out of her eyes. Need a trim, she thought as she strolled through the dim living room toward the front door.

She opened the door before he rang the bell. Like any good detective, her old partner was standing just off the wide porch looking things over.

"You lost?" Her voice was as steely as ever. She hoped he didn't know how difficult it was to make it sound that way.

His blue eyes met her brown ones. "So it's true. You've gone native."

"Shh." She put her finger to her lips. "Don't tell my attorney. He thinks I'm still at my desk."

Detective Woody James stepped up on the porch and enveloped her in a stiff hug. "How's it goin', boss?"

"It's all right. Been better, been worse." She extracted herself from his clumsy embrace and ushered him into the house.

About the Author

Ann lives in Texas with her handsome hubby and several rescue pets. *Lilac Lane* is the second book in this Romantic Suspense series, the first being *Stutter Creek*. Ann's very first book with 5 Prince Publishing was *All For Love*, a heartbreaking story of ill- fated romance.

She is also the author of *The Phantom Series*. Book One is *Stevie-girl and the Phantom Pilot*, Book Two is *Stevie-girl and the Phantom Student*, and Book Three is *Stevie-girl and the Phantom of Crybaby Bridge*. Ann has also published short fiction in the anthologies *Timeless* (paranormal love stories) and *Tales of Terror* (horror) as well as a speculative short story, *Chems*. Her current work-in-progress is book three set in Stutter Creek. The new novel is called Copper Lake. Read on for a short excerpt at the end of this book.

Ann has also written a horror novel that is not yet published. Watch for it to be coming out in 2014 or 2015. When she isn't writing, Ann is reading. Her to-be-read list has grown so large it has taken on a life of its own. She calls it Herman.

If you enjoy Romance Suspense
5 Prince Publishing would like to
introduce you to author
Denise Moncrief.
Enjoy an excerpt from her novel
Crisis of Identity.

Crisis of Identity

Chapter One

The room had already filled five times with sea-soaked bodies. The dead lay head-to-foot, column-by-column, row-by-row, ten by twenty. Victim 973 had scrawled her Social Security number down her left arm just as she'd been instructed. I noted the number on my log and moved on, trying hard not to think about the person, concentrating only on the morbid job some pushy cop forced on me.

Across the high school gymnasium, a man worked the other end of the column. As his stealthy glances trailed me around the gym, the acid in my overwrought stomach churned every time our eyes met.

"Want to take a break?" His sudden question reverberated throughout the cavernous space.

I curled one tendril of hair around my left ear. "Sure."

I followed him into the locker room, grabbing a foam cup and filling it with tepid coffee. The man did the same from another urn. The burnt brew left traces of bitterness in my mouth. I rubbed my teeth over my tongue in a vain attempt to remove the acrid leftovers.

My mind turned off for a few precious moments as I ignored the makeshift morgue on the other side of the wall. The man's strong, masculine bass invaded my mental hideaway. "They're starting to smell ripe." He gulped down another ounce of artificial stimulant, staring at me over the rim of his cup.

My insides flipped. "It's been four days."

He nodded. "Most of these don't have numbers."

"Makes it harder to identify them."

He leaned against a locker. "This group must have thought they were invincible."

"Doesn't everyone?" I tossed my cup into the

overflowing trash. "Think they're invincible, I mean."

"Certain death. How do *you* interpret that? I think it means, 'I stay. I die.' Must not have sunk in until it was too late." His sarcastic attitude unsettled me, made me want to defend the dead.

"They've been warned before and nothing happened." When the locals ordered an evacuation two years before, it proved to be a false alarm. The residents of the Texas Gulf coast weren't so easy to convince this time. It seemed no one learned a lesson from Hurricane Katrina. "And…we're not dead." Our eyes locked.

Someone's presence warmed my back. The site supervisor stood over my shoulder and repeated his prerecorded rant for the millionth time. "Mandatory is mandatory. The dead ignored the warning to their own peril. If they wanted to stay put, the least they could do is write their soc number on their arms…just like they were told to do. How many times did the news people make that announcement? Write your number on your arm if you plan to stay. How hard is that?"

I shifted away from him. I didn't dare write my number on my arm.

"Suppose the two of you take a few. You look wasted, and these guys…" He waved his hand toward the gym. "Aren't going anywhere."

***

I dropped onto the cot at the far end of the locker room, struggling to remove the stained smock the state so generously provided. Forget about sleep; it wouldn't come. I had too many memories that begged to become nightmares. I closed my eyes anyway.

The springs in the cot next to mine creaked. "I'm Jake." Why had it taken him so long to introduce himself?

I released an internal sigh. "Tess." I told the truth,

because I had to say something and I was out of lies.

"Tough job."

"Yeah." I wanted him to shut up and leave me alone.

"Why would someone like *you* volunteer for this?"

I opened one eye and glared at him. "I didn't volunteer. I was strongly encouraged to help. Why are you here?"

He hesitated. "I'm a U.S. Marshal. It's my job. Part of the oath and all that."

I opened the other eye and assessed him. "Why would you move here—" He smiled, cutting off my question. "I can tell from your accent you're not from Texas."

"I followed a fugitive here from Illinois." He leaned forward, his knees not quite brushing mine. "She's accused of murder."

"Murder?"

"Stabbed her boyfriend…in the back…in cold blood."

My reaction gushed from my mouth. "How can you be sure it was cold blood?" I sucked back a gasp at my gaffe. My question probably seemed strangely timed and oddly constructed. "I mean…it could have been self defense."

He offered me a cold, hard stare with unblinking eyes. "I just know."

"That's…awful."

"I guess I followed my lead at the wrong time. I got trapped riding out the storm…just like you."

"What makes you think I got trapped?"

"If you'd had any choice, you would have left."

My brother Tony forced me to stay, but he left me. A storm surge so strong it pulled the house out from under us knocked him into the sea. The Gulf of Mexico spit me back onto the beach as if the ocean didn't like the way I tasted.

I survived, but I had no time to grieve. The realization impaled my heart.

Jake stretched out on his cot. "There's a boat out of

here tomorrow. It's taking volunteers back to the mainland." Galveston was in ruins. The thin strips of concrete that once connected the island to civilization lay scattered on the beach looking somewhat like a child's building blocks.

"There is?" I tried not to appear too interested.

"You didn't know?" A different question danced in his eyes—a challenge of sorts. "So how long have you lived in Galveston?"

"Not long. My brother found a job. So I moved here a few months ago to be with him."

"Where's your brother now?"

I blinked at him. "He's gone."

His stern countenance wavered, but before I could embrace his presumed compassion, his expression settled into severity once again. "Now you'll have to start your life over…again." His eyes captured mine. A shiver of dread slithered down my spine. It was as if he *knew* me, even though he didn't seem to *know* me. "Are you going to sleep?" He nodded toward my pillow as if he didn't think my conscience would allow rest.

"I never sleep."

Within minutes, he emitted soft puffs of breath, in and out, obviously lacking any guilt to keep him awake.

The shadows lengthened and receded over the locker room, drifting in and out of the grimy, shattered windows as if the world was still revolving around its axis on schedule. But I was sure it had stopped turning. I was the fugitive he sought.

***

The unrepentant sunshine streamed through the cracks, jubilant in its victory over the storm. Only five days since the devastation of Hurricane Irving and the sun acted as if nothing had ever happened. I turned away from the brightness with an ill-tempered snort.

Jake caught up with me on the gym floor. "Did you get any sleep?" His question hit me as a trifle vindictive.

"No. But you did."

"I snore." He grinned. Then his smile faded. "I thought you'd be gone this morning."

"Why? I have to finish the job."

"That's…admirable."

The thought that pestered me all night erupted from my mouth. "What happens to that woman when you catch her?"

"She'll go back to jail." He stopped by the double doors and folded his arms over his chest, blocking my path "Then she'll go to trial."

"What if she did what she had to do?"

"There was no evidence it was self defense."

I stared hard at his implacable façade. How could the man be alternately warm and cold, compassionate and hard, flexible and unyielding? I stepped around him and entered the gym. There were already bodies lined up waiting for our initial inspection, so I began the task of collecting information from my column of the dead. The hours passed as I searched pockets and noted identifying characteristics on those with no papers or markings. I glanced toward the open door as two men begin loading the last group onto a waiting truck.

One more victim to notate. I squatted next to her. Even in partial decay, her features were enough like mine it pushed me back on my heels. I lifted her arm. My breath hitched. Her Social Security number was so nearly like mine. I scanned the gym. Jake, the one man who might care if she became me or I became her, was absent. With a few strokes of the pen, I could die and live again.

My heart pounded with the possibility I might get a

chance to start over without the baggage of my past dragging me down. I changed her identity with a few swipes of a permanent marker. The number went onto my log with an unshaken hand, and I was free to escape the woman I used to be…the woman I didn't want to be any longer.

***

I raced across the remaining bit of buckled concrete toward hope, barely reaching the dock in time to scramble aboard the last boat for the mainland. Glancing around the small craft, I relaxed and settled into my seat. Jake was not on board as I worried he would be. Even though I left him arguing with the site supervisor, I still feared he would stop me from leaving.

Peering toward the far shore, my goal in sight, I sucked in one ragged breath as the boat headed into the bay. But just a glimpse of movement drew my attention back to the island. I turned to see Jake rushing toward the ramshackle dock and pulling himself up short when he reached the edge. Across the gently slapping surf, his eyes met mine and I was certain the chase wasn't over.

Other titles from 5 Prince Publishing
www.5princebooks.com
~~~

Crisis of Serenity *Denise Moncrief*
The Porcelain Child *Jessica Dall*
The Acceptance *Bernadette Marie*
The Annunaki and the Dragon Court *Katrina Sisowath*
The Letter Drawer *Sarah Galloway*
How to Have an Amicable Divorce *Lindsay Harper*
The Ice Goddess *Hannelore Moore*
Indomitable Spirit *Bernadette Marie*
A Heart Forever Wild *Sara Barnard*
Desperado *Sara Barnard*
The Copper Witch *Jessica Dall*
Home Run *Bernadette Marie*
Blissful Tragedy *Amy L Gale*
How to Have an Affair *Lindsay Harper*
The Soul of Jesus *Doug Simpson*
The Girl before Eve *Lisa J Hobman*
Courting Darkness *Melynda Price*
Owned By the Ocean *Christine Steendam*
Sullivan's Way *Wilhelmina Stolen*
The Library *Carmen DeSousa*
Rebekah's Quilt *Sara Barnard*
Unforgiving Plains *Christine Steendam*
Love Songs *Bernadette Marie*
Little Spoon *Sara Barnard*
The End *Denise Moncrief*
On Thin Ice *Bernadette Marie*
Through the Glass *Lisa J. Hobman*
Indiscretion *Tonya Lampley*
The Elvis Presley I Knew *Robert C. Cantwell*
Finding Hope *Bernadette Marie*
Over the Edge *Susan Lohrer*
Encore *Bernadette Marie*
Split Decisions *Carmen DeSousa*
Matchmakers *Bernadette Marie*